CW01212232

GRANDFATHERS' GIFTS

John Hargreaves

By the same author

FICTION
Doctor Clegg's Machete

NON FICTION
Harvests and Harvesters

GRANDFATHERS' GIFTS

JOHN HARGREAVES

Published by Tangible Press
Market Drayton, Shropshire

ISBN-13: 978-1517188962

To the memory of my grandfather
Private Frederick Clegg, South Staffordshire Regiment

And a gift to my grandchildren
Ella Hargreaves and Moss Hargreaves

DAY ONE

IT BEGAN WHEN a young journalist called Emily Wray phoned him a week before his sixtieth birthday and asked if she could pop round and have a chat. She'd heard that as he reached each new decade he received a unique birthday present from his long-deceased grandfather. She said it would make a fascinating story.

More accurately, it began on his tenth birthday – the twenty-first of August 1960 – when his grandfather gave him eight chess pawns carved from wood that looked bloodshot. He'd asked if they were made of California redwood and his grandfather said no, they were made of French chair leg.

Stephen supposed he could even say it began one spring day in 1918 when Private William Oakley foraged through a shell-wrecked farmhouse near Chambrecy and salvaged a piece of cherry wood, the carving of which he believed would see him through the war and bring him safely home to his bride and the baby she was carrying.

Who could say how far back you had to go to find the true beginning of things? The endings in his life were so often depressingly definite.

He looked round the living room of his flat with

dismay. He could close the doors to his two bedrooms – one as unkempt as a single man's sleeping place could be, the other crammed with the detritus of a lifetime's passing enthusiasms – with confidence that they would not be opened. He could wash two cups and prime them with instant coffee in the reasonable hope that she would not follow him into his unsavoury kitchen. Young bladders were astonishingly elastic and it was conceivable that she would be finished and away before needing the bathroom. But she would want to sit down to take notes. She would look around his living room and see what it said about the way he lived now. She might even think his end was in sight already.

It had been so long since his door bell had rung, it sounded like an alarm. She was an hour early.

"Hello – Emily Wray. You're expecting me, sort of." Her smile broke into cheering dimples at its extremities. "I came early on purpose in the hope I might catch you as you really are, not as you think I want you to be."

"Stephen Oakley," he said, so disarmed that he vaguely offered his unshaven cheek in case she went in for those little air kisses that people seemed to do nowadays.

"Pleased to meet you." She held out her hand for an old-fashioned shake.

"As you want me to be." He led the way down the hallway corridor between jumbled footwear and old coats bulging from pegs on both sides, anxiously closing doors as he passed.

She stepped into his living room and moved swiftly to the piano before he could offer her his sunken armchair. She swivelled the upright seat away from the keys – several of them missing their ivory, he registered with fresh eyes. He registered also her practical flat shoes, bare legs and cool cotton dress. He found it encouraging that there were still pretty young women who chose to breeze comfortably through life with bare legs in summer frocks.

"Do I pass muster?" She gave him the smile-with-dimples again and he noticed also a blush of mid-summer freckles bridging her nose from one cheek to the other, which pulled him up for some reason he didn't fathom and made him determined to behave himself.

"Sorry. Lovely to have a visitor so bright and early."

He watched her take a small electronic device from her shoulder bag and place it on a stack of books on the coffee table in front of her. She clipped another gadget onto a miniature tripod with flexible legs and fastened it to the corner of the table after relegating half a dozen old magazines to the floor. She aimed a metallic eyeball at the sagging armchair into which she clearly expected him to sink, and then produced a notepad and pencil.

"You don't mind if we multi-media do you Mr Oakley? Or can I call you Stephen? I want to make sure I capture everything you have to say about your fantastic story and let you roam at will without having to interrupt, because my shorthand is coming along but it's not quite there yet. Plus the recorder catches all the pauses for correction and the webcam doubles up for security as well as capturing the body language, and that can be so instructive don't you think?"

Aware momentarily of his body language he felt himself ease back in reaction to a puppy journalist who seemed to have quite enough energy for the two of them.

"Should we start with a nice cup of tea?" he asked.

"Because you're a little nervous and you think it will relax you? Or are you being ironic and subtly trying to take control of the interview?"

"I would say you have given some thought yourself to the matter of taking control of the interview. I thought you might be thirsty. How far have you come?"

"From Willesden."

That delightful little smile again.

"Short bus, long tube, a fifteen minute walk. Coffee would be lovely."

Before he was out of the room she had pulled a laptop from her bag and started tapping the keys.

He came back bearing a bottle of milk, an open packet of sugar, and two mugs of instant coffee on a cutting board.

"I didn't know you could still get milk in bottles," she said, pouring for herself after a quick sniff at the neck.

"The past lingers in odd ways. My neighbours seem to be mostly young professionals keen to lower their carbon footprint. They think recycling glass is better than recycling plastic."

"Are they right?"

"I've no idea. But the corner shop in Ham is pleased to oblige."

"So how come you live amidst young professionals?"

"Why are you asking me about milk bottles?"

"I was distracting you while I closed my laptop. You were reading my words."

"You're right, I was. Trying to. Isn't that natural?"

"Perhaps. But not acceptable. I'm a professional journalist and you need to trust me. This is my story."

"I rather thought it was my story."

"And I'm trusting you."

"You are?"

"To tell the truth."

"I wouldn't dream of anything else."

"The whole truth."

"Okay. My father gave me this flat years ago, on condition I never asked him for another penny. The deeds forbid me to turn it into cash and I'm in ever-increasing debt just trying to pay the council tax and service charge."

"You're telling me something about trust?"

"You asked how I come to live in a building full of young professionals. The flat below is on the market for over a quarter of a million. I believe that's a snip for a young professional."

"Not for a young journalist it isn't."

"Perhaps you're in the wrong profession."

There was even something a little puppy-like about the way she scrutinised his face. Eventually she said, "I can't tell whether you're smiling or smirking."

"It's a smile. They're dimples at each end, not the wrinkles of age and grimace. And now that we're both charming each other with our smiles and dimples, are you going to show me what you were writing?"

To his surprise she opened her laptop and passed it to him.

"It's just background; I won't be filing it as copy. And if you are flirting with me, please stop. It's inappropriate."

He lives on the fourth, top, floor of a modest set of flats at the end of a residential cul-de-sac in North Kingston, on the edge of Richmond Park. Dating from the 1930's at a guess – there's just a touch of art deco about the bay window with its wrought iron frames. There's something a little touched about my subject too. He looks like he has lived every moment of a full and eventful life but has little to show for it. He already has an older man's face, with greying stubble on a craggy surface. It's more decently weathered than gone to seed though, and framed by a thick shock of hair which he sweeps over his ears occasionally while he's talking. His corduroy trousers, sweatshirt, and crumpled linen jacket, like his body, look well lived-in. His room too, is showing its age. He has burgundy velvet floor-to-ceiling curtains round his bay window, faded to pastel pink down the edges where they've caught the sun – the room faces south, overlooking a communal parking area and neighbouring gardens, sideways to the park. His furniture looks nineteen seventies, but more Salvation Army than retro. In fact, it looks as though he might have got it from The Salvation Army in the nineteen seventies. He has a cathode-ray-tube television with a tiny screen and a one-piece sound system which seems to prioritise vinyl. Yes, there's a stack of LPs below his books, which are all cheap paperbacks, looking tatty and not organised by size or any other criteria as far as I can tell. Black-and-white prints on the walls – Escher tessellations and rock psychedelia – are attached by drawing pins but curling at loose corners. Piles of junk on the floor. A room full of stories, perhaps. Undusted. But all of that is about to change.

"You type quickly." He gave the laptop back.

"You have a slow kettle."

"The furniture came from my extended family, since you profess to be interested in the truth. Not the Salvation Army. The Oakleys like to find a good home for their cast-offs."

"No offence intended. I would never ordinarily share my thinking with my subject."

"I'm not used to being someone's subject."

"Except your father's?"

He stopped to consider this briefly, then shrugged his shoulders in the direction of the webcam. "I come from an odd family."

"Me too, I guess."

"Look. Do I have any reason *not* to trust you?"

"Listen," she said. "I'm not sure we've got off to a very

good start. Do you mind if we re-wind?"

"Please do start again. Anywhere you like."

"Are you married?"

"No."

"Children?"

"No."

"Siblings?

"No. Not normal ones."

"So why did your father buy you out, as it were?"

"I thought you said you wanted to start over?"

He waited and noted that she knew when to remain silent.

"But I'm happy enough to tell you that I have both step-brothers and sisters and half-brothers and sisters. A modern family, I suppose. Nowadays these children of multi-married parents can be very clannish, don't you find? But back then it was different. My parents packed me off to boarding school and orphaned me before they remarried. We didn't communicate much. The Oakleys in general on the other hand, in the guise of my multiple second cousins and relations once removed, are a huge old-fashioned clan, as I suppose you know. It must have been one of them who told you about my grandfather's unusual gifts."

He leaned forward ready to launch himself from the sagging armchair. "I'll fetch them to show you."

"No," she said decisively. "I want to keep that for later. After lunch would be good, and just one at a time. I'll file a teaser for the West End Final then follow it up in the slip. My editor wants to pace this story over the week to your birthday and let it build momentum."

He thought she was showing off with the jargon. Easily done in the early days: she was young enough to get away with much worse. Not young enough to cope with beans on toast though.

"I'm afraid I wasn't expecting you for lunch."

"The paper man at the station said the Norbiton and Dragon does a good Thai curry. Exactly the same food in the bar as in the restaurant but half the price, he said. So my expenses will cover us. You must call me Emily, by the way. And we'll be walking close to the park gates so we can pop inside and take a few pictures. Something a little wild and outdoorsy will give us a more romantic hook for the web than a head-and-shoulders in your flat. No offence."

He hadn't been to the Norbiton and Dragon for ages.

"So give me the big picture," she said. "About your grandfather and your inheritance."

He had never thought of his decennial gifts from his grandfather as an inheritance. But he did fancy stepping out for a good lunch alongside this attractive if rather combative young woman with her unlikely sense of journalistic mission.

"The Oakleys were a family firm of builders from points northwest of here. Still are, though they've splintered in all sorts of ways. My grandfather William grew up in the original Oakley yard, in Market Drayton. He liked to whittle scraps of wood with a penknife and over the years he developed a flair for it. On my tenth birthday he gave me something he'd carved many years previously. Something of no monetary, artistic or utilitarian worth."

"And yet you valued this special gift hugely?"

"Yes, I suppose I did. You'll see why after lunch."

"And then?"

"He died. Just a few weeks later."

"You were very close?"

"Within two feet of each other actually. He was giving me a driving lesson in his Zephyr Zodiac on the beach at

Bolton-le-Sands. I was lurching and stalling, trying to get the hang of letting the clutch out smoothly and he was laughing his head off and then he just pitched forward and sort of folded in on himself and died. I knew what had happened straight away, and funnily enough I suddenly realised I had the thing going smoothly with my foot just so on the accelerator and I went round and round in a huge circle for the longest time. I pretty much learned to drive and lost my best friend at the same time. And then ten years later, on my twentieth birthday, out of the blue, another present from William, along with a letter telling me about it."

"Do you mind?" She opened her laptop with its screen like a barrier between them and tapped away as she asked him where he was and what he was doing on his twentieth.

He didn't mind at all; he felt the barrier gave him permission to gawp. "I was in San Francisco. Sort of managing a band."

"How did he do it? I mean posting stuff from the grave?"

"I assumed it was forwarded by my Great-Aunt Mary – William's sister-in-law. We were both staying with her that summer when I was ten. I spent most of my holidays from school with William, and he often stayed with my great-aunt. I thought she was William's go-between, but she died long before my thirtieth, and William's presents kept on coming."

"Amazing."

"He must have pre-paid a solicitor or something. Hard to imagine Royal Mail offering that kind of service."

"No, I mean just look at this." She turned her screen towards him but he couldn't make sense of it. "It's Bolton-le-Sands," she said. "I'd never heard of it before but it's right there on the edge of Morecambe Bay, where those Chinese immigrants drowned picking cockles, and this road just tips out onto the beach and look at all those cars!"

"People drive out there for picnics."

"Google Earth picked a fine day."

"You're checking my story?"

"Just being a nosy journalist. I like to be thorough. Tell me where you lived in San Francisco and we can see if the house is still there."

"I must have lived in twenty or more places, not counting all the motels when we were on the road. We'd be here all day."

"Okay. Big picture."

"The third one came when I was thirty. That would be August of nineteen eighty. I'd done my bit for world music by then and let Peter Gabriel take over. Done my own little stint as a journalist too, which ended badly. I think I was living here already. The gift just came in the mail on the day, in plain brown wrapping. No return address. Postage paid."

She tapped away and he paused to let her catch up.

"The fourth must have come when I was up in Staffordshire. I spent the late eighties up there. They were happy times: prison, artists' colony, househusband."

"Goodness!"

"That was doing pottery workshops in prison, not time."

"We can fill in the details later."

"I don't know how the package found me but my father's lawyers got hold of me easily enough. I'd leased this flat and was living off the rental and they said that was breaking the terms of the leasehold. A week later the woman I was living with told me I was pretty unlikely father-material for the child she had decided she wanted and kicked me out. So I came back down here and began my entrepreneurial period. I identified a niche product in the snack market – mixed nuts and seeds roasted in tamari. Addictive but healthy – the dream product – and so obviously my silver bullet I decided to do the manufacturing and marketing myself. In Kingston, if you can imagine. So I was here for the fifth present, in 2000. It was not long after Concorde went arse up in Paris. The present arrived bang on my birthday. And I've been here ever since. The last one will come at the end of the week."

"Why do you say the last?"

"Well they're not going to go on forever, are they? William was sixty when he gave me the first; I'll be sixty on Saturday. I suspect he knew he didn't have long to live and I reckon he figured by the time I reached the same age I'd be starting to focus on... well, let's say the big picture."

He stopped talking and watched his interviewer's face as she worked on her copy. Her eyes tracked the words her fingers produced on screen as though she were reading a piano score but the greater part of her was anticipating the music ahead. She smiled to herself even as her lips puckered slightly in concentration; a clumsy phrase, perhaps, or a sentence that was too long. And her eyebrows lifted periodically; pleased with the pace perhaps, or with an idea for a strong ending. She was obviously managing to craft a story from the bare bones he had provided. Her fingers slowed and she leaned towards the laptop as if over the ivories, heading for a delicious resolving cadence.

With a prancing tap of her fourth finger she hit a solitary key in a final flourish. "Sent! And just made the deadline. Let's go take some pictures."

THEY ENTERED THE PARK by way of Ham Common and zigzagged their way up to Pen Ponds, into the fenced enclosure of Isabella Plantation where the hydrangeas were in full bloom, then back through High Wood and Coronation Plantation where deer were grazing.

Stephen had a little experience behind the camera himself – though not this kind of camera. He'd sold a few photo-stories to the music press way back before bands had marketing managers, when egos were flattered by just letting them be themselves in everyday settings. He still had an everyday sort of ego himself, he reckoned, and in front of the lens he found it easy enough to act like a minor band personality from the early seventies who thought he was still interesting to look at. He posed astride a fallen oak, in mid-stride on stepping stones over a stream, leaning dreamily against a wispy adolescent birch, lying in deep grass gazing at the drifting clouds. Emily snapped away without directing and without laughing. Then she held the device between them and flipped through all she had taken. Her thumb twitched furiously before coming to rest on a head-and-shoulders where she'd zoomed in to catch him looking, yes, a little wild and windswept, in the heart and soul as well as the hair and whiskers. This was the one she liked best, she said. Her thumb moved again and then she held the device to her ear and said "Gerald? Hello, it's Emily. I've just sent you the perfect image. To use for the whole week. Of Stephen Oakley. I've got a feeling the story's going to be magical."

They left by the Kingston Gate and strolled on to the Norbiton and Dragon. He felt exhilarated. He hoped he wouldn't wake up the next morning full of regret. She talked about how much she loved London; the solid feel of it, despite the diversity and the endless surprises. He told her how much the place had changed. She had a vegetarian stir-fry on jasmine rice that smelled like San Francisco and a glass of red wine that looked like half a bottle. He had a Guinness and what might have been called a Caesar salad if Constantine had kept going east another two thousand miles.

They followed the road back to his flat and fell into a comfortable silence as they walked. He pictured the eight slightly-irregular chess pawns he would soon lay before her and told himself he'd better make it a good story. Best leave the 'magical' to her. He'd concentrate on trying to tell it right. He wondered where to start and thought as good a place as any would be the crack in the wall of the Burnet breakfast room.

YOUNG WILLIAM OAKLEY had never heard of the game of chess until the long hot summer of 1914 when the clay soils of north-east Shropshire dried and shrank causing subsidence to the foundations of the western wall of Burnet Hall and a crack to appear in the wall of the breakfast room.

The building was not about to collapse but Lady Burnet believed, unfashionably, that western civilization might very well. Her son was at annual training near Aberystwyth with the territorials of the 4th Battalion The King's Shropshire Light Infantry. It was like a holiday for most of the men but her son took it terribly seriously. He'd followed a long line of Burnet males into the local yeomanry or militia, and joined the Wem and Whitchurch Company as soon as he was eighteen. If war came, he told his mother, he expected to be in charge of a crucial length of coastal defences. And now a long diagonal crack had appeared across the internal wall of her breakfast room and she was convinced that it was an omen portending great danger. She summoned Frederick Oakley, the builder from Drayton, to advise on making it safe, and he took his youngest son William with him.

Frederick had dealt with similar cracks in the hot, dry summer of 1904 and knew it merited no alarm. But Lady Burnet was in a state and he thought it prudent to dig a few inspection trenches, take some measurements, and probe the plasterwork the full length of the crack before telling her that the foundations were giving way no more than one hundredth of an inch per annum and that once the crack was cut back and re-plastered she would never know that it had ever existed. William helped carry his tools from the cart and then got in the way, so when a young lass about his age said she wanted help, Frederick gladly shooed him away.

"Come with me," she said, pulling William by the hand when he failed to move adequately by himself. She led him indoors and though he managed to pull his hand free, he meekly followed. He supposed this was the kitchen, though there was no sign of a cook or any food. It was cavernous and spotlessly clean and he was struck with horror at the idea that she would make him take off his boots and usher him through to a parlour in his stockinged feet. But she stopped at an enormous butcher's block on wheels, pulled up high stools on either side, and removed a dust cover from a chequerboard laid with finely carved wooden pieces.

"I don't bite," she said. "At least not hard. I'm Ada Doley and I need someone real to play chess with."

William didn't feel at all real. He found he couldn't look at this Ada who bit softly, so he stared down at the board.

"Well? Can you play?"

He asked if it was like draughts. He said he sometimes

played draughts with his brothers.

"That's because you're an artisan. Draughts is a game for artisans. Dominoes is for workers. And chess is for intellectuals. My father doesn't play any games, but he knows what chess is because he has to know about these things. I'm going to be an intellectual. You can be one too. It doesn't matter that your father is a brick-layer or that mine is a butler. But we have to study."

She sat down and opened a small leather-bound book which lay next to the board. William stood opposite her.

"Lady Margaret says that even though I'm only fourteen and finished school two years ago, I have the most orderly mind and the neatest hand of anyone she knows and she has asked me to index and catalogue in alphabetical order her whole library. In the front page of every volume I have to gum a picture of the Burnet crest and I have to include all the books in the house and there are volumes in every room including Master Herbert's. He's been mobilised to his war station at Barry Docks which is in Cardiff which is in Wales and he's left behind his Boy's Guide to Chess and H G Wells only I didn't stick anything in him because I'm certain Lady Margaret would not approve. The front pieces are called pawns and they can only move forward and only by one square, or two on their first move if you prefer. You're white so you start."

William wilted under her scrutiny.

"You can move any one you like."

He waited until he realised that she was not going to abandon the task, nor breathe fresh life into him. He moved the little piece on the extreme left one square forward.

Ada read from the Boy's Guide: *"According to Benjamin Franklin, by playing at chess we may learn, One: foresight, which looks a little into futurity, and considers the consequences that may attend an action."* She struggled to articulate *futurity* and *consequences* and the game progressed slowly.

"He's not a bricklayer," William said, making his first voluntary contribution after many minutes. "He's a builder."

Ada liked that. Their eyes met for the first time and William saw that he had her attention. She made him promise to play again when his father came back to fix the fissure in the breakfast room.

And so began their young courtship. For some time Ada insisted that she tolerated William's attendance on her because a flesh-and-blood opponent made learning chess easier than playing both sides herself, book in hand. She always won, and was occasionally quite cruel in her commentary on the working of his mind. Increasingly, though, his flesh-and-blood presence came to make a broader impression on her and sometimes misled her into making foolish moves herself.

"By playing at chess we may learn, Two: circumspection, which surveys the whole chess-board, or scene of action – the relation of the several pieces, and their situations," she read from Benjamin Franklin again at their second game, while William's father cut back the cracked plasterwork on the wall of the breakfast room.

"My mother has taken the boot maker from Nantwich to the village school to measure the children. The labourers pay into Her Ladyship's Shoe Club and if they have a full card before the new school year she adds interest plus two shillings and sixpence and sends for Amies so every club child has two pairs of well-made shoes for the year. But I don't agree with it. I think Lady Margaret should keep her two-and-sixpences and the workers should be paid a proper wage. So does Mr Wells."

William went out to Burnet again with his father's plasterer. He moved his pawns forward more boldly and Ada attacked without mercy. *"By playing at chess we may learn, Three: caution, not to make our moves too hastily."* She put her book down and smiled condescendingly. "The pawns do all the hard work and get no glory. Just like in real life. They shuffle forward, they block, they hold the dangerous ground for the powerful; and they can be sacrificed at any time. But when you sacrifice a pawn, William dear, you've got to make sure that it gives advantage to a more important piece. This is why I am biding my time with Lady Margaret and learning to play chess. I am developing foresight, learning to be circumspect, and being cautious – so that I am prepared for my big move."

By the time the breakfast room was redecorated and its mirrors rehung, William had himself become something of a fixture at the hall. Lady Margaret first became aware of him traipsing round the library at Ada's heels on the very day the 4th Battalion The King's Shropshire Light Infantry sailed from Southampton for Bombay. The territorials were releasing regular army units for active service in France and Herbert was heading for routine garrison duty in a relatively civilised part of the Empire, thank goodness. Lady Margaret told William that he had come on cue as a talisman, assuring her son's safety, and that he must come often.

Ada being the very last in the order of things at Burnet, she enjoyed having an assistant at her beck and call and soon began to picture marriage to an artisan as an effective and pleasant enough route out of service. Her mother and father found William courteous and kindly and admired the way he absorbed the headstrong and sometimes radical impulses of their maturing daughter without himself seeming to chafe at his station or show disrespect to others. William thought nothing of the forty-minute walk from the wood shop in his father's yard, where he was working his apprenticeship under relaxed conditions, to the even more relaxed pleasantries of Burnet with its obtuse conversation, the certainty of cake or a bar of chocolate from Lady Margaret, and the possibility of a parting kiss from Ada Doley.

William knew, too, that his father was only too happy to have him out of the way, learning about the gentler pleasures of life in a well-chaperoned place that might protect him from infection with his older brothers' rabid patriotism. Heaton, just turned eighteen and always itching for a fight, had been ready to sign up as soon as the Germans invaded Belgium. It was going to be over by Christmas, everyone said, and if he didn't go now he would miss the fun. Frederick made him promise to his mother in front of the whole family that he would not sign up without her blessing, and then made the whole family responsible for holding him to it. After the defeat at Mons in September, Albert and Arthur joined Heaton in wanting to enlist. They knew by then that war was potentially dangerous and men could be killed but the Germans had become a threat to their family and their home and it was their duty to fight.

Frederick said it was his duty also to protect his home and family.

"It sounds like the great powers themselves, posturing and manoeuvring," Lady Margaret said when she asked William about his brothers. "We must make sure you are not cast as the Archduke Ferdinand."

"Heaton says taking the Derby pledge will be a fair compromise," William said, hoping he wouldn't be pressed because he wasn't entirely sure what the Derby pledge amounted to. Taking a pledge sounded like a noble undertaking, but his father said the Derby pledge was no more than a cheap trick.

"Promising to serve only if eventually needed will prove to be as final as enlisting, but with a few weeks' grace."

"I believe my father thinks likewise. He took the train to the Kent's Lane colliery and Silverdale ironworks to bid for work. He said making repairs to tied farms and cottages for the likes of the Burnets would hardly be considered vital war work. Begging your pardon, ma'am."

"He's perfectly right," she said. "And I believe I can be of some assistance." The 4th Battalion The King's Shropshire Light Infantry had been ordered to Rangoon and then on to Singapore, which Lady Margaret believed was even more civilised, and she told William that he had become not merely her good luck charm, but positively the guarantor of her son's safety.

William learned from Ada that Lady Margaret played bridge – a game of the gentry – with the wife of the Lord-Lieutenant. The Lord-Lieutenant, Ada said, was the king's top man in the entire county.

To his surprise, Frederick Oakley not only won a contract to repair a pipe fitter's workshop in Silverdale, but was invited to submit an estimate for laying brick for an extension to a munitions factory near Crewe. By the time conscription was finally introduced in 1916, William's older brothers were all in lodgings and laying brick for the defence of the realm. They were automatically given exemptions by the local Military Service Tribunal.

On his sixteenth birthday, William asked Mr Doley for permission to marry his daughter. Mr Doley consulted Lady Margaret, who was alarmed at the prospect. Mail from The 4th Battalion The King's Shropshire Light Infantry took a long time to reach home, and she read

Herbert's rather casual accounts of suppressing two mutinies by native troops long after the participants had been rounded up and executed. She supposed they were more easily intimidated than the Bosch. And knowing the last scene of a drama a mere sentence or two after its beginning did take the worry out of it. Now he was going to Hong Kong, which she supposed was as far as she could wish from the tragedy unfolding in the fields of Flanders. The safer her son appeared to be, however, the more determined Lady Margaret was to keep her young talisman close in her own stewardship, not Ada's.

It was inconceivable that Mr Doley would consent to his daughter marrying into a Methodist household, Lady Margaret told William. When his face crumpled, she said that there was a way round this problem, and that even though the pair were very young she would bless the marriage herself once he had accepted confirmation into the Church of England.

"And you agreed?" Ada was incensed. "Old Pudsey only runs classes after Easter, and they take forever! He cancelled two out of three because of his gout when I was doing it and then closed down for months because of some pox or other. He'll be dead as a doornail before you're ready for the Bishop."

In the event, Reverend Pudsey lived on several years after Ada, whom he buried in his churchyard just two months after the war ended, when the Spanish Flu swept through the country in a devastating second wave which proved fatal for so many young and otherwise healthy souls.

"I have to go to classes?" William said in amazement. "I thought I just had to promise. You know, to be the right kind of Christian."

"What did you promise Lady Margaret?"

"That I would."

And Ada had learned that when William made a promise, he kept it.

The following Easter, William began confirmation classes with Reverend Pudsey, tramping across the fields to the vicarage every Wednesday evening after work. The Oakley yard in Drayton was moribund, with Frederick away on the train most days pitching for contracts or keeping an eye on the sons who were delivering them. Oversight of William's apprenticeship fell to Old Armitage, which fuelled family jokes because the seventy-year-old could barely see the end of his nose. He could make panel doors and window frames by touch – Frederick said by smell – but there was little demand and mostly scavenged materials to make them with. William learned the discipline of sharpening tools and oiling them, keeping each and every one ready in its ordered place. He helped keep an exceedingly tidy workshop. His mother cooked a substantial dinner midday – payment for local jobs now being made mostly in cheese, eggs, and game – and Old Armitage took a nap after it most days.

In the Autumn of that year Reverend Pudsey's confirmation class was learning by heart the catechism in the Book of Common Prayer when the 4th Battalion The King's Shropshire Light Infantry was brought back to Southampton from the far east and without so much as a day's leave was re-directed to Le Havre. Over eleven-hundred strong, the battalion drilled in a makeshift camp on the north side of the harbour, the men still in their tropical khaki. As soon as their new uniforms arrived they were sent to Flanders and pitched headlong into the battle of Passchendaele. In three years in the east they had lost six men, to illness. On their first day on the Ypres salient they lost 130.

Old Armitage told William to bring a course saw and axe in the handcart and led him out to a copse on the edge of the Burnet Estate where he said there was some nice fruit wood. He found plum and cherry and told William that he'd had a nod from Mr Doley himself so not to worry about trespass and foraging. William hauled the cart back with all the wood Armitage said they needed.

"Pay attention now, young William. Keep looking and stay curious, because there is no end to seeing, and you and I are going to bodge a rocking chair for Ada."

"But why?"

"Because she's going to be married."

"But why a rocking chair?"

"Because as you get older, the more you become who you really are. Everyone should look forward to getting old. And she'll thank you for it when she's nursing your baby."

William had never thought about a baby. He paid close attention as Armitage set him to work cutting wood into billets for legs and shaping them with a drawknife; watched him run the flat of his hand along the wood for the runners, then his nose; fetched boiling water from the kitchen to steam the green wood and start to give it shape.

Herbert Burnet now sent frequent postcards to his mother who asked for William directly they arrived. She poured tea, gave him biscuits on a plate, and read her post aloud.

"Halted in a quiet spot well back in reserve this morning and rigged up a super bivvy under a tree. Had a capital wash and a shave in a stream alongside. Then with a clean face and a clear mind I had a good sound sleep which is just the sweetest thing on earth. Woke up feeling quite bucked again.

"He never writes about keeps or revetments and all the other mediaeval things the Times' correspondent goes on about. Nor of the casualties or the wounded, enumerated daily in the leader columns. He seems inordinately concerned with sleep, young William. Sleeping and bathing and eating and drinking. What do you think we should make of it? Do you think he's quite all there?"

In the spring of 1918 the Germans launched another great offensive. When they started their all-out attack along the Somme Herbert wrote to his mother, *The birds are singing. I've heard them for real – I don't just mean in my head. It's quite astonishing. I expect to see fish jumping any day.* He wrote this several times, embellished with his memories of fishing in the Tern and the Duckow and when she asked William how he could possibly write such things, William didn't know what to say, except that he supposed the Somme was a river too.

"It's no such thing," she said.

"It will be different this time, Ma'am," said Mr Doley, who was also listening.

But Lady Margaret didn't see how anything could ever be different again. "My poor boy is stuck. It is going to go on forever. Forever and forever. Why doesn't he come home on leave? It's only a day or two by train. His letters arrive in two days, for goodness sake."

William worked hard on the rocking chair. Each joint became a labour of love, each turned spindle a miracle of composure.

"We shan't use a drop of glue," Armitage said, "but work with the wood's own tightening as it dries, so one part hugs the other just as firm as you could ever wish. And as this cherry ages, it will darken to a deep, warm, red. It will go on getting richer long after I am gone, lad."

William kept the tools sharp and the shop tidy.

The German push on the Somme petered out in April and they renewed their offensive towards Kemmel. The 4th Battalion The King's Shropshire Light Infantry was sent there too.

Without telling Armitage, William carved a tiny, neat heart on the base of the seat of the rocking chair, with 'A' and 'W' inside. Armitage read it with his fingertips.

Herbert Burnet's Company was sent back from the front again and put on reserve duties bringing up materials for the repair of communication trenches. He wrote about the sheer heaven of sleeping on straw in a French barn. He described how the Medical Corps did them proud before a foot inspection, with half a dozen tin baths in a row filled with hot water from a boiler outside, passed in buckets down a chain of laughing men, the air steaming like a Turkish bath, and the sweet sweet smell of soap! He assured his mother there was nothing like it when you haven't been separated from your clothing for twenty days and nights. And then at last, a postcard showing a Parisian burlesque on one side and *Leave granted. Home soon* on the other.

The Lord-Lieutenant told Lady Margaret they were recruiting in Shrewsbury for the 4th Battalion and the timing struck her with the force of a message from above.

"You are going to enlist, William dear. It's time. Herbert is coming home and you must go back with him. You will keep Herbert safe and he will keep you safe. I see it clearly."

"You will do nothing of the sort," his father told him. "You're not eighteen yet. They don't let you enlist nowadays without a birth certificate."

"You're seventeen-and-three-quarters going on twenty-five," Lady Margaret told him. "The Lord-Lieutenant will take my word for it . He's asking for young men to rally round Herbert. Tell your father the Lord Lieutenant will have his way, William. It's your time. The time has come. Your father will understand my meaning."

"If he's seventeen-and-three-quarters going on twenty five, we could marry first," Ada said.

"Of course you could," said Lady Margaret, seizing the opportunity of winning William's compliance. "I believe they have an army chaplain on hand at recruitment for just such eventualities."

"No. We want a wedding right now, in our own church, don't we William? And a married life together while we get everything agreed."

Old Armitage helped William polish the rocker. "The reason we have wars," he grumbled to himself in William's hearing, "is that women like men who'll fight."

The Germans concentrated their forces on the weaker French sector in Champagne. The British decided to support the French with two army corps, including the division in which the 4th Battalion The King's Shropshire Light Infantry was serving. The Battalion travelled by train to Rheims via Paris and enjoyed a very pleasant few weeks while waiting for their new recruits to make up numbers. Herbert said that it would be like being back at Raffles and the lads would hardly notice that he wasn't with them for ten days.

Frederick Oakley told his son that the Americans had landed in Western France in great numbers and had been training with their new French weapons for months; soon they would be swelling the ranks in the front line. He told William that the tanks the War Office was building would change everything; he'd met a chap who built the factory where they put together the Mark V with Walter Wilson's epicyclic gear steering and were turning out hundreds of the things, ready to drive all the way to Berlin. He said anyone signing up now, with twelve weeks basic training, then a week or two in a transit camp getting organised, then getting across the channel – they'd likely need to turn round and come straight home again because the whole thing would surely be over by then. He had no other course to offer his youngest son. The Military Service Tribunals were now run by determined civil servants with a single brief: to make up numbers in the front line with all urgency.

Old Armitage walked out to Burnet Hall where William lodged briefly with Ada after their marriage, in a little room above the butler's pantry.

"I want you to have something," he said, after Mrs Doley had revived him with mint tea. He laid a small hand chisel on the table, pushed it towards William, and quickly withdrew his arm as if to avoid a temptation to take it back.

"They'll be giving me a gun, I expect. A gun with an attachable bayonet, it being the infantry I'm joining."

"It may save your life in a different way. Every one of us is frightened, lad. But if you can keep doing what you love, you might come through."

William was moved. He held the tiny carving tool and felt the balance of it, wrapped his palm around the smooth, three-inch handle – boxwood, he thought, cut by Armitage himself to take the tapered tang of the tool – then slid the short length of tempered steel from its leather sheath and felt its cutting edge with the flat of his thumb.

"It's a fine gift."

"Right. Only keep it to yourself. That's why there's only one, not a whole belt. Don't let anyone know you work with wood or they'll put you with the sappers making tunnels underground, or laying duckboards in the filth.

No good ever came of working with wood underground or underwater. Wood needs to breathe, same as folk."

William slid the chisel back into its sheath and hid the tool away in his inside pocket.

By the end of May, after training drastically reduced because of the dire circumstances on the front line, William was in Chambrecy, in the heart of Champagne. It wasn't a hellish landscape of mud and desolation, like Lady Margaret had described from her reading of the Times. The trenches were disconnected shallow slits in a pastoral landscape, with ripening corn knee high in many of the fields. Row upon row of tidy grapevines, their new growth pruned once already, lined the hill slopes. Occasional roses flowered among the vines, positioned purposefully like coal miners' canaries to give advanced warning of threats to the grapes.

On the 28th the Germans attacked with great force and the 4th Battalion The King's Shropshire Light Infantry was pushed back in a fighting retreat which reduced them to 350 men. In the midst of this, William scavenged through the wrecked furniture in a shelled-out farmhouse in which his platoon sheltered briefly. He found a handsome chair leg which he believed was cherry wood. He volunteered to make safe the outbuildings and while doing so found a rusty saw with which he hurriedly reduced the leg to smaller pieces. After *stand-to* each evening, however exhausted, he would huddle in as private a place as he could find and as if repeatedly reading a letter from home, or staring at an intimate photograph, he would wrap his hand around Armitage's chisel so it was almost hidden, and begin carving his set of chess pieces for Ada Doley.

On the night of June 5th the Shropshires were huddled in the hamlet of Chaumuzy ready to support the North Staffs and Cheshires who were being pounded by German shells on Bligny Hill. Early the following morning the Germans attacked and by 8am wounded British, many of them gassed, fell back to where William and his battalion waited. They were not a pretty sight. They did not make encouraging sounds. By 9.30 the Germans had stormed the hill and the remainder of the British were fighting their way down its slopes towards the Shropshires. The 4th Battalion was ordered by Brigade HQ to counter attack and retake the hill. They would be assisted by a brief artillery barrage at 12.45.

The covering barrage never came. From his trench near Chaumuzy William clambered up to ground level and launched himself - squinting in the brilliant sunshine and sweating already in what felt like tropical heat - across open fields and through knee-high corn, in clear view of the Germans on the hilltop a mile away. He was neither at the front of the two hundred remaining Shropshires nor in the rear, on the left flank or on the right, but he felt no protection from any quarter as shrapnel hailed down swiftly from above. He reckoned the thinning body of men around him had halved by the time they reached the bottom of the hill where they sheltered briefly in a small area of dead ground out of the line of German fire. It was crowded with the bodies of severely wounded men, the remnants of the earlier retreat. He was drenched in his own sweat and the blood of someone else - the lance corporal, he presumed, who'd been jogging along close to him one second and not the next. Everyone newly arrived in the dead ground was doubled up panting for breath and it would have been easy enough, he thought, to fall to the ground amid the half-dead Cheshires and North Staffs. They were almost neighbours back home, after all. But when the handful of remaining officers, all subalterns, rallied the Shropshires, William rose to his feet. He was neither the first nor the last to do so. He looked to no man, for either comfort or instruction, but a smiling wink from Second Lieutenant Burnet found him anyway. Then came a desperate rush up the final slope, over open ground, facing machine gun and heavy rifle fire. William would remember nothing of firing his own rifle, only of running. Later he would be described along with the rest of them as a strapping labourer fresh from the Shires – fast on his feet, unwavering, eager to get the job done. William himself had no description for what happened when he found himself in among the Germans as they staggered up from their shallow slit trenches. He would retain no memory of stabbing at bellies with his bayonet or swinging the butt of his rifle at an enemy jaw, only of bending in on himself with a painful stitch, gasping for air, his eyes smarting as sweat dripped down his forehead. In any case, the hand-to-hand fighting was soon over and the Germans either fled or surrendered.

Within thirty minutes William came under bombardment again, not from a German counter attack but from the British barrage which should have preceded the Shropshires' attack at 12.45. The few dozen men who were left hurriedly dug themselves in, scrambling for the shallow holes dug by earlier occupants of the hill. William frantically cut turf with his bayonet and scooped out the chalky soil with his bare hands to deepen the hole he found himself in. Then at 6pm a runner arrived with an order to retreat down the hill so that the French could mount a full scale attack on the position. It would mean exposing themselves again to German shelling. William decided he wasn't moving. He couldn't hear the commanding officer's response but thank God he didn't move either.

All evening they faced incoming shells and sniper

rounds, one of which killed Second-Lieutenant Burnet cleanly through the head.

William lay on his back in his shallow trench and stared at the sky. Darkness had been a long time coming. There was a new moon. His sweat had long since dried. It was pleasantly warm. He very carefully eased a chess pawn from his pack that lay beside him, and felt its shape and form with satisfaction. He slowly worked it with his gouge, entirely by touch like Old Armitage. He made tiny scrapes, massaging the wood with his fingertips after each one.

Shortly after midnight the Shropshires were relieved by an advance party of Northumberland Fusiliers. They left the hill in darkness and reached the Brigade trenches, exhausted, just as day broke.

Later that day, William received his first letter from Ada. She said it was early days but she was past her time of the month and in any case she could tell from the way she felt: she was expecting their child.

He was making good progress on his first chess piece. He thought, if he made one piece each week, he would have the set finished just as the child was born. Thirty-two pieces. Eight months. And the child one month along already. Thirty-two weeks and he would be home with his wife and child, because the Americans had surely learned by now how to use their French weapons and would be arriving in huge numbers any day, along with the new tanks his father told him about, with their epicyclic gear steering.

He took care to keep his chisel and his chess pieces close and safe, just as Lady Margaret had kept him close and safe.

He finished eight pawns on schedule. But after the night on Bligny Hill, he found that his hands simply would not fashion a king or a queen, a bishop, a knight or his castle.

THE YOUNG JOURNALIST picked up one of William's pawns, looked at the base of it, and asked him in a thin voice if they were numbered.

He was pleased to see that she was not as tough as she pretended – she was barely hiding the emotion from her voice, fiddling with the pawn to buy time before making eye contact. So he had told the story well. That gave him pleasure too. His grandfather had taken him for a walk on Arnside Knott on the evening of his tenth birthday and they had rambled around for an hour or more until the light was fading before William sat him down on a slab of weathered limestone and began talking about the chess pieces. His ten-year-old self had pictured the ruined Pele Tower to the south as a bombed-out French farmhouse; had reinvented scrub mountain ash, battered by onshore winds, as mortar-shelled stumps of oak in no-man's land; had imagined the limestone screes with their struggling tufts of marjoram and thyme as endless vistas of bomb-puddled clay where red poppies volunteered and flourished.

"No," he said. "I'm pretty sure he didn't number them."

"This is the most irregular. The least symmetrical, I mean. Do you think it was the first one he made? The one on Bligny Hill?"

"Perhaps."

"Do you think it saved his life, as he cowered down in his little hole? Not by deflecting a bullet, obviously. I mean psychologically?"

He felt touched: the way she had been drawn into his storytelling.

"I wasn't there to interview him. And I was barely ten

years old. In fact, I don't recall asking any questions. It was the only time my grandfather talked to me about the war, and he only did so obliquely. He talked of his chess games with Ada; making the rocking chair; being given the chisel; and finding the piece of wood. I hung on every word, and never thought of asking for more."

"So you invented the charge up the hill and the hand-to-hand fighting? The British guns that shelled their own men?"

"No, I didn't need to. Bligny was a key position, the highest in the area. A French General watched the whole thing through binoculars and described the action in his commendation. He awarded the Croix de Guerre to the entire battalion, though to my knowledge William never wore the colours. And there are other accounts. I read the details in the regimental museum in Shrewsbury."

Emily opened her laptop and Stephen was dismayed to think of her checking up on Bligny and the 4th Battalion. Then his doorbell rang and she shot to her feet.

"I'd better get it," she said. And then casually, "Just in case."

He glanced equally casually at her screen. It listed half a dozen emails, all recent and unread. From Gerald; from Roberto; three in a row from Ade; Gerald again. All with the same domain name – presumably her paper's. The subject line was straining with imperatives, each one referring to himself: *re s.o. answer your phone... you still with subject?... where the hell?... stephen o going ballistic! —call in now!*

He heard her calmly explaining to someone at his front door that if he didn't go away she would have him evicted for trespassing.

Looking out of his bay window, he saw a van in the livery of the local radio station. A man carrying a recorder over his shoulder emerged from the outer door of the flats, sauntered towards the van, and conferred with a man in the driver's seat.

"Don't mind if they see you," Emily said, returning to her laptop. "A visual will sharpen their appetite nicely. But no talking."

He couldn't remember the last time his visual had sharpened someone's appetite.

A few minutes later a larger van with multiple antennae on the roof pulled up alongside the radio car.

"Rover G Cripes!" Emily articulated slowly, staring at her screen. "There's two hundred and thirty seven comments under my teaser online!"

"There seems to be a camera crew down there now."

She came to look, and then pulled him back from the window. "They're more aggressive. I'll give them a quick reminder of the law. Once they know I'm here and that you're not talking... at least they should stay outside the building."

As soon as she left, he started reading the comments under her online introduction to the Stephen Oakley story.

Wogus Bogus wrote, *Wow! Your granddaddy plans something as careful as that, you bet he made a secret investment. Wonder how much ten grand would be worth now, with compound interest over fifty years?*

Cyn#6789 started with a quote from the article: *'There's something a little touched about my subject.' Dead right there is, darling. He's been rummaging around his odd-sock drawer and come up with a few old knick-knacks he can hang a story on to claim his fifteen minutes of fame and a few free drinks.*

Sad Math Man wrote, *The amount of money accumulated by compound interest over time is given by the formula* $A = P(1 + r/100)^t$. *A principal sum of £10,000 invested at the 1960 bank rate of 6% over 50 years would therefore become 10,000* $(1 + 6/100)^{50}$ *which by my calculation works out at a handsome £184,202. Like the man said, 'compound interest is the eighth wonder of the world.'*

Next, someone who called himself Pound4Pound with a profile picture of Harold Wilson in his Gannex raincoat smoking a pipe, wrote: *Get real. The interest rate set by the Council of Building Societies Association for personal deposits in August 1960 was 3.25% and inflation has averaged 4% over time. So ten grand invested in 1960 would actually be worth £7,783 now. Maybe the guy should hang on to his Sally Army furniture from the 70's.*

"And *I'm* the one you described as *a little touched*," he said when she came back from talking to the TV crew.

She grabbed her laptop but he could see her quickly reject the idea of lecturing him for invading her privacy. "You've heard of the silly season, I presume? We're well and truly in the middle of it. And there's not much competition at the moment."

"*Victor Meldrew found in space*," he said. He'd seen it on a newsstand once and actually bought the paper.

"It's all rape, murder, and celebrity voyeurism. You're going to be the antidote to all that."

"When a single lottery ticket can win ten million?"

"That's chance: a machine choosing at random. This is human. It's about a grandad's love for his grandson and what he's done for him."

"You set all this up, didn't you? Hinting at a secret inheritance?"

"I certainly did not. I want your story to fly, yes. But with just you and me in the cockpit."

She read from her phone. "They're tweeting too:

Modest flats end of cul-de-sac North Kingston, edge of Richmond Park. How hard to find?

"When you rang you asked if you could just pop round for a chat. You never said anything about flying."

"Yes, well things have moved on. I think you should throw a few clothes in a suitcase and come with me before it's too late."

"I'm not sure I do that kind of thing anymore. Anyway, I wouldn't give them too much credit, if I were you." He nodded at her laptop. "You'd think my grandfather was a Rothschild from the fantasies on there."

Emily switched from phone to laptop, and scrolled down. "I want to learn all about sad Grandfather William and the wife he barely knew," she said.

"There were other sadness's in William's life; others he barely knew who touched him deeply. But I can assure you there is no secret ten grand to learn about. He didn't even own a roof over his head."

"Too bad. One of these guys says forget about compound interest – the average house price in 1960 was two-and-a-half-thousand pounds and today is £167,000. If William had bought four houses..."

"With his fantastical ten grand..."

"You'd be in line to inherit well over half a million."

"And who would have been collecting the rents meanwhile? Not to mention fixing the holes in the roofs, putting in central heating and re-styling the kitchens and bathrooms every ten years for the last half century?"

She beckoned him towards the window and held him half behind the curtain so neither of them could be seen from below. There was a man on a moped and two teenagers with bikes, talking to the two from the media.

"With a smartphone everyone lives just round the corner," she said. "I want to feed the world this lovely story decade by decade, day by day until your birthday and if we don't leave soon we're going to be trapped in here sending out for pizzas, and I'll have to sleep on something the Salvation Army passed on before glam rock was invented." Another car pulled up as she spoke. "We should get away quickly while they're setting up their tripods and telescopic lenses and lose them in the traffic on the way to my place, where there's a spare room with a comfortable bed."

When the promise of comfort didn't work she tried the opposite: "Come on, where's your spirit of adventure?"

He could go down right now and tell the handful of people on his doorstep the plain truth. He could hold up his grandfather's simple gifts for the camera. He supposed it might make a thirty-second quirky end-piece on the local news. Then they would all go away. But she would go away too.

Then she played her trump card: "I'm sure the paper will pick up your expenses. Think of it as a week's paid vacation."

He paused for thought. "You said you came on the tube."

"So I did."

"So how would we lose them in traffic? I sold my last car the same time as I acquired my furniture."

Emily contemplated the sunken armchair and what it would be like sleeping in it. Then the state of his kitchen, as he ushered her through.

He pointed from the kitchen window to the high wall surrounding Richmond Park. "You see the oak with a big limb reaching over the garden of the house with the conservatory? A pair of teenaged lads have a rope ladder tied to it. They hook it down with a clothes prop. I've seen them do it. Must save them twenty minutes going round via the Kingston Gate." He could see her imagining the manoeuvre necessary once the limb was reached, and the height of the drop on the other side of the wall, and resisted the temptation to repeat her line about the spirit of adventure. "I reckon if we can manage that together we can probably survive six days in each other's company."

"I need twenty minutes to file the story of your first present. They want to start a special blog today."

"My story? Or your story?"

"It's about trust, remember. And teamwork. And it's William's story too, of course – the sacrificial lamb sent off to the trenches as payment for keeping his brothers safe at home."

While she wrote, he unburied his old rucksack, rummaged around to find some clean socks and underwear and a half-way decent shirt, and then looked for the other four presents from William. By the time they were both ready, the crowd outside had grown larger. They hurried downstairs and he knocked on the door of flat number one.

"Hey man? What's going down? Someone having a party? Someone died or something?"

"I live in flat 16 on the top floor and I need to get away from those hacks outside. They want to fill the airwaves with some bull about me and my non-existent millions. So the deal is, we climb out your kitchen window and you give us fifteen minutes to get clear by being a media star, right? You tell them what a nice guy I am and how we have a drink together every now and then and a good laugh, okay?"

"Sure, sure, I can do that." The man let them in, and they brushed past, heading straight for the kitchen. The place was messy, but smart under the surface. Plush carpet. Space-age kitchen with shiny hygienic surfaces, built-in dishwasher, microwave and a dozen other gadgets on the walls. Stephen pulled a chair up to the window and went out first, the drop to the ground causing a stabbing pain in his left hip, with its touch of arthritis. Emily passed his rucksack out, then her shoulder bag, into which for some reason she had stuffed her shoes. There was gravel beneath the window and he held his arms out to take her weight as she came, but instead she turned round on the sill and used her own arms to lower herself gently to the ground.

"Hey mate, what's your name?"

He answered truthfully, and received both thumbs up and an exaggerated wink.

They hurried round the side of the adjacent house and knocked urgently on the back door. Emily peered in the kitchen window and declared nobody home. He grabbed the wooden pole which held up an empty clothesline and hurried to the end of the garden. He tucked the straps of his rucksack into the notch at the top of the pole, raised it over the wall, and dropped it into the park. When he motioned to Emily for her shoulder bag she looked at him with horror and instead used one strap to tie the bag shut and the other to hang it round her neck, leaving her arms free.

The bottom rung of the rope ladder was hooked over a large nail in the base of the limb back towards the trunk and when he knocked it free with the pole the wooden rungs came at them viciously. Emily fended them off with both hands then insisted that Stephen lead the way: he was the one who'd seen how it was done.

A few minutes later he had made no progress at all. He was swinging wildly only a few feet from the ground, his body almost horizontal and his arms like jelly. Emily looked over her shoulder, expecting to see the cameras that would reduce her heart-warming story to farce. She swapped places.

On the third rung she tried holding the rope between the rungs instead of the rungs themselves, and found the ladder shifted less. "It's counter intuitive," she said, "but it's easier if you hold the rope sides." She moved up rapidly, then paused for breath, her body automatically inclining to the horizontal. "My arms feel like they're done for." She used what strength she had left in them to pull into the ladder, and wrapped her elbows round the rope above the next rung. "That's better. You can rest your arms like this." And then she climbed again. "I think the trick is to push yourself up with your legs, not pull yourself up with your arms. And try to keep your arms bent, and the ladder close to your chest."

He was impressed. "You've done this before, haven't you?" Her head was already level with the top of the ladder. "When they reach the branch, the boys stand up on it and just walk towards the trunk," he said.

Once her feet were on the tree, he tried again. He paused after each rung, tucking his elbows round the rope. And slowly but surely he made it to the limb, where she waited for him.

"No," she said with a tremble in her voice. "I haven't done this before, or anything like it. I don't like heights." And he remembered again what it was like to feel part of a team.

"I'll go first," he said. "And I'll find something to hold on to all the way. You follow me, and if you need to look down at your feet, don't look beyond them. Think of the branch as the floor."

They made swift progress, and soon reached the trunk. The oak was low-branching and though the trunk was well inside the park, the ground rose steeply on that side of the wall and they only had a drop of five feet back to earth. He collected his rucksack and they hurried away from the wall without looking back.

When they reached Queen's Road, Emily pulled a pocket A to Z from her shoulder bag. "We can walk to Richmond Station and catch a train direct to Willesden Junction."

"Or we can hitch. Should be a doddle catching a ride from here to Richmond with a pretty young woman like you on the team."

Emily stared him down.

"Okay, I know hitching is a bit nineteen seventies. But give it a try for a couple of minutes while I get my breath. When someone pulls up, just tell them you've got your dad along with you." He stepped away from the road and turned his back to the oncoming traffic.

Within half a minute they had a ride.

"Richmond Station?" Emily said through the passenger window. And then, as she slipped onto the passenger seat, "I've got my grandad along with me."

He climbed in the back. He sat in silence as the two up front made small talk and felt suddenly a deep sadness for all that was missing in his life.

DAY TWO

HAVING AN OVERNIGHT GUEST was a novel experience for Emily.

Her house was clean and tidy, if not obsessively so. She always had fresh bed linen and towels in the airing cupboard because she liked to change them often, on impulse. And there was usually food in her kitchen because although she kept her body trim, she mostly cooked for herself and liked to eat well. So she could offer hospitality with confidence. But she lived in a detached bungalow; isolated from the world outside, intimate within. She heard Stephen's every toss and turn. She heard his snoring. She heard him get up to use the toilet and registered that he hadn't flushed. Was that the routine of a crummy old man? Or a responsible water conservationist? Perhaps, even, of a thoughtful gent concerned not to wake her?

She pondered the options while giving him time to fall back asleep. Then she got up, dressed in shorts and T-shirt, hurried through her routine of stretches, and tip-toed past his door into the box room where she kept her treadmill.

When she started running, she forgot about the noise

problem. There was too much to remember and her head struggled to keep up. She blamed the wine he had poured before, with, and after the linguine arrabbiata she had made when she had finally got him back to Willesden. He'd followed her like an old dog from one room to another, bottle in hand; fiddled with her place settings on the dining table; leaned against the fridge in the kitchen watching her work; topped up her glass every time she took a sip. He'd asked what kind of peppers was she using and then told her all about Naga Bhut Jolokia, the strongest pepper in the world. She liked radicchio in her salad? He told her how in Italy they feed it to livestock because it kills internal parasites. She pounded the tread. He'd poured forth an endless stream of anecdotes and had an opinion about everything, but it was difficult putting them together to make anything like a picture. Her pulse rose as she picked up speed. The complete irrelevance of Helmand Province. How the French managed to lose the battle of Agincourt by a hundred to one. If she challenged, he simply dropped it. Open her laptop to check he wasn't spinning a yarn and he reminded her no media – that was the deal. Clever. She started to sweat. Okay, but just for the evening, that was what she'd agreed, and he said evenings plural. And she'd fudged that too because she knew she mustn't come on too intense and frighten him away. She watched a fat pigeon belly-flop on her single blueberry plant in the pot by the back door and leaned forward to bang on the window. He was actually surprisingly good company. But he steered away from himself whenever she probed. She wondered if it had been a mistake to take him away from his flat, with all the prompts it contained. She should have thought it through. Running in the box room, ideas came on their own. No distractions except the pigeon raiding her blueberries. Just her feet pounding on the tread and her brain doing its own thing, like one of those little machines they use for measuring wind-speed – whizzing round and round filled with whatever came at her. It worked a treat once she got going. Like right now... yes... this could be her strategy: it could work just the same for the two of them... they would run together... Run away!... She would hire a car and take him north to where he came from, rich with prompts, and let whatever happens, whatever he responds to, get him whizzing. She slowed the machine and stepped off with a clear head, resolved to put her plan into action.

She grabbed her laptop on the way to the shower and added her postal address to her Linkedin page.

She noticed as she passed the loo that he'd lowered the seat at least. She flushed it. The plumbing made a racket, but there was still no sign of him when she came out. She ground coffee beans, filled the cafetière, and toasted a bagel to try and draw him to the kitchen. She supposed bacon would have done the trick, but it wasn't an option. Nor was taking him breakfast in bed.

Eventually he knocked on the kitchen door.

"Can I come in?"

"Course you can." She closed her laptop. "Have some breakfast. I thought you'd never wake up."

"I've been awake a while, actually. Noisy place. I thought you might have a boyfriend who works unsociable hours."

She didn't know what to make of that. Then she couldn't stop herself from blushing. "I work out on my running machine first thing every morning."

He pulled up a chair and poured himself coffee. "Course you do."

"It's where I do my best thinking. But it has a bit of a thump to it."

"Same as my thinking."

"And makes me pant."

"You don't find it easy to let things go, do you?"

"There is no significant other in my life." And then because she thought it came out sounding sad, she added quickly, "At the moment. And I'm pleased to be able to inform you that they've found a hotter pepper than yours. It's called the Trinidad Moruga Scorpion and it's eight hundred times hotter than tabasco sauce, as against only four hundred times for yours."

"You snore, too, did you know that?"

"Nonsense. And if I did, I don't think it would be very polite for you to make a point of it."

Stephen helped himself to a bagel.

"Especially given how much *you* were snoring."

"It's not my fault if you live in a nineteen-thirties bungalow with paper-thin walls. It's the kind of place you expect to find an elderly female relative living on her own. Reminds me of my auntie's place in Ormskirk."

"It was my grandmother's house."

"Well there you go."

"But she didn't live on her own. Tell me about your auntie in Ormskirk."

"Certainly not. You said this was going to be like a vacation, not a week-long interview. I haven't even had breakfast yet."

She offered him butter, cream cheese, and honey, and watched in amazement as he spread all three on his bagel. Then he waved it in her direction.

"Contrary to received wisdom, the bagel was not made in the shape of a stirrup to celebrate King Jan Sobieski's victory over the Turks at the Battle of Vienna."

"That's got to be in the running for the most useless piece of information I've ever heard."

He held the thing that was nothing to do with a Polish king's stirrup in mid-air and looked hurt. She couldn't help smiling at him.

"Sorry. Someone once told me I do that when I'm nervous: barrage them with useless information."

"Why would you be nervous?"

"I don't know, but you have that effect on me. Despite the charming smile."

Someone had once told her that she smiled when she was nervous. But instead of sharing that with him, she smiled again and that set the bagel moving towards his mouth.

Not wanting to watch him eat, she waved a remote control at the wall. "Do you mind? The local news will be on in a minute."

Images of clouds moving across a crude map of south-east England appeared on the screen she had mounted herself, cleverly she thought, between two of her grand-mother's larger pastoral canvases. A voice explained the effects of a deep low out in the Atlantic.

A teenage girl missing for three days was urged to phone home. Her family and friends were patrolling the neighbourhood wearing tee shirts that had been printed with her photograph – she looked drunk outside a bar, Emily thought – asking *Have you seen our precious little baby?*

Four lads had gone swimming in a notorious clay pit, long surrounded by barbed wire and danger signs, and only three had come back. The council was being blamed for not draining it.

"Plus ça change," she muttered.

"That'll be Jean Baptiste Alphonse Karr. Nothing silly season about *his* journalism though; he edited Le Figaro. Sorry, I'm still doing it aren't I?"

"Here comes our contribution." She pointed her remote at the screen and raised the volume to hear the man on the ground floor in Stephen's block of flats.

"All I can say is that whatever is going down, it couldn't be happening to a nicer guy." He was standing on the doorstep of the building, beaming at the camera. "I mean, me and Stephen go back a long way, let me tell you."

"How long would that be, exactly?"

"Yeah, years and years. Best flatmate a guy could ask for. I mean the stories I could tell you about the size of that man's heart."

"They've edited it heavily," she said. "There's a full ten minutes on YouTube. He goes on about the time you climbed out onto the roof to rescue his cat. And when you paid for the sewage people to empty the sceptic tank and look for his girlfriend's engagement ring when she'd broken with him and flushed it down the loo and then made up again when you'd got them both round your own kitchen table and talked things through."

Stephen looked aghast at the screen on the wall as the camera panned slowly up the wall of the building to the bay window of his living room.

"Generous? To a fault, I'd say. Sometimes me and a few mates would go up to his place on the top floor on a Friday night and the cocktails would come at us like hits in a paintball park. If we went to the pub, you had a fight on your hands to get a round in."

"You also promised to pay for his band to cut an album," she slipped in.

The interviewer asked, "And did you ever talk of his remarkable birthday presents?"

The man from the ground floor hesitated and seemed to be getting his wind back while thinking how to turn another brick wall to his advantage. He put his finger to his lips and winked at the camera. "Ah ha," he said. "But you wouldn't be asking me to break a confidence with a friend as good as that, would you?"

It was a lovely note to end on, and the television duly cut to adverts. She turned it off.

"In fact, he went on to say that his band was playing in some pub on Saturday night and he fully expected Stephen Oakley to be their special guest, when he was certain more would be revealed."

"So there'll be a price to pay for all this?"

She knew there might very well. "Not necessarily of the kind you expect."

"You know my block of flats is on mains drainage? And strictly no pets? Are we all going to be exposed as frauds?"

"I think I'm taking a bigger gamble on that than you are."

"Let me show you my second present from William. You can draw on his unique benevolent fund."

"Please." She wanted to give him a genuine smile because though she was eager to hear the next episode of his story she was worried that he thought she was being too pushy. But she didn't want him to think she was nervous either, so she concentrated on pouring them both another cup of coffee.

He returned from the spare bedroom carrying a little cloth bag. He untied its drawstring and tipped onto the table six large coins. They looked like coins. She imagined they might be guineas, or doubloons, except that they were made of wood and were clearly carved by hand.

ADA OAKLEY TRAIPSED ACROSS THE FIELDS to Drayton one morning towards the end of October. She was blooming with rude good health and enjoying an easy pregnancy but was nagged by a growing fear.

The Oakley yard was quiet and when she banged on the house door the whole place sounded hollow. She sat on the doorstep and pondered what she should do. It was fortunate that though she could think of no option other than returning to Burnet Hall, which filled her with dread, she worried her problem so thoroughly that she was still sitting there an hour later when William's sister-in-law returned from a long ordeal queuing in the cold outside the grocer's, the baker's and the butcher's.

Mary fumbled through her shopping basket looking for her door key, berating Ada all the while for scaring her to death because she looked like she'd frozen to stone she was so still and pale. She hurried her through to the kitchen and pulled a chair up to the range. She riddled the fire, which she'd damped with slack before going out, and soon had enough flame to add more coal. She pulled her father-in-law's tartan rug down from the creel, where it was warming ready for his own cold return later in the day, and wrapped it round Ada's shoulders.

"You've had news?" she asked eventually, her stomach in her feet.

"Lady Margaret says the war will be over soon. Any day now, she says."

"Good. That's good news. It's what they're saying here, too." She filled the kettle and put it on the hob.

"Lady Margaret doesn't like to see me, my father says. She stopped me working in the library soon after Master Herbert... soon after she heard about Master Herbert. So I'm kept at the back, doing laundry mostly. But I see her watching me secretly and it frightens me."

"What do you mean, you see her watching you?"

"I see her in the shadow of the shutters, upstairs in Master Herbert's room, when I'm hanging up washing outside the scullery or fetching milk from the dairy. I don't look up. But I can feel her there staring down at me, with a blank face. Blank or worse."

Ada shivered and Mary knelt beside her, took her hands between her own and rubbed them vigorously. "You mustn't imagine things, Ada."

"It's her does the imagining. She thinks they've made a mistake and when the war is finished, Herbert will come back. I know she does. Only it's William who will come back."

"Yes, he will."

"And I'm scared of what she'll do then. There's no knowing. But I feel how she looks at me. I feel it like a dagger."

Mary stood and pulled Ada against her breast and rocked her gently.

"Aimed at my babby."

Mary said she would light a fire in the attic bedroom which used to be William's. She would look after her. And William would be home soon.

But the process which had begun on the 5th of October when the Germans asked the American President to negotiate terms was stalled for weeks. Neither the Germans nor the English nor the French liked the American 14-point peace plan. Then German sailors mutinied and the revolt spread rapidly.

On the 4th of November the 4th Battalion The King's Shropshire Light Infantry attacked the German rear-guard southeast of a place called Valenciennes and captured the position but suffered heavy casualties. Three days later the Kaiser abdicated and a German delegation crossed the front line in five cars, was escorted for ten hours across the devastation of northern France to the Forest of Compiègne, and sued for peace. Even then, it took days until on the 11th of November an armistice was finally agreed. It was signed at 5am. Soldiers of the 4th Battalion The King's Shropshire Light Infantry, who had advanced a further nine miles to Taisnières-sur-Hon, heard at 9.30 that hostilities would cease in an hour and a half.

Across all armies there were over ten thousand casualties on that last day of the war, of which more than two thousand died. Many artillery units continued to fire on German targets to avoid having to haul away their spare ammunition.

William wrote to Ada at Burnet Hall and her father bore the letter across the fields, his wife two steps behind all the way, to an Oakley yard which looked busier since the return of three sons and their families. They swept past stables occupied again, if with bony, spiritless nags, and into the house where everyone quickly gathered. Frederick Oakley said to go through to the parlour and Mary made tea for everyone. Ada, sitting on a straight-backed chair in the centre, was given a moment to read the letter to herself. Her mother and father stood solemnly on either side and both noticed Frederick top up his cup of tea from a silver hip flask, even though he was a Methodist.

Then she read aloud: *Dear Ada the men all talk about getting a good kip, now the guns are silent, but there's not many of us do, I'm sure. It's an eerie silence, and I imagine all the time I can hear wiz bangs coming over, and shells, landing close, I think it might take a while longer for our ears to settle to the silence. And the NCO's keep us at it, whether it's madness, or necessary, I know not. We've been out from dawn to dusk, saving provisions, making inventries, and carting kit, back to regimental stores, there's whole cities worth of clobber out here in the fields and it seems like we're going to be rescueing as much of it, as we can. None of the men think it will start up again, but an army division is like an ocean liner, thats a fact, no one can stop it on a say so. The other thing is, they're saying the conscripts will be sent home first, then the regular volunteers, so us territtorials, with our obligations, how we'll fit in the scheme of things, I cannot say.*

"His spelling's a touch wayward still," Ada said. "And since I pointed out that he seems not to believe in the usefulness of commas, he scatters them all over the page and they don't all land where they ought. Anyway, then he says how much he misses me but that bit's private."

Her mother snatched the letter from Ada's hand and read the last part to herself. She blushed and thrust the piece of paper back at Ada.

Frederick grunted with satisfaction.

Mary wiped tears from the corners of her eyes.

Frederick's son Albert thought salvage. He could picture it well enough: whole cities worth of clobber out there in the fields. He thought of surplus flat-back army petrol lorries that could carry bricks and tiles and drainage pipes down the lanes of Shropshire just as well as artillery shells in Flanders.

William's battalion marched from one billet to the next, arriving at Villers L'Hopital in the middle of December. They were there until early May the next year, when the battalion finally left for England, eventually arriving at Southampton on the 18th. At the dispersal centre he was given an advance on his final pay, a warrant for a train ticket to Market Drayton, and a demobilisation ration book which he would exchange for an emergency card at his local food office, where it would eventually be changed to a civilian ration book. He developed an immediate fondness for the word 'civilian'. He opted for a suit of plain clothes instead of the clothing allowance of

52 shillings and sixpence which most men chose – he wanted to return home looking like a civilian, not in uniform carrying a steel helmet.

William was discharged into Army Reserve Class Z. It meant he was liable to be recalled in the event of a grave national emergency. But the 4th Battalion the King's Shropshire Light Infantry was disbanded, to be reconstituted as part of a new Territorial Force the following year. So he would not be required to attend regular local drill and annual camp.

When he saw William sidle into the yard and edge towards the house in his cheap, ill-fitting suit, Frederick Oakley knew that his youngest son was wounded for life. He never spoke of it, for that was not his way. But he never turned his back, for that was not his way either.

If he had let Mary write about Ada they might never have got William back at all.

But Frederick's face could not hide what he shrank from saying. He dropped his gaze.

From the deserted hallway, William saw the ashen face and recognised at once the meaning of it. He nodded in the direction of his father who stood with his back to the mantelpiece in the parlour. Frederick returned the nod without stepping forward and William climbed the stairs to his old room.

Mary was rocking gently in the chair as she fed the baby milk from a bottle.

William sat on the edge of the bed and watched her.

Eventually she put the bottle down on the floor, still rocking with the baby fast asleep in the cradle of her arm, and she whispered softly like a lullaby: "Shhhh, now. Shhhh, now. Shhh, now."

"When did she go?"

"In January. It was the Spanish flu, William. Your father

said you'd be home soon and you'd learn for yourself."

"She wrote to me when the baby came. She said we should name him George after the King."

"It just took her so quickly and none of us knew what to do. Billy Fletcher who was at school with our Arthur came back with a leg and a lot more missing, William. Father said if we wrote and told you in a letter we might lose you too."

"But you did write."

"I knew you would want to know about little Georgie. We thought you would come home any day. The Wiggins boys came home. Then Twelfth Night came and went. Then Candlemas, and Albert went off to France and bought his first lorry and I told little Georgie he might bring you back with him. I did want to write about Ada, William. But your father said best not, and it's been such a terrible time."

"It has."

"Do you want to hold him?"

"Best not. He looks settled."

And so Mary, who had run the house, being the oldest female, since her husband Freddie and Freddie's mother had died in the accident that was never mentioned, was confirmed in the role of mother to William's baby son and the better the job she made of it, the easier for William; and the easier for William, the easier for everyone else; so that the family accommodated to the new circumstances almost without words.

In the first spring and early summer after the war there was a great noise of business in the Oakley yard. The newspapers talked about the government wanting to build homes fit for heroes and a few municipal corporations jumped the gun and began clearing their worst back-to-backs. Oakleys was well placed with its fleet of three lorries and for a while it looked more like a haulage business than a builders'. Heaton, Albert and Arthur worked alongside demolition crews, salvaging roof tiles and timber and bringing it back to Drayton, filling every inch of the yard and spilling over to rented space wherever they could find it. They made up loads on the outward journey from the market gardens of Whixall Moss, carting Brussel sprouts, broccoli and savoy cabbages to Merseyside and East Lancashire; then Shropshire carrots and early potatoes to wholesale markets across the north-west.

The family grew louder; Heaton and Albert had three children each and Arthur two already, and their wives were competitive – in the kitchen, in the scullery, in the yard where their children played among the heaped-up salvage from northern slums, with runny noses and scraped knees, making noise that so quickly turned sour as they squabbled over their corner of it, racking up the sound levels until it seemed that no one talked anymore without shouting. Except for Mary, who kept George up in her room with her, a mummy's boy without a mummy, and William, who drifted through it all like a ghost, almost still a boy himself, but with fading hair.

And where was the house-building boom? The Oakleys' capital was spent, just like the country's. They had borrowed heavily and run out of credit, just like the country. As tempers shortened the noise developed a rough edge. The working sons needed to get out of the house – their enormous end terrace on Chester Road with three floors, six bedrooms, and a cellar beneath, with the yard right there with the lavvy at the far end, and piles of brick and heaps of sand, with the wood shop and the three lorries and all the stacks of old timber with rusty nails and roof tiles in different sizes, many of them broken, that bunged up the stables now the horses had gone. They escaped to the pub and the beer gave their noise a violent edge. Albert wanted a bigger share of the haulage money, since it was his idea. Heaton was angry and let him know he wasn't having it. Heaton's wife learned it too, though she said she'd fallen downstairs.

William's capital as a returning soldier was as quickly spent. He rose early, went to bed early, and made little impact on the space in between but even so the wives in particular came to resent him. They started to whisper about the food he ate, when he put nothing in the housekeeping; about his shirts in the wash when he did no laundry; about his mucky old greatcoat on a peg by the front door when he never stood in the yard to keep an eye on the babbies.

Frederick had a quiet word with them: "He's a simple lad, with simple needs."

Years later William would have friends who were also Friends with a capital F, that is to say Quakers, who taught him a song from America that started 'Tis the gift to be simple' and he would sing these words to himself sometimes – not with pride, for he was truly a simple man – but with something like affection for his father.

In the yard they heard only that William was a bit simple, and though his brothers would never repeat it verbatim, the word seeped around the timbers and tiles and lodged in the family's consciousness quietly and aimlessly, rather like William himself.

It was a new joiner called Harry Jackson who befriended William one day and called out to him from the wood shop.

"Why don't you get yourself in here out of the rain?"

Old Armitage had long since gone and William didn't want to.

"Look lively, lad. I'm getting soaked holding the door open."

"I don't..."

"Get yourself in here."

There were three men making roof trusses and William sat out of the way in a corner. Harry poured him a cup of tea from his flask and then left him alone.

After a week, Harry said: "I reckon you know how to sharpen a saw?"

William shook his head.

When the men had gone home, William gripped Harry's saw in a vice and took a file from the rack of tools above the end bench. He worked his way down one side on alternate teeth, taking off just sufficient metal to remove the shine and leaving a constant gullet between each tooth. Then he worked his way back up the other side and finally he made minute adjustments to the bend of two or three points.

By the end of the month, every saw in the shop was in perfect condition. William moved on to the Jack planes and the Bismark planes. Then the chisels. He worked in the evening when the men had left. In the daytime he watched. Harry gave him a penknife, and sometimes he whittled scraps of rough wood aimlessly.

When did he start on his first coins? Who knows, for he almost certainly made them in secret, in a corner of the yard on a fine day perhaps, or in the wood shop after the men had left, by the light of a paraffin lamp. They were crude creations, made from sawn-off sections of half-inch dowels. Harry was puzzled when he first found them. But William had identified a strong new undercurrent in the disquietude of noise and he became increasingly driven by it.

After Sunday dinner, he heard his father and his oldest

brother in the parlour:

"Cut wages by two shillings in the pound and we'll have trouble, Heaton."

"If it's not two shillings now, it'll be four shillings in six months."

"Close the wood shop and we'll be out of house-building. The Oakleys will be jobbing bricklayers again."

"I'm not talking about closing anything. I'm saying wages are being forced down everywhere you look. We don't have any say in the matter."

"We have a say about how we do it, Heaton. There'll be government money for new housing sooner or later, there's got to be. We need to keep the joiners. Sack your navvies. You can get them back from the workhouse whenever you need them. Get your brothers some big repair jobs and turn Albert's pile of scrap back into coin. Cut the joiners by one shilling in the pound and get them work wherever you can find it."

On the Friday, William listened as Harry Jackson explained himself to the joiner they called Fishplate:

"We've got to look out for ourselves because the Oakleys look out for the Oakleys, pure and simple. They'll send a joiner to the workhouse as easy as a ditch-digger when the time comes."

"They'd send you today, if they knew you was in a union."

"It's not a union. It's a Friendly Society. It's called the Independent Order of Foresters because it was started in the Middle Ages by men who worked in the royal forests. You won membership by combat with quarterstaffs. Does that sound like a trade union?"

"It sounds like socialism."

"It's no more than a way ordinary working people like me and you can insure themselves and their families. I pay in thruppence a week. If I'm out of work through no fault of my own, they pay me ten shillings a week for as much as fifteen weeks – 'til I get another job."

"It'll sound like socialism to Mr Oakley I guarantee."

"I'm just saying you can join if you want. I can put your name forward if you want."

Next William heard a group of women wearing wooden clogs and tattered shawls, with silent babies in their arms and gaunt toddlers by their sides pleading with Heaton and then with his father. They were the wives of the men who dug trenches for foundations and sewage pipes, destined now for the Poor Law Institution on Buntingsdale Road. After hearing Heaton their faces were pale and drawn. After Frederick, who closed the door on them, they sat in the dirt and wailed.

William made coins with increased urgency. They bore no royal imprimatur or denomination. The head looked straight at the bearer, and smiled. The tail was a stylised bird, or fruit, or flower. He gave them milled edges if he could find no fluted pegs, as if to guard against clipping by counterfeiters. They were rough-hewn because he was carving into the grain of the wood. He knew they would split and buckle. He called them his honest coins.

Six months later, Oakleys won the best part of a contract to build a small row of new corporation houses in Bunyard. They were to be remarkably well built – all with three bedrooms, parlour, scullery and indoor bathroom; with gas and electricity; and with a sizeable garden to the front and rear. The high rents they would command meant they were to be houses for the skilled working class. Working class heroes like Harry Jackson, who had served at Gallipoli and in Palestine.

But soon after work started, Harry's wages were cut again, by a further two shillings in the pound.

William turned every scrap he could find into honest coinage.

Harry told Fishplate not to throw them out.

"Right you are. We'll be taking them home to feed the fire and keep the babbies warm the way things are going."

"Perhaps they'll buy us joy in the coming cooperative of international fellowship," Harry joked.

Work on the corporation houses was paid for in stages up front, all laid out in a legal contract, and Heaton ploughed the profit straight into three plots on Chetwynd Road, where he was going to build for sale on completion. Arthur thought it was rash. Albert accused Heaton of feathering his own nest. He said they'd be hard put to sell all three, and Heaton was planning on making one of them his own. Money became tighter than ever. Frederick saw that the family would have to spread out, before they came to serious blows. But that needed capital.

This time it was Heaton who said there'd be trouble if they cut the wages again:

"I think we've got an organiser in the wood shop."

"Who? What makes you think it?"

"I'm not sure, father. Fishplate keeps dropping hints. I think it must be Harry Jackson."

"Best get rid of him."

"The last thing we need now is an agitator."

"Though he's a good joiner."

"There's something smug about him. And I don't like the way he is with William."

A few days later Heaton stopped Harry at the door as he was leaving for the day and told him to put down his bag. Harry said he was dog tired and in no state for playing games; it was well past time he was getting home to his family. Heaton pushed him inside, closed the door behind them, turned the key, and put it in his pocket. He strode towards the end bench and the wall where all the tools were kept obsessively sharpened and systematically stored by his youngest brother. A set of chisels was displayed like a row of shiny new dentures, with a gaping hole as if one rotten incisor had been pulled.

"Show me the inside of your bag."

"I'm borrowing it, that's all."

"To lend on to the pawn shop."

"To bring back with me in the morning."

"You're not coming back in the morning."

"I've been borrowing it every night for a week. You can ask your William. I'm making a little doll for my daughter's birthday."

"Then you're seven times a thief. And using Oakley's wood too, no doubt. Give me the chisel."

Harry took it from his bag and put it back in its place in the set. "I got the wood from God's Acre."

"Well it may all be God's in the long term. But right now it's mine, and you're thieving."

"I scavenged the wood from the Churchyard."

"I'll send Mary to you in the morning with wages owing. You can be thankful I'm not pressing charges."

William sat in the corner of the wood shop the next day and heard the timorous mutterings of the two remaining joiners. He listened to Heaton's swaggering account when the Oakley men gathered in the parlour. And when he went up to Mary's room to sit while George slept, she described to him the scene with the missus and nine children in the Jacksons' cottage when she took Harry the three shillings and sixpence he was owed. She was wet-eyed through the telling of it, and at the end she said simply that she had to get away. She was going to take little Georgie away from all this as soon as she could and William could come with her if he wanted but she knew he would always be provided for by the Oakleys and she didn't know how she was going to feed two mouths let alone three.

William quietly selected the finest sheet of lime wood the Oakleys possessed. He asked Fishplate for the cup from his snap flask, placed it upside down on the wood, and drew around it. He cut out the disk with a jig saw, sanded the edge, and with the gouge given him by old Armitage – which he took away with him each night – he began carving a beautiful set of coins. These coins would not split or buckle. He gave both the obverse and the reverse a raised rim, and around the edge – the third side, he called it – he carved the inscription JOY IN FELLOWSHIP.

Somehow word got around, and one by one the Oakleys came to look. Occasionally a child would stay and watch for a while, and people assumed he used them as models for the striking reliefs of children at play which he carved onto the face of each coin. Some of the wives thought it proved he could use a tool and should be working for the firm, but mostly they rolled their eyes. Word had also got around that Mary wanted to move but didn't know what to do about William. They assumed that William was minting his own money to pay his way and shook their heads with forbearance.

But William was making the coins as a gift for Harry Jackson. JOY IN FELLOWSHIP: it was William's benevolent fund. When he had finished, he asked Mary where Harry lived.

He found the house deserted.

"They left quietly in the night without telling the landlord," the woman over the way told him. "On foot. With not much more than the clothes on their backs. And all those young 'uns."

* * *

SHE WATCHED as Stephen toyed with one of the coins, and toyed herself with the notion of telling him what she knew already. "On the back... " she said.

"There's an odd motto: A GREAT PIECE FOR CIVILIZATION."

And the moment was gone.

"He was mimicking the '14-'18 War Medal which said on the back THE GREAT WAR FOR CIVILIZATION. He wrote in the letter that came with them that his spelling wasn't so good in those days. He said he'd meant to carve A GREAT PEACE."

"So the coins never reached Harry. Did he end up in the workhouse?"

"Who knows where Harry ended up. But the coins came to me, a few days after my birthday in 1970. I've lost the letter but I remember William wrote movingly of his friend Harry Jackson. And he wrote of Harry's friendly society – the Independent Order of the Foresters – though at the time I didn't understand all of it, or even very much of it. He wrote about prudence being an admirable quality, but spending being important too. At first I thought he was telling me something about the parable of the talents. He said the giving and taking of coins is one of the most powerful ways we connect with each other, and it calls for kindness and consideration. Money is actually all about cooperation, he said."

"But he never gave them to anyone. At least not in his lifetime. Not even to Mary, who was raising his child."

"He tried hard to give them to Harry. He wrote of days spent trudging the highways asking for him. He walked to Stoke, then Wellington; to Shrewsbury; to Wem and Whitchurch and Nantwich. By the time he'd given up, Mary had left."

"And taken your infant father with her?"

"Yes. North, to Lancaster. The others drifted north too,

eventually. Except for Heaton, who sold two of the houses they built in Chetwynd Road and moved into the third himself. Albert went to Crewe first, where he'd worked during the war, then on to Fleetwood. Arthur moved to Ormskirk. Albert's eldest went to work for Arthur when he fell out with his father, then set up on his own in Bolton le Sands."

"What a shame they all went north."

"What do you mean?"

"I mean grim. Dark satanic mills, pitheads, and all that. Market Drayton to Stoke sounds bad enough. Please don't do that."

"Do what?"

"Put the butter on your knife back in the butter dish."

"Sorry. Would you like me to take it out again?"

She took the dish away and watched him lick the end of his middle finger, dab up crumbs from the eating of his toasted bagel, and transfer them to his mouth.

"Grimy D H Lawrence stories. And The Road to Wigan Pier. The Loneliness of the Long Distance Runner."

"So you read English Lit at Sussex. But we had a middle class up there as well, you know." He rubbed his finger dry on his trousers.

"I'm not sure I've seen the evidence."

"It's true that the Oakleys went north because they believed that's where people made things," he said, missing her reference to his table manners. "The only one to head southeast was my father, who never valued the making of anything. Except money."

She waited patiently but nothing more came. Eventually she said, "Tell me more about your father."

"You tell me more about your grandmother. Are those her paintings?"

"Yes. You like them?"

"They don't look like the work of an elderly lady."

"Not much about my grandmother did."

"Except her house. How long have you been living in it?"

"Almost all my life, as it happens. My parents died in a car crash when I was a baby."

"Ah. An orphan, then. Like me."

"Not quite."

"And your grandmother died...?"

"Just six months ago."

Her door bell hadn't rung for almost that long, and when it did so now it sounded like an alarm. Someone had been quick to spot her address on Linkedin and track her down.

She opened the door on a lanky youth with the unlikely claim to be the writer of an award-winning arts and crafts blog who wanted a few words with the birthday presents man. His moped was by the kerb. When she tried to close the door on him, he put a foot between it and the jamb.

"You can't do that."

"Who's going to stop me? Birthday presents man coming to the rescue?"

"Keep back, Stephen! He just wants your picture. He's breaking the law." She opened the door wide and slammed it harder against his foot.

"So he *is* here." He took a phone from his pocket and threatened her with it. "One call and you'll have a pack of us down here."

She wasn't used to people not following the rules and for a moment was flummoxed. He'd turned up so quickly, and one way or another there would be more soon. Her plan had been to hire a car and have it ready on the doorstep. Then she spotted Peter Tomkins coming out of his house on the opposite side of the road. She repeatedly whacked the door against the foot wedged in it, yelling as she did so, "Get! Out! Get! Out!" She saw Peter rush across as the foot finally withdrew and the door slammed shut.

She turned quickly to Stephen: "Round up your things. Get your backpack."

"Another cliffhanging escape via the kitchen window?"

"Everything all right in there, Emily?"

"Thank you Peter. Yes. I think so. Is he still there?"

"I should say so. I've got him by the collar. Do you want me to teach him a lesson?"

"No! Thank you. Just hang on to him for a second while I think what to do."

She scribbled a note to Peter on the pad she kept by the landline: *Please take Stephen to Merry Kettle. The sec I bring paparazzo in front door leave out the back. Look after him until I get there.*

"That's not strictly correct. Paparazzi chase celebrities."

"It's spot on, Stephen. For the next few days at least. As soon as I'm free, I'll get a car and pick you up."

"To go where?"

Best not to overdramatize. Not 'underground' or 'to a safe house'.

"I don't know. North of Watford. I'm going out to negotiate terms. I'll send Peter in."

"What if I don't want to go?"

But she didn't think he could stop now. He loved his grandfather too much. He wanted to tell her more.

SHE HUMOURED HIM when he argued against the GPS on her phone. It said to turn off the M6 onto the M54, and he said he'd never heard of such a road. Playing the aging technophobe. Or more likely, she soon realised, engineeering lunch at the Royal Oak in Eccleshall.

When they had eaten she spent half an hour drafting

the story of William's coins. She read sections aloud in a nook of the bar and was impressed by the way Stephen made constructive comments while avoiding the impression he was giving his approval. He made a good sounding board.

"I like the way you've managed to avoid describing William's – how should we say? – 'special status' in the family without being untruthful."

"But mine isn't the story of William, is it? It's the story of his gifts to you."

"And you describe his coins beautifully. You've given *quantitative easing* a positively spiritual dimension."

"I don't know what our financial gurus will make of it. Look at this." She turned her laptop to face him and scrolled back to the speculation about the best return William could have realised on a £10,000 investment made in 1960.

Equities always outperform cash investments in the long term. The stock market annualises 10% over very long periods. That would turn ten grand into £1.17million in fifty years.

"They've forgotten about inflation already," Stephen said.

Not if it found its way to Laker Airways or Polly Peck, mate. Might as well give it to a one-armed bandit.

"Not to mention Maxwell Communications."

Betcha someone who'd lived through the Wall Street Crash and the Great Depression would go for gold. $35 an ounce in 1960; $1225 an ounce last time I looked. Gold sovereigns under the mattress would have turned that ten grand into £350,000.

She stacked the six wooden coins, which she had spread on the table to inspire her writing, to make a bank teller's neat cylindrical pile.

"You've made a rouleau," Stephen said. "I love dedicated words like that, don't you? Words that have such a specific purpose in life? Did you know that the droppings of otters have their very own word?"

"Feeling nervous again as we approach your old haunts?"

"Will your paparazzi be there waiting for us?

"I think we're a couple of days ahead of them now."

"They're called spraints. The droppings of otters."

"I prefer plain English. How did whoever sent you the coins know where to post them?"

"Anyway, you're the one who should be nervous, leaving me in a tea shop with your 'no-significant-other-at-the-moment' for an hour and a half. He was a talkative chappie."

She smiled despite herself. She'd pictured them having a cup of tea and a bacon butty. Fifteen minutes max. "Peter is a neighbour. Or more accurately, his parents, with whom he still lives, are neighbours. I haven't spoken to him for months."

"He as good as called you his old flame."

"We went to school together. I was not a party girl."

"I can buy that. And I can answer your question. Mary knew where I was because I used to write to her, believe it or not. Not to my father. Or to my mother. But I used to send trite little formal letters, fortnightly, to Aunt Mary ever since prep school, where we had to produce them under supervision: 'Yesterday I had a lovely walk across the common, stopping to watch the ducklings on the pond. I have finished the Dickens you gave me at Christmas and found it a very good read. I hope you are keeping well.' I kept it up through university and for a month or two after I dropped out, until the haze got too thick, or she died or something. I really can't remember."

"What did you read at university?"

"Not Dickens, that's for sure. Mostly I wrote poetry – terrible poetry, full of fake existential angst – and lyrics for friends who'd learned three chords on their guitars and wanted to woo the ladies. I dropped out after one term and went to San Francisco with the vague idea I might meet Allen Ginsberg."

"What else did he talk about? Peter?"

"He said you were frightfully clever. Actually I think clever and a bit frightening was the way he put it."

"Peter is unreliable if you must know. Unreliable and a little bit creepy."

"Yes, he said as much himself. Waiting to be rescued, I'd say."

"So did you ever go back to get a degree?"

"No, but that didn't alter the impression I made on the Oakleys. I told them I'd matriculated and that was good enough for them. For ages they called me *Prof.* Not with respect, but with jokey affection. Whereas with Aunt Mary they'd been unpleasant. When she walked out of the big house in Drayton the Oakleys' books got in a mess that no one else could sort properly. She was hired to teach primary school when my father was old enough and when she adapted to the role by lengthening her vowel sounds the Oakleys called her *Miss Priss.*"

Emily slid her rouleau off the edge of the table, into the bag. Then she paid the bill. She was eager to get a look at one of these Oakleys.

Just before they dropped down into Loggerheads, with the Cheshire plain before them, it started raining. "This is why it's grim up north," he said. "It's always bloody raining."

It took her a while to find the switch for the wiper, which performed meanly.

"Though we're not up north proper yet," Stephen said. "More the heart of England I'd say. There's a point close to here where rain can either flow east into the North Sea, south into the Bristol Channel, or northwest into the Irish Sea."

"And now you're going to tell me the word for it."

"I don't think there is one. But we could make it up. William used to play that game where you invent collective nouns: a herd of cows, a gaggle of geese..."

"An exaltation of larks."

"You know it. What would it be for coins, he'd say, or journalists, or windshield wipers?"

"I don't see him playing word games, somehow."

"You will once I've shown you what he sent me on my thirtieth. I think for his generation the notion of never-ending, meaningless warfare lodged so deeply in the consciousness of people with intelligence and feeling, they *had* to invent The Charleston and flap around setting up a League of Nations, and create fantastical notions like William's benevolent fund."

For a horrible moment she thought Stephen might have invented William as an allegorical figure. "What are you saying – in plain English?"

"It doesn't matter because once the Oakleys had labelled William a bit simple, a bit simple is all they saw: a grown man playing silly word games."

BY THE TIME THEY REACHED DRAYTON, she was desperate to stretch her legs. She suggested a walk, even though it was still drizzling. He said they could park by the old Oakley yard and walk through the new estate to the three houses Heaton built in the twenties. One of Heaton's grandsons still lived there last he knew. One of his solicitude of second cousins.

"I mean a real walk. Do you ever walk far enough and fast enough to raise your pulse?"

"We're not in the Lake District yet. This is north Shropshire. The land of muddy fields and cows."

"You need to start doing some regular exercise. At least you don't smoke. I don't think I could have done this if you smoked."

Where did that come from? He looked so taken aback she had to tell him not to worry. She said she tended to put on her earnest side when she was working but she was surprisingly playful underneath and knew how to have fun. And she instantly regretted that too. She could feel him plotting how to put her to the test.

She followed his directions to Berrisford Road and parked beneath the aqueduct that carried the Shropshire Union Canal. She sprinted up the sandstone steps and waited for him on the tow path.

"Did you count them?" he asked, out of breath, as they set off towards the locks at Tyrley. She jogged carefully down and up again.

"Thirty-nine."

"The start of my love of reading. I'd forgotten. When you don't have children you don't reinforce the key experiences that brought pure joy to your life. I mean things like making dens, inventing secret writing codes, hoarding food for a midnight feast. William did all those things with me."

"And the thirty-nine steps?"

"He set me a treasure hunt that brought me here. He made clues with a puzzle. He'd give me a map and say *I'm at 654321 – or* whatever the reference is for the aqueduct – *and people call me forty steps. But you know better. Take 1 away from me and divide by 19 to get the first of your clue and an incentive to read John Buchan.* So that would give me a 2, see. Then he'd send me to the churchyard to get a number from a certain tombstone, or to a phone box where I'd have to add up the digits in its number and take the square root. When I'd worked out my six figures I'd find the treasure."

"I've never read The Thirty-Nine Steps."

"Best left to ten-year-old boys. The delicious bit where she has to take off her wet nylons while he's handcuffed to her isn't in the book. Hitchcock realised sex was entirely missing and added all the best bits himself. Buchan met him after the film, and told him he'd improved it no end."

It had stopped drizzling by the time they reached the bottom lock, which was closed and full of water. A narrow boat arrived just behind them and Stephen asked the man at the tiller how long it would take to get through.

"A good forty-five minutes start to finish if there's no one coming down but my wife looks lively on the gates."

"I'll buy you both an ice cream from the shop at the top if my young friend here can't knock five minutes off that."

It hadn't taken him long to call her bluff on playfulness. She looked at the stack of locks in dismay.

"You're on." The man at the back of the boat thrust a heavy iron bar into her hand.

They didn't have locks on the bit of canal behind the zoo in Regents Park. She hadn't a clue where to start.

"Slide the socket on the end of that key onto the end of the axle on the winding gear by the side of the gate there, and crank like hell," Stephen said, in a rush so eager to win his bet she didn't have the nerve to say no.

"Now the other side."

She shuffled along the narrow ledge that ran across the top of the gate.

"You'll have to move faster."

She had the other paddle up in seconds and water

gushed out of the lock chamber.

"Lucky for you, the paddles are down on the top gate. Get ready to push on the balance beam to open the gate."

She pushed. Then saved her energy. Then pushed again. It wouldn't move an inch until the water levels were even on both sides.

"Now the other gate!"

She looked across the half-open entrance to the lock. Was she supposed to leap?

"Run round the lock and cross over the top gates. Move!"

She ran, then pushed the second balance beam. The narrow boat moved swiftly and smoothly into the open chamber. The pilot wasn't going to give her an excuse for losing.

"Now close both sides of the gate and lower the paddles with your iron."

One closed, paddle down. Run round. Close the other. Paddle down.

"Top gate, now. Quick! You know what to do."

She heard the woman on the boat say she'd never do it. Paddle up. Paddle up. Water filling the chamber. Boat rising. Push the gate when the levels are even. It was simple enough – she just had to follow the logic. The boat pulling back a few feet. One gate open. Run down to the bottom, cross over, open the other side. She was out of breath. The boat pulling out. Close the gate. Wind down the paddle. Her arm aching. Round again. Don't fall off. Third lock. Fourth lock. Don't get cocky and miss a step. Adrenaline making her smile. Nerves or fun? They're all egging her on now. Even the wife. Especially the wife. Gate closed. Paddle down. Over to the other side. Then dash to the top. Level water beyond for as far as she could see. Raise the last two. Water filling the final lock and lifting the boat. The wife on the tow path reaching to take back the key and when she gives it she nearly loses her balance and topples precariously at the edge of the water, out of breath. Congratulations bellowed from the boat. Applause from Stephen. Loud cheers from a group of lads further along the towpath who haven't a clue what's going on.

She punched Stephen's shoulder and then – adrenaline still flowing – wondered if she hadn't hurt him.

"Sorry. That was supposed to be playful."

"Fair enough. Pulse raised and all that. You did it with ten seconds to spare."

"I don't believe it. You cheated in my favour."

"Why on earth would I cheat for you?"

The sun came out for their walk back to the car and she found herself happily firing off questions about the canal: when was it built and who by and did they have dynamite to cut through the sandstone and why didn't the water go stagnant? He knew all the answers, or if he didn't, he made something up that sounded convincing. He went on about Cadburys running a pony express to get milk to Bourneville. Years ahead of the US mail, he said.

When they arrived back at forty steps she asked what his treasure was, at the end of the treasure hunt William laid.

"You mean other than being turned on to a great boys' adventure story, even if devoid of sexy scenes with nylon stockings? I'm not sure I can remember. The fun wasn't about the prize, any more than the fun you had at the locks was about avoiding buying ice cream for two holiday-makers."

"I'd like to bet you remember very well."

"The clues gave me a six-figure map reference and that took me to a village north of town called Adderley. I peddled out there on my bike, to a corner shop where they were expecting me. He'd called in and pre-paid for my treasure. An ice cream, as it happens."

They drove back into town and pulled alongside a silver Mercedes in the driveway of the house that Heaton built on Chetwynd Road in the nineteen twenties. She was introduced to an ancient Fred, grandson of Heaton; to Charles, son of Fred, and Charles' wife Julie; and to two of their sons whose names she didn't catch but one of whom was a dealer in second hand cars, hence the Mercedes. The other sold used furniture from the same premises, and she gathered that it was many years since an Oakley laid brick in Drayton. Charles would be offended if they checked into a hotel and Julie wouldn't have them eating in a pub, and neither of them would hear of them helping in the kitchen or making up beds. They found themselves thrust outside again with instructions to get some more fresh air and come back in an hour with a good appetite.

They walked round to the old Oakley house on Chester Road, where the first Frederick had spawned the family and the business. The yard had long disappeared. There were three bungalows on it now, tidy and quiet behind wrought-iron gates and privet hedge. The old house had a for-sale sign in its small front garden. Dandelion and dock had gone to seed around a lacework of buttercup and crazy paving, trapping the odd beer can and plastic take-away tray.

"Empty for a while, by the look of things."

They gazed through the parlour window side by side, cupping their hands round their faces to block out the strong evening light and give them sight inside.

"This is where the males gathered and nattered about the state of trade for hours on end," Stephen said. "When William was a boy and when William was nearly sixty, the same. He would sit in the corner and not say much. I'd sit on the floor next to his chair, all ears. Strange how fascinated I was, when you think about it. I'd soak up gossip about rival firms and moans about the price of labour; boasts about some dodge that meant so and so used pine and got paid for oak; fond stories of Frederick in the old days boasting about when he took the train first class to London and was measured for a suit by a proper tailor in Savile Row, Heaton having afternoon tea at a Lyons Corner House, Howard going to see the Windmill girls on his honeymoon. They were great talkers, the Oakleys, even if most of it was swanking about themselves and their business and what it bought: Isaac buying a caravan, Douglas a sailboat, Jim a timeshare in the Algarve. Not a lot of culture in there, unless by way of snide comments about people who put on educated airs – though they never said "like Aunt Mary" if William was in the room. I was hearing all the family lore going round and round, the Oakleys' accumulated oral history, one generation's memories talked into the next, and I grew up absorbing it like an orphan's birthright."

Stephen was absorbed in his recollection but she saw that they had both stepped back a pace from the window, which now acted like a dirty black mirror. She saw the two of them side by side in reflection and noticed that she was leaning in towards him as he lectured her about the family. He was looking at all those old, male faces, she supposed. She felt drawn to put her arm around him, though she resisted easily. She wondered if he would even have noticed.

She imagined simple William Oakley putting his arm round his clever grandson and it came to her in a flash: "What if he set you the granddaddy of treasure hunts?"

"What?" Stephen swept his hair over his ears with his

fingertips, one side first and then the other.

"William liked to set treasure hunts, you said. And when he knew he was going to die he set one for you that would last a lifetime."

"Nonsense."

"Each present comes with a story, its fragment of John Buchan. But they're telling you much more than that. They're giving you clues."

"Nonsense," he said definitively.

"They're leading somewhere. It's obvious."

"Nonsense," he felt obliged to say for the third time.

DAY THREE

SHE WAS RIGHT, it was just the kind of thing William would have loved to set up.

The thought had not kept him awake; he had slept well, despite two stumbles to the loo and back down a corridor he remembered from his youth as dangerous. The house was built like a Victorian castle. It absorbed every sound but had odd steps up and down in unexpected places. He woke to a deeply comforting smell of bacon which nevertheless soon triggered alarm.

Emily wouldn't eat bacon. Emily, who was driving him northwards, prompting him, goading him, milking him to feed her silly-season journalism.

Emily would write up her treasure hunt nonsense on her blog.

"Where's Emily?"

Julie didn't turn from the Aga. "Emily strikes me as a very nice young woman, Stephen. I do hope you're not... complicating things for her."

"Rather the reverse, I think. Where is she?"

"She's run off somewhere."

"That will be for her cardio-vascular health and clarity of thinking. Her early morning routine. She'll come back."

"The boys will be back too, any minute."

"I don't think she'll do justice to a proper breakfast."

"I saw her picking at her plate last night. Is she a vegetarian? I've done fried tomatoes, fried mushrooms, fried eggs, fried bread."

"I think so. But I suspect it's not as simple as that. She's... singular."

"You mean like one slimming biscuit?"

"No, she's far too sensible for that. I'll go and look out for her. When I'm back I'll eat for both of us."

He leaned against the substantial brick gatepost until she came round the corner, cheerfully pulse-raised and asking if there was time for a shower before breakfast.

"If you're quick. The men will be back soon. The Oakleys always work for a couple of hours before breakfast."

"Just like the nineteenth century. I love these enormous meals with loads of family round a big table, all talking a mile a minute. Last night was fabulous, and they only called that *tea*."

"I don't want you stirring up this treasure hunt idea."

"It was the Shropshire equivalent of one of those big feasts they have in Tuscany or Provence that go on for ages, like you see in the movies."

"For one thing, William wouldn't like it."

"It's too late. Sorry."

The Aga provided plentiful hot water and Charles had never seen the point of showers. Emily said she thought that was quaint; the idea of starting the day with a deep hot bath sounded heavenly.

It was an odd thing to say, he thought, given that since rising for the day she had already run a fair chunk of a marathon and started a new discussion thread in her drip-drip account of his birthday presents. He was mopping up the juices from his breakfast plate with a piece of toast when he thought to ask if they had Wi-Fi.

"Bit of a sore point," Pete said.

"Charles won't allow it, out of respect for his father," Julie said.

"I won't have it, out of common decency," Charles said.

"That's rich. It was you who started the calendars. When me and Tom were still in short trousers."

"My calendars were tasteful."

"Grandad's ninety-two. A bit of sauciness might be just what he needs."

"What the elderly need is respect. Not wrap-around pornography."

"Language!"

When the Oakley hubbub finally subsided, he thought he heard the front door click shut. Over his last cup of coffee he learned that generations of Oakley office girls had been compelled to pose topless for the annual calendar or risk losing their jobs; that in homes with Wi-Fi the airwaves were filled with pornographic images that filled your lungs and saturated your brain just as surely as if you downloaded them on a computer; and that Emily had bathed, dressed, and quietly slipped outside.

He found her in the town library, seated at what was now its dominant feature – a large table with multiple stations providing free, high-speed broadband.

"Too late?" he said, in a way intended to express both accusation and disappointment. But his heart wasn't in it and he knew she knew it.

"Too late now, because it's done. Too late before, because my mind was made up. I'm sorry, Stephen; some ideas are just too good to let go. Sorry."

"I'm sorry too, because I can see you're getting carried away by your own imagination and when you finally have to come clean on this blog of yours, this is going to look like an exceptionally silly silly-season. Before I show you the next present I'm going to take you north in the wake of the fabulous Oakleys and show you a few home truths on the way."

He didn't physically take her hand and pull her away from the computers, drag her back to the house on Chetwynd Road, tell her to grab her bag, and cold shoulder her into the passenger seat, daring her to speak. But she responded as if she was being treated like that, and it made him feel better. As he drove north from Drayton, careless of whether or not he was listed as a driver on the car-hire agreement, he turned on Radio Three and she didn't even demur at that.

Bartok accompanied them through Audlem and Wybunbury. They entered Crewe by the Mornflake oats plant and he rattled off the manufacturing record of the town to Sibelius' Karelia suite. Huge locomotive works, Rolls Royce now Bentley, BAE global combat systems. A place where they made things. He stopped briefly on the edge of a new retail park: "This was Albert's yard. His son Jim built a little row of houses over there somewhere. They'd already gone when William showed me the place in the late fifties. They were on a slope and Jim in-filled the foundations with slag the Oakleys were paid to haul away from the steel works at Shelton. It took three years for it to swell up enough to push out the walls but the first complaint about a floorboard buckling was warning enough. When the lawyers caught up with him they found a jobbing bricklayer with nothing in the bank, living in a house owned by his sister Frieda."

They heard an entire Walton symphony as they drove on to Ormskirk. "Aunty Frieda ended up here," he said, pulling alongside a modest nineteen-thirties bungalow clad in grey pebbledash. "William used to stay with her occasionally, and I did once – soon after Uncle Harold died. Harold was a hired labourer who lost an arm in an accident with a faulty hoist in another Oakley yard, and became a serious liability. It was Heaton's idea, as senior Oakley at the time, to buy him off by marrying him to Frieda, whose strong tongue had put off other suitors."

"This is sublime," Emily said softly, unperturbed by any home truths about the Oakleys. They were playing one of the Bach cello suites.

He drove out past the church. "That's the only one in the country with both a tower and a steeple side by side."

She gaped at it. "Unique maybe. Sublime it is not."

"I didn't think you would appreciate Bach."

"Does that mean we're friends again?"

It occurred to him that she may have feigned a fondness for the cello suite to win him over. He felt flattered at the thought. And then ashamed of himself.

His little lecture about manufacturing in Preston as they skirted the town on the motorway was more pleasantly expressed and he made no mention of the Oakleys. Then they were on the lip of the Trough of Bowland, with the grey sweep of the Pennines beyond, and he felt his spirits lift. He pulled off at Forton Service Station and jiggled round the barrier on the service road as he had done many times; drove across Pilling Moss and hustled Emily onto the Knot End ferry which was just leaving, determined to show her some Oakley handicraft at its best.

"This was the first Victorian planned town, created out of the sand by Peter Hesketh-Fleetwood. The Oakleys up here acted as though their wings had been clipped, just like Fleetwood's were when his agent fleeced him. The new wisdom at Oakley gatherings was that subcontractors bled your profit; the work you did yourself was the work you made real money on. And the work the Oakleys liked best was laying brick." He walked Emily up the street William had shown him when he was ten. He explained to her the difference between a Monk bond and an English bond and showed her how the bricks were laid in different patterns for different effects. He found a garden wall built in Sussex bond and a Flemish diagonal bond that incorporated Staffordshire blue bricks to make a diamond pattern. He showed her a strong saw-toothed decoration on a gable end, and contrasted it with a weaker dental course facing it on the next house. "Look at the finish on that chimney stack: see how it stands out from every other one on the street. That's an Oakley chimney. It's in perfect proportion to the height of the house and the pitch of the roof; bold and graceful."

"You sound proud of it. Even the way you're standing – you look like an Oakley chimney."

"I'm pretty sure William never laid a brick in his life, but I think he took pride in showing me these houses. He didn't like the word pride himself. He thought its associations with king and country made it culpable."

"I fancy he might have thought the Oakleys were fairly culpable."

"He said in one of his letters later that he thought virtue in life came from honest work and an appreciation of beauty, and that you can find both in the most unlikely places."

LEAVING KNOT END, he was aware of surrendering the airwaves. She turned down the volume on the radio and tuned into a station playing country and western.

"So tell me about your time in San Francisco. Managing a band and living in twenty or more places not counting all the motels when you were on the road."

"Sort of. I said sort of managing a band."
"What was it like?"
"I wasn't the guy that got the gigs and the record contracts. I was the bloke who finally located Gizzie in the john, buckled up and crying into his vomit, ten minutes after he was due on stage."
"Who was Gizzie?"
"Gizzie was bass player with The Salsifies. But it could have been JoJo or Raz. It could have been anyone from half a dozen bands."
"Why was he crying?"
"I don't know: stage fright, a bad trip, his goldfish had died."
"So how did you get him on stage?"
"God knows. But whatever skills were involved must have been thin on the ground at the time, because people came to rely on me. I probably gave him my shirt, for one thing."
"But they paid you well, right?"
"Not really. More a matter of them letting you join the family, taking you under their wing. I fixed the sound sometimes, too. You'd be amazed how clueless rock musicians were back then."
"You could have made a good career as a sound techie."
"If I'd stuck with it."
"What about girlfriends?"
"I tended not to stick with them either."
"Why not?
He looked across at her in amazement. "For your blog?"
"Course not. Just curious."
"We didn't have girlfriends. We were 'with' someone. Usually briefly, I'm afraid. And I'm not talking Grace Slick."
"Who's she?"

He drove in mock shocked silence for a while. They both knew she would find out for herself soon enough.

"Your mate Peter-who's-only-a-neighbour told me a lovely story about a playground skipping game. We must have been on the third cup of tea by then. I had time to learn the words and join in, though we didn't work out a harmony. Let's see... you were doing the skipping and the girls on each end of the rope sang in unison:

Here comes Emily down the street
Who do you think she's hoping to meet?
First comes love, then comes marriage
Then comes Peter with a baby carriage.

She tried to poke him with her elbow, across the handbrake. "I told you he was a creep. I didn't even know what it meant."

"He told me he bribed them to do it. He spent all his pocket money trying to woo you and the result was you wouldn't speak to him for months."

"And I didn't read English Lit at Sussex," she said, presumably to change the subject. Then perhaps because she sensed he was still picturing her skipping to Peter's lyric, "I was on a four-year liberal arts course at Keele, like at an American college. Majoring in music. Except I dropped out in my second year."

"So we're a pair of drop outs."

"So I guess you were a hippy? Free love and all that?"

"*Hippy* is a much misused term. Ever since at least 1969. And the notion of an *English* hippy is a contradiction in terms."

"I think my grandmother was a bit of a hippy. I dropped out to be with her when we learned she was dying."

He gave this the moment's pause it deserved and then mumbled about there being more selfish reasons to drop out. "So will you go back to finish your degree?"

"So why does Ormskirk Church have a steeple and a tower next to each other?"

She did this mini time-warp thing in conversation, he was learning. It gave the impression her mind had a review mode she never switched off. Ormskirk was miles back. Well she can look that one up for herself too, he thought, though he knew the answer. And so it went, all the way to Lancaster.

"But you were *with* hippies, right?"

And perhaps because he was coming through Aldcliffe and dropping down to White Cross and Penny Street Bridge, where the road crossed the Lancaster canal and he used to play in one of the Oakley yards, he gave a little more of himself to the conversation: "I believe I have often acted selfishly in my life. Especially towards women."

"But you swapped your clean shirt for Gizzie's soaked in vomit, right?"

After the Infirmary, he turned off the main road and pulled up alongside a small paved area by the canal. He said, "You're like a dog, you know that? You don't like to let go, do you? You're like a dog with a bone."

"And you're like a cat. You play with people, play with things that amuse you, like a cat with a mouse. But you never make anything of it, do you? Your flat is full of things that have amused you at some time or other, that you dumped in a corner to turn into skeletons."

Did his memory work like that – as a depository for things that amused him at some time or other, his memories of William dumped in a corner to turn into skeletons? Was it conceivable after all that she might organise them into something more?

And then he reminded himself that when it came to cats and dogs, the dog was the predator.

* * *

THEY CHECKED INTO THE KING'S ARMS and Emily caught up with messages across various media. She knew this annoyed him, so she stayed in the lobby to do it, and sent him up to his room for a rest. On reflection, shoes off and spread-eagled on a double bed, head level with the tea-making kit – tiny plastic pots of UHT milk and twin-packed ginger biscuits – he found this even more annoying. He put his shoes back on, went down to the bar, and ordered a pint of Guinness on her room tab.

"Someone's opened a Facebook group called William's Treasure," Emily said. "And it's got four hundred and fifty members already."

He sat down opposite. Let her interpret what was going on.

"Yes! Of course – why didn't I think of that? There's a post from someone called Cartesia. She says William is giving you a six figure map reference, decade by decade." She was so focussed on her screen she didn't register his expression of dismay. "Each present gives you a digit. Eight pawns. Six coins. Six presents will give you a six figure map reference. So on your sixtieth birthday you'll get your last present, Stephen. Stands to reason they're not going to go on forever.

"No, no, you're so wrong."

"The hunt is on, Stephen. Everyone else gets it – they're buzzing. Boy, there's actually a lot more about geo-caching here than you ever want to know. Not to mention benchmarking, letterboxing, and orienteering. Not a lot on offer in terms of genuine hidden treasure, though. Diving in the Bermuda Triangle and random metal detecting don't count because they're not intentional treasure which is why they're so excited about William. Someone's tweeted about plastic lunch boxes versus old

60mm ammunition boxes. Ammunition boxes appear to be the gold standard for geocachers. If William buried his treasure he was sure to have used an am-munition box, they say. That makes it eminently detect-able from the surface."

"Can I get you a drink?"

She nodded, eyes flitting furiously across her screen.

He brought her a large glass of Shiraz. Then he loosened the drawstring on a cloth pouch and tipped onto the table a heap of small square tiles made of wood.

"And this is why they're all wrong, Emily. Not coins this time, though each is carefully hand carved. But as you will see, there are twenty-three of them. Twenty and three. So no convenient map-reference digit from my third present from William, I'm afraid." He felt quite as pleased as a cat dropping a dead bird at the feet his mistress.

She picked up one of the tiles. It was about an inch square. A hard but light-coloured wood with a fine grain. Plain on one side. A bold letter E carved in relief on the other. She spread the pile flat and turned over some of the tiles. They all bore a letter.

"There's got to be some explanation," she insisted. "Some ideas are just too good to let go of. There must be an explanation. Let's hear the story. Maybe the answer is in the story."

MARY OAKLEY FIRST HEARD of the Bela River camp from one of her pupils. Derek Newby said he hoped the prisoners would be Nazis, in which case his gang would camouflage themselves and creep up on their bellies like commandos and attack them with pea-shooters and cat-apults, and make their lives altogether miserable. But his father told him they were going to be Eye-ties, which would be no fun at all.

Less than twenty miles from the Bela River camp, at Grizedale Hall, behind a double perimeter fence and surrounded by ground cleared of rhododendrons to give clear shots from the watchtowers at anyone trying to escape, the army ran the camp they labelled *number one*. It held Germans whose record and attitudes during interrogation put them in the category *black*, as opposed to *grey* or *white* Nazis. They included high-ranking officers. They were delivered to Grizedale in vehicles with blacked-out windows after being driven round the tiny lanes of north Lancashire in circles to disorient them and conceal their whereabouts. Observant neighbours soon worked out what was going on, but word of it did not reach Derek Newby.

Bela River, camp number 104, was a different matter. Derek Newby's father sold his milk to Libby's at Milnthorpe, where it was condensed and canned, and the factory was acutely short of staff: a camp full of free Italian labour just down river would provide an ideal solution. It might come in handy on his own farm too, when it was time to make silage.

Mary told William, who lodged with her more frequently after George joined up, that the inmates had no doubt come from the hot, dry deserts of North Africa and would likely freeze to death, if they didn't dissolve in the rain and wash out to sea first. Instant concern knit William's brow and Mary, still cautious with William after all these years, thought it necessary to assure him she was joking.

"Perhaps we can help."

"Gracious, William, as if we don't have enough to do helping our own."

But she said this with a light touch, too, because in truth this war had lifted more burdens for her than it had imposed. She had struggled for years to support herself and George independently of the Oakleys, on the meagre earnings of a primary school teacher. Now George was making his own way in the world and she had the respect of everyone, bar the Oakleys. She had been much put-upon at her Lancaster school by a bully of a headmaster half her age who was currently being taught manners by the British Navy. She was blossoming under Makepeace Whittaker, a stalwart in the Society of Friends and former educationalist coaxed out of retirement by the Education Committee's persistent appeal to his sense of duty. Makepeace found it difficult to maintain discipline in his classroom; he spoke softly and wielded no big stick and he suffered arthritis in his hands which made writing on the blackboard both painful and embarrassing. But he was a charming man with a generous intelligence. He became a close friend and advocate for Mary, who derived much satisfaction from being the real leader of the school.

As George had been in the Officers Training Corps at Lancaster Grammar, he was given an emergency commission in the Royal Corps of Signals. He was based over in Catterick, which wasn't so terribly far away. He seemed to be quite enjoying himself and wrote home – not often enough – telling her how he'd learned to ride a horse, and then a motorbike. She pictured him on top of a Yorkshire moor practising semaphore to pass a message from the hill below to the hill above, like a Tudor yeoman warning of a coming Armada, and it reassured her. He told her this wouldn't be like the Great War. Churchill would never let the British Army get bogged down in Flanders again. He'd poke around in the soft underbelly of Europe, and let the Russians get on with it in the east, and wait until there were enough Americans on the ground to make an invasion of France a pushover before he did anything rash.

George took an individual view of things, Mary thought. He never sounded belligerent or jingoistic but he seemed quite keen on the war and spoke cheerfully about the inevitability of it all.

Makepeace Whittaker said hc supposed a second world war was considered necessary to mend the terrible consequences of the first.

George said that war was not necessarily all bad. It was a stimulus to the economy for one thing. And it encouraged enterprise. He said Britain would again take on huge debts, but other countries would have huge surpluses. And that meant opportunities,

Derek Newby's father kept his son home one or two days every week, *to help with essential farm duties* he said. He always sent a piece of raw cheese, wrapped in a page of the Westmorland Gazette the next day. George said it was worth at least a pair of lamb cutlets. Whenever George visited he brought Mary a nice piece of pork or beef. He carried cartons of cigarettes instead of currency.

Makepeace said he supposed a third world war might be necessary to mend the consequences of the second. He said he hoped for a better world at the end of this war but was gloomy about the chances. He said he thought this was perhaps an unworthy concern but it was supported by the behaviour he witnessed daily in his classroom.

Increasingly, Mary felt she had some unworthy concerns of her own. She wondered, for instance, though she loved him dearly, whether she actually liked George very much. She wondered if he wasn't becoming a bit of a spiv – a dealer with the sharpness and ambition of an Oakley but without any of the bricks and mortar.

William took Mary's bicycle the next time Makepeace gave her a lift to school, and without a word rode fifteen miles up the A6 from her home in Skerton to Beetham and then down the tiny lane to Hang Bridge, which carried the road from Milnthorpe to Holme over the River Bela. He leaned the bike against the parapet and sat next to it, dangling his feet over the river.

The sound of the water was forceful but soothing. The river was young still, though only a mile or two from its mouth at the top of Morecambe Bay. It swept confidently round the west side of the new huts, dived beneath him under the bridge, and disappeared into thin woodland to the south. The banks were lush with green vegetation. No mud. And no shell holes. A short goods train puffed and rattled its way along an embankment running up the the eastern side of the camp. No flying sparks. No inferno of flame and smoke. And then it was blissfully silent. He could still hear the flowing water, and birdsong, and some muted domestic clatter from within the huts, yet it sounded to him like silence. He could come here every day, he thought, and sit on this bridge outside the camp, and feed this sense of blissfulness. That must surely help.

"Don't do it, mate! It's a lot colder than you think."

William swung his legs back over the parapet, stood, and stared towards the single wooden beam that constituted the gate into the camp. Beyond the barrier, two army lorries, parked and empty. Some hammering in the distance. And then he saw the glow of a cigarette end. Beside the barrier there was a tiny windowless hut with an open door, and a man in the dark inside, sitting on a bench perhaps. A sentry box. He walked towards it.

"And I wouldn't leave your bike behind if I was you or one of this lot'll half-inch it."

William went back for Mary's bike, and wheeled it towards the gate.

"Whisk it away quick as a wink they will, and be giving midnight rides to the farmer's bricks an' mortar. Before you can say 'nine months' we'll be overrun with little Guiseppes."

William dealt with his discomfort by looking at his feet. Then he saw the man's rifle, lying casually on the floor of the hut, and he became agitated. The soldier threw his cigarette down and stomped on it and the sudden movement made William lean away, lose his balance, and drop the bicycle. He fell awkwardly, and the soldier's attempt to pull him to his feet made him panic and yell.

Ten minutes later William was sitting in the office of Major Selby, the camp commandant.

"So you have a medical exemption," the Major said. It was a statement which allowed for contradiction, but did not accuse.

"I think it was seeing the rifle that threw me a little. It was exactly like mine."

"The Lee Enfield has been standard army issue since 1895. So you bore arms in the Great War?"

William considered this question, and the kindly way in which it had been asked. He found himself wanting to tell this army officer about Ada Doley and Lady Herbert; about his father and the family firm; about the little chisel Old Armitage had given him. The Major, who looked old enough to have been in the Great War himself, waited patiently. In the end, William simply nodded.

"And you want to help here. So we must make use of you."

Major Selby was a pragmatic man. He would oversee the custody of thousands of Italian and then German prisoners of war, from the summer of 1942 right through to new year's eve at the end of 1947. His regime would not brutalise, or humiliate, or threaten, and the respect he earned would enable him to motivate and manage a huge volunteer workforce which helped put food on the nation's tables at a time of desperate need.

An orderly put a mug of sweet milky tea on the table in front of William.

"The fence round this camp is not to keep the prisoners in, but to keep the cows out. I make sure they understand that as soon as they arrive. Self-discipline keeps them in, and common sense, and these Italians have got both. They are pleased to be alive and out of the war, though they are not cowards. Nor will our local farmers find them slothful or dishonest, once they get to know them."

William sipped his tea.

"But they tend not to have much English." Major Selby took a small yellow booklet from his desk drawer and placed it carefully in front of William. "English–Italian phrase book. It's War Office issue, for the use of local employers. Full of frightfully useful translations into Italian of things like *clean out the stable* and *pick the fruit without bruising*. Our farmers prefer sign language."

William picked up the booklet. "My sister-in-law is a teacher."

"There you go then. We don't send the men out to work for the first few weeks after they arrive. You can help them with their English."

William swiftly put the booklet down.

"You needn't think of it as teaching. I don't mean the finer points of English grammar and syntax. You can wander about and have little friendly chats. Introduce them to a few courtesies like please and thank you. Hello and goodbye. That would be splendid."

William repeated the word frequently during his hour-and-a-half ride home. The sun on his face was splendid, the occasional wisp of breeze stirring his hair was splendid. The uncut hedgerows white with lacy flowers were splendid. He arrived home just as Makepeace pulled up in his Morris, dropping Mary off on his way home, and they all went in for tea.

"Well that does indeed sound rather splendid," Makepeace said.

Mary was alarmed that William had taken himself off without telling her where he was going and made amends for what she saw as her lack of protection by wrapping him in practicalities: "I'll get you some sticks of chalk, William. You can label beds and chairs; floor and ceiling; doors and windows. Then you can get them to make up sentences on the walls, adding a word each in turn. You'll have to take some cigarettes with you, so you can give a prize for the team that makes the longest one." She sketched out half a dozen language games he could organise.

Makepeace smiled and nodded. "You may be right, Mary, you may well be right. But rural Italy is a feudal backwater you know. These men will very likely know how to plough with a mule, butcher a pig, and dig drainage ditches. But they may not know their alphabet. If they can't read and write in their own language..."

"...They can learn to read and write in ours."

"He'll need to get them on his side first."

"Cigarettes are a good idea. And a pack of cards."

"But not dice."

"And a cricket bat."

"I hardly think so, Mary. A football perhaps."

"Yes – William can referee, and insist that he will only listen to appeals in English."

William rode up to the camp the next morning without football, cigarettes, poker dice, cards or chalk. He gave his name to the soldier at the gate, who seemed to be expecting him. He leaned his bike against the outer wall of Major Selby's office. Introduce a few courtesies, he reminded himself. That was his brief.

He walked cautiously up the main avenue between rows of huts, and saw no one. He doubled back towards the gate and was drawn towards a lorry under which someone was working, flat on his back beneath the engine. He was whistling a playful tune. Opera, probably. Italians loved their opera.

"Good Morning. My name is William. I am very pleased to meet you."

The whistling ceased. A greasy muscular arm, holding an enormous spanner, emerged from beneath the vehicle and then the legs swung sideways and a similarly muscular and greasy torso, naked from the waist up, emerged into the light and lay absolutely still.

"And I'm the bloody Queen of Sheba, mate."

"Ah. Not Italian, then."

"No more than you're a mechanic, I'd like to bet. But you've got two hands, I see, and it would make my life a sight easier if you'd give me the loan of them for five minutes."

William was on his back under the Bedford three-tonner for much of the next three hours. He emerged a good friend of Private Bob Hackett, who would borrow his hands many times over the coming weeks and in return would teach William how to drive the lorry. They were so short of drivers for delivering the men to and from the farms that Major Selby talked about recruiting suitable prisoners to do it. By training up William, Bob would delay the evil day a little. "They're not bad sorts, but it doesn't do to let them get ideas above their station. When their own kit falls apart, they get issued with ours, but they have to sew diamond patches on the back of the shirt and the knees of the trousers. So everybody knows who they are, like. We're not supposed to fraternise, see. Everybody knows that. But how can I not fraternise with someone and then hand them the keys of my little babies?"

William's introductory line had achieved an excellent result first time out and he decided he would stick with it. Bob said he'd find plenty of Eye-ties in the cookhouse. The shed with the multiple chimneys.

There was more opera inside, with random percussion from passionate operations with pots and pans. "Good afternoon. My name is William. I am very pleased to meet you."

Emboldened by his experience under the Bedford, he continued his roving monologue unperturbed by the lack of response in any language.

"*Potatoes.* In English, we say *potatoes.*

"*Good afternoon.* My name is William. I am *pleased* to meet you.

"*Potatoes.* Or you could say, *spuds.* You are *spud bashing*. That is, you are *peeling potatoes* for tea.

"*Hello.* My name is William. I am *very pleased* to meet you.

"*Thank you.* Thank you for letting me watch you potato bashing.

"You work very well in the kitchen. *Thank you.*

"*Hello.* My name is William. I am *pleased* to meet you.

"Ah. You like to smoke? You want a cigarette? I am sorry, *my name is William* and I do not have any cigarettes."

Mary said he was lucky they didn't make him finish peeling their potatoes.

Makepeace said he was lucky they didn't give him a black eye.

After he'd spent a few days in the camp, prisoners

would call out to him “Buon giorno, Signor Potato.” He would smile warmly, make a pleasant observation about the weather, or ask if they were well, and bid them good day.

Then one day a young man on the crew building more huts asked William to write something for him in English. It was clearly a letter home, with the date at the top and a greeting, Cara Mamma e caro Papa. There were three or four short paragraphs in large, child-like print which had been crudely erased and written-over in several places. He gave William a pencil and pointed to the foot of his Italian text. “Gooduh afternoon-uh,” he said, jabbing at the paper. “Gooduh afternoon-uh, Signor Potato.”

Makepeace said how splendid. He said the letter might be three months on the censor’s desk and then a month getting to the Red Cross in Switzerland and then two more months getting through to Mama and Papa in Calabria or wherever, and it probably didn’t say much more than ‘I hope you are well, don’t worry about me, I am safe, but I am worried about my brothers’. But this was the young man’s heartache, and he had asked William to grace it with his English.

Mary glowed with pride.

Soon all the Italians wanted some English words at the end of their letters. They queued up with their pencils and scraps of paper.

“It helps make it real for them,” Makepeace said. “It’s a way of sharing with their nearest and dearest something real of this unnatural experience.”

Mary thought it was time William started with his ABC’s.

“It’s actually quite unreal,” William said. “All the Italians are A’s, B’s and C’s: There’s a Ferdinand Abate, a Mario Bruzzi, a Salvatore Citino. I’ve seen a roster –

there's hundreds of ABC's and not a single D,E or F. Maybe *they're* all in Bridlington. And the GHI's are in Llandudno."

On the Sunday, William rode his bike to nephew Joseph's yard at Penny Street Bridge and sharpened half a dozen saws. In return, he begged a few ends of Oakley floorboard and cut them into dozens of tablets an inch square. He couldn't see himself teaching with chalk on a board, or pen on paper. But perhaps this lovely thin maple with its light grain would be different.

The next day he sat in sight of the building crew at Bela River and quietly began chiselling in relief the letter A on the first of his little tablets. Eventually some of the men wandered over.

"Hallo Signor William-uh."

"Good Morning. It's a lovely day today. The sun is warm. The sky is blue."

By the time he'd finished the A and started on a B, the men who came to look at what he was doing were clearly impressed. Impressed but mystified.

"I" – William tapped his little chisel against his chest – "I am a carpenter. *A carpenter*. Like you. Like Jesus. *Jesus was a carpenter.*"

"Gesu!"

There was a simultaneous gasp and William blushed deeply. He quickly emphasised with shakes of the head and chisel that he was not Jesus. But the carpentry did work miracles, and when he had enough letters to spell out *please* and *thank you* he found the Italian prisoners soon learned the words and used them aggressively to insist he next make the letters that allowed them to spell out their names. Before long he had dozens of characters which he carried around in a canvas bag which Mary made specially, embroidered with 'ABC's for ABC's'.

The day Bob Hackett had been preparing him for arrived sooner than either of them expected. William was asked to step into Major Selby's office and was told it was time to graduate. He would be duly honoured – any correspondence from the Major's Office would include the letters 'ABC' after his name. William didn't get the joke until Mary explained it to him later.

"Not only can you drive the Bedford three-tonner," the Major said. "I understand you also know how to free the throttle when it gets stuck and engage the top gears despite the best efforts of its wayward gearbox to prevent you." He spelled out the terms of the driving job and said he would issue him with a valid licence. The next day William was on the road.

He was on the road a great deal longer than he should have been, as all the signposts had been taken down to confuse the enemy. The sunken lanes of the Lyth Valley and the twisting switchbacks over the crags towards Kirby Lonsdale thoroughly disoriented him. He had a camp guard in the cab with him for the first few miles, his Lee Enfield leaning casually against the dashboard making William nervous.

"Don't worry mate, there's no bullets. It's just for show, to keep the girls happy."

He dropped his first half-dozen men in Meathop. The Ministry of Agriculture had ordered the ploughing of Meathop Marsh in May, and provided a tractor and Australian disc harrow to do it. Land Army women and other volunteers had planted vast quantities of seed potatoes, turnips, beetroot and swedes, and were now desperately trying to keep on top of the marsh grasses and mosses that were growing back with vigour. The guard, empty rifle slung on his shoulder, started his Italians at one end of the strip to be weeded, and the women from the Land Army and the Lancaster Land Club started at the other. William could see that the Italians were excited by the challenge ahead.

After that he was on his own in the cab. Three men to drop at Whitebeck Farm where they were going to be picking apples and plums. Two others over at Brigsteer to clear bracken from a fell-side field for a farmer who had to double his milk production. And so it went on. The later drops were behind schedule, and the farmers showed their annoyance. One was waiting in the road and without a word scowled at his man and tapped vigorously at his watch. Derek Newby's father was ready with pitchforks for his two. He pointed to the top of his silage tank and the cart full of grass waiting alongside and shooed them into position thrusting at their backsides and yelling *pronto! pronto!* until they'd scrambled up, when he tossed them their forks.

The last man on board was due at a smallholding in Arnside over an hour ago. William felt terribly responsible. He waved him down from the canvas-covered back of the lorry, and when he jumped over the tailboard William motioned for him to get in the cab.

"Hello. I am William. Sorry I am late. I will go faster."

His passenger shrugged his shoulders nonchalantly.

William focussed on making the best speed he could, more confident in taking bends now he had no men standing in the back. His passenger whistled merrily, and he relaxed a little. Major Selby was right: these men were not cowards. This one, at least, awaited his fate calmly.

The young man casually pointed left or right as they approached a junction or crossroads, and William shouted 'Thank you' over the noise of the engine. Then the man picked up William's bag of letter tiles, loosened the draw-string, and rummaged inside. When the lorry finally pulled up outside the house with the sign *Donne Roaming*, he spelled out on the dashboard MICHELANGELO.

There was no angry farmer waiting at the gate, and Michelangelo seemed in no great hurry to get out.

William turned off the engine and then with both hands pulled back the stiff handbrake lever. "It is a nice day. The sun is hot. The sky is blue. I am sorry you are late."

"Si, Signor Potato." He slumped back in his seat and seemed to sigh.

There was a tapping sound outside and William lowered his side window on its strap. A woman was trying to get their attention from inside a bay window down the side of the house, and when she had it she gestured for them to join her.

"You're just in time for a cup of tea," she said, opening the back door as the two men approached. She wiped her hands on her apron and then held one out to William.

"Jean Wellington. Thank you so much for delivering our Angel Michael."

They sat at a scrubbed oak table where tea was mashing in a Wedgewood pot and were promptly joined by John Wellington, who also proffered his hand for shaking.

"Chop my head off and I'm still a duke."

William looked nervously round the table and could have sworn he saw the young Italian roll his eyes.

"Don't worry. I set crosswords for a magazine. Wellington was a Duke. Take off the first letter and you're left with Ellington. Another Duke."

Michelangelo took from the thigh-pocket of his tattered British-army battledress, complete with diamond knee patches, a small brown-paper package. He slapped it down on the table and slid it forward. Jean reached out and pulled it towards her.

"What have they sent you out with today?"

She opened the small parcel to reveal two stale slices of bread the colour and texture of compressed sawdust. She raised the corner of the top piece and peered beneath.

"Another red jam doorstop. You go feed that to the hens right now and I'll make you a proper sandwich as soon as the bread is out of the oven."

"It's his reward for letting us take Tobruk," John said, as soon as Michelangelo left the kitchen.

"Now, John. He's only a boy still. Just think if our Jack was captured and put to work on an Italian farm. Wouldn't you want the family to look after him?"

"Our Jack isn't a fascist."

"No more is Angel Michael. He doesn't even know what the word means."

"He joined The Party for goodness sake."

"So? Our Jack joined the Socialist Party without a clue what it stood for."

"He knew what the Peace Pledge Union was about though."

"You know very well he joined both of them because Helen told him she'd break off with him if he didn't. It doesn't mean if he's shot down he should have to eat doorstops, does it?"

"I have a son," William said.

"Don't mind us, William Oakley."

Michelangelo came back grinning. He laid on the table the letters spelling out his name. "Is the tea ready for Michelangelo?"

And this William did mind. "I didn't know you could speak English."

"Yes, a bit. Jean and John are teaching me."

"You misled me."

"I mislead them too. I tell them I am fascist when naturally I am communista."

"Why did you do that?"

"They socialist. I give them sinner to convert. So they very good to me."

John Wellington said, "He's doing it again. He's never read a word of Marx in his life. He's a street urchin."

"We're both Labour Party, right down the middle," Jean said. "John does love a street urchin. It makes John Donne such an interesting challenge."

"And who is John Donne?"

"Oh dear, William. I'm afraid you've just given my husband another challenge. There's no going back to the camp for you. We'll have to keep you hostage."

John Wellington leaned across the cluttered table and rearranged Michelangelo's letters while talking about his favourite poet. William read: 'GALLEON CHIME'. Then the hands reached across the table, shuffled the letters again, and as if by magic withdrew to leave 'ALL CHIME GONE.'

He had no orders for the middle of the day. He had assumed he would go back to Bela River and talk polite English to new arrivals. But he had graduated: he had letters behind his name. Now he was in the driving seat, so to speak, and he thought he might very well stay here with these forward, friendly people, until it was time to pick up the men at the end of their day's work. He would learn how to read poetry and then face the consequences. He would help cut out the raspberry canes that had finished fruiting, and tie the new shoots to their wire frame against the onshore winds. He would see with Michelangelo how many short words they could make from the letters of his name – and both would be amazed by the number. He would learn how to layer strawberry runners to double the size of next year's crop. He would return to the poems John had shared with him, and read them again and again, and take something new away every time. He would enjoy making anagrams out of his own name, clean out a hen house, sharpen a scythe, turn the contents of a compost heap, fall in love with the poems of Edward Thomas.

"The other drivers they sleep, Signor Potato. The Ingelish soldiers, they like the long siesta. They lie on the seat where they drive and they sleep all day."

"Don't believe what my husband says about the Italians, William – running away when they saw us coming. Their little tanks were out of date before they came off the assembly line."

"My wife will get us into trouble the way she feeds Michelangelo. The NFU has told us we mustn't be nice to the Italians."

"Don't you think it takes courage to sit inside a tin can whose engine keeps breaking down, facing guns you know can easily penetrate your flimsy armour and set you on fire, at a range where your own gun is useless?"

"They said if you give A a few cigarettes for a good day's graft, or B a couple of biscuits to go with his army-ration sandwich – X, Y and Z will want the same and they'll start fighting among themselves over who goes where, and before you know it the whole scheme will fall apart."

Michelangelo said for sure if they only knew, his friends would be scratching each others' eyes out for the chance of listening to Signor John Donne. He closed his eyes when John Wellington read poetry to him. He said he was soaking up the Monteverdi of it whatever that meant but William would notice his head nodding and cough loudly when he thought he was about to snore.

Michelangelo said he'd never been near a tank, thank

goodness. He'd worked on the docks at Tobruk, unloading rice and blankets from ships. John taught him the word *stevedore* which he loved and used frequently in describing himself.

And, one miserably wet and windy day towards the end of September when the smallholding seemed more than capable of looking after itself, they discovered that Michelangelo was an artist.

He asked for pencil and paper, and Jean responded with the bounty of a fairy godmother. She had coloured pencils, she had wax crayons. She had charcoal sticks. She was sure she had a box of children's watercolours somewhere. Even better – her daughter Hilary had dabbled with oils the summer she went to Woodcraft Camp in Tolpuddle. They'd be up in the attic somewhere; she'd send John up. She never threw anything away. She had paper and hardboard, and a little fold-up easel. He could take it outside and paint the landscape, or she would arrange some flowers, or fruit for a still life. Yes, how perfect for a prisoner of war: a still life. How liberating!

As it turned out, Michelangelo was more interested in Hilary herself than her old paints. He stuck with the pencil and paper, and asked if he could lift down the studio portrait that hung above the piano. The absent daughter of the house, in her green summer uniform with the red badge of the WVS on the breast pocket, had a fresh, innocent look about her that was at odds with the dramatic mood suggested by the strongly contrasted lighting. Michelangelo copied her again and again. In some of his drawings she looked like she had been hustled into the studio fresh from a long walk on the fells. Others he drew in a style that seemed to have more in common with the images of young women William had seen on postcards in the Winter Gardens arcade in Morecambe.

As the days passed, the darts in the front of Hilary's dress became more acute, pulling in the waist; the padded shoulders became bolder, the gathering at the seam more lavish. Michelangelo unfastened the buttons from the neck, drawing by drawing, peeling back the material to reveal a tiny crucifix above the first hint of cleavage. Her lips, too, seemed fuller, her eyes more knowing.

In the drawings he showed her parents, Michelangelo moved Hilary out of doors. Her cheeks became flushed, her hair windblown. She looked so carefree Jean cried sometimes. When that happened, Michelangelo always insisted she keep the picture.

Jean bought paint for Michelangelo to take back to camp. He was going to paint a mural. The photograph of Hilary went back on the wall above the piano. They were busy outside lifting potatoes, drying onions, planting out leeks and sprouting broccoli.

On Meathop Marsh the Italians and the Women's Land Army lifted eight tons of potatoes from each acre they'd planted. They no longer needed a guard from the camp, armed or otherwise. Nor did they work apart, at opposite ends of the rows. The Italians' English improved. Their vocabulary became more colourful and expressive. They bagged the harvest in hundredweights, in hessian bags, and always lifted the full bags for the women. There were opportunities for gallantry and for flirtation. One or two bags went missing: the prisoners unpicked the threads and made themselves slippers for the winter ahead.

Michelangelo asked William if he would help him draft a letter.

"I want to say: when I look at your face, something happen deep inside me. I – Stevedore – am melted with Puccini, with Rossini, with Verdi. I am become a lightening conductor!"

A love letter then.

"You will help me, please, to make the best impression? Good afternoon, it is a very nice day? The sun is shining? The sky is blue? Thank you, Hilary?"

"To Hilary? I don't think so. I don't think you should."

"Ah. But have you ever been in love, Signor Potato?"

"It wouldn't be fair to Jean. To Mrs Wellington."

"But I am not in love with Mrs Wellington."

And when William could bear looking at the silent, crumpling face of his young friend no longer he said, "I was in love once. We learned to play chess together. But you're mixing two ideas. Lightening conductors are for electricity, not opera."

"But my heart swells for Miss Hilary – my love for her is my opera! I will sing my story for her and she will sing her story for me. We will make duet! Because when I think Hilary, I feel l'incantesimo, I feel electricity, I feel jump start the soul!"

"Perhaps you should start a little more subtly. That's more the English way. Perhaps you could start with the warm glow you feel when you draw her face."

"Yes! A warm glow, like the sun. *You have set my heart on fire*."

"Or by describing the mystery of your attraction to her."

"*I am attracted to you, appassionato, like the mystery of the heavenly bodies*'"

As far as William was aware, Michelangelo never received a response from Hilary Wellington whose postal address, discovered by stealth on an envelope in the waste bin of their hosts, was in Sutton Coldfield. But for weeks they listened keenly to the poetry John Wellington put their way – to seek inspiration, to plagiarise, and to feed the fantasy of themselves as cooperative versifiers of the heart.

Michelangelo took up basket weaving in the winter and stopped drawing – though William heard shortly before Christmas that he had completed a mural on the end wall of his hut at Bela River. Major Selby said it was very popular with the other inmates because it reminded them of home, and because of its *adult* content. "It gives the impression that female Italian farm workers all live in a renaissance painting by Bellini."

William went to take a look midday, when most of the prisoners were out working. It was a bucolic scene with healthy young women engaged in a range of chores – feeding hens, scything grass, picking fruit – under a Calabrian sun so hot they had all casually unbuttoned their WVS-style uniforms to the waist. In every woman, whatever her expression, William recognised the face of Hilary Wellington. In the middle distance, one of the Hilarys was crossing a stream on a row of stepping stones. At the far side, a man with red diamond patches on his knees and a bag of potatoes on his shoulder – I, Stevedore – waited for her. William stepped up close and peered at the stepping stones. They were painted in the shape of his letter tablets and each was inscribed with a letter, spelling out W – I – L – L – I -- A – M.

HE HUMOURED EMILY as she moved his beer and her wine to the adjacent table, spread out the letters in front of her and turned them all face up. There was no M for Michelangelo and no W for William. "Aunt Mary used to put them under her plant pots, to stop them staining the window shelf. These were probably all that were left."

"But your grandad loved word games, right? He learned to love them when he stayed with John Wellington, and later he used to play them with you, right? So..." She jumbled the tablets around on the table, pulling three or four letters out at a time to construct a word. "I bet he taught you how to play Scrabble."

"Yes he did as a matter of fact. But not with these tablets. Scrabble didn't arrive in England until the mid fifties."

"Come on, aren't you curious?" She moved the letters around frantically.

"You can hardly accuse me of not being curious. How do you think I put together the tale I just told you?"

She abandoned her attempt to make sense of the letters and sank back in her chair with a sigh. "But you don't give me endings. I want stories with a beginning, a middle and an end. I want to know what happened to Michelangelo and Hilary."

"Well I can tell you that in general the Italians at Bela did enjoy the attentions of a number of local ladies. They were blamed for bringing syphilis from foreign parts but I found a retired doctor who'd dealt with it at the time and he said it was clearly a local strain. He said local prostitutes gave it to the Italians. The Italians passed it on to the girls in the Land Army. The Land Army girls gave it to the farmers. And the farmers gave it to their wives. The Italians just stirred it up a little."

"What am I supposed to make of that?"

"You could make a great deal of it at the time. Fraternization regulations allowed co-operators to enter into friendly relations with local people so long as they didn't become amorous or sexual. So while English soldiers were bringing back Italian wives by the boatful, an Italian co-operator who fell in love with a Lancashire lass could be reported by a jealous rival or a nosy neighbour and get two years in prison with hard labour. Many did."

"Who would have reported Michelangelo?"

He grimaced as she took her phone from her bag and started thumbing the screen. "And you don't explain William at all. You make him sound so detached."

"You're going to phone a friend? I told you I don't think Michelangelo ever met Hilary. I've no idea what happened to either of them."

"I'm going to put the bare bones on the blog. I'll flesh it out later."

"As for my detached grandfather, yes, he stopped working at Bela River. When Mussolini fled and Victor Emanuel surrendered in the autumn of forty-three, Italian prisoners were given a choice. Some who came from the north, which was occupied by the Nazis, were afraid for their families and daren't be known as co-operators. They were moved to secure camps. Those from the south gladly changed status and mostly lived on the farms where they were working. Mary told me William stopped going to the camp when the first German prisoners arrived. He said it felt like the earth was dropping away again in front of him. She took him to a Christmas service in Beetham church in 1947 and they found to their surprise that there were still German prisoners at Bela River. The back of the church filled up with them and when the service was over they sang Silent Night in German. Stille Nacht, a cappella and breaking into two-part harmony after the first verse. The congregation burst into applause at the end. All except William who had tears rolling down his face."

Emily stopped fiddling with her phone and repeated his words quietly, "It felt like the earth dropping away again in front of him. Yes, I know that feeling. Like standing alone on the edge of a precipice." For a moment this young woman to whom he had become attached in such a peculiar way seemed unaccountably vulnerable.

She reached over the pile of wooden tablets and put her hand on top of his.

"It's helpful that we're developing a real relationship," she said.

He eased his hand away and reached for his beer. "I think a real relationship has to have content. More than a few stories about old birthday presents." He took a long draught. "I think we would need to relate to each other *about* something. Something that matters to both of us."

"Hang on a minute." She focussed entirely on her phone.

"I'll get us another drink."

"No. No!" She waved him back down into his chair, one thumb busily working the phone. "Call out the letters to me. One by one. Someone has read my post already and wants to know what they are."

He slid some of the letters apart from the rest. "There's five S's."

"He says he's got the best anagram solver ever."

"Four E's."

"Why didn't I think of that?"

"Two N's, two A's and two T's. The rest are all singles: an X, a K, a P. No, there's two H's too. An O. An R. And an I." He'd managed to get the E's mixed in again, and counted them a second time. "Did I say four E's?" But the answer had come back already.

"Amazing!" Emily picked out an S, then an H and quickly spelled out the solution. "Shakespeare's Sixth Sonnet."

He read it upside down and was mildly impressed.

"It makes sense, Stephen. These letters date from the time your grandad was learning to appreciate poetry."

"It makes for an amusing coincidence."

"But above all, it gives us a *six* – for the third digit of our map reference!"

He was not so much interested in the six. Or in Shakespeare's sonnet. He focussed on the *us* and the *our* in the language of this excitable young would-be problem-solver who was undoubtedly bringing a fresh sense of fun to his sixty-year-old life and guessed that whatever content they might create, they were going to spell trouble.

DAY FOUR

SHE COULD ONLY IMAGINE TWO REASONS why Stephen would take such gross advantage of a buffet-style, eat-all-you-want full English breakfast: either he was reverting to native Oakley or he was anticipating a thin day ahead without her.

"You're thinking, there can only be two reasons why someone would pile his plate as high as this, right? Either he has known serious hunger at some point in his life or, whatever his habit at home, he has a profound understanding of breakfast as the cardinal meal of the day – to be savoured slowly, one page of the morning paper at a time, with newly-made toast delivered at regular intervals and multiple refills of freshly-brewed coffee. But I can see you struggling with this so here's something to distract you while I eat." Stephen placed a single item made of wood on the table beside her bowl of muesli.

She picked the thing up. It was nine inches long and an inch in diameter, tapering to a stubby point at one end and with a rounded knob at the other. A rich grain swirled up its length. It was smooth and highly polished. She held it flat across the open palms of her hands. She cupped one hand over the rounded end and swivelled it. She balanced the thing across her index finger, the rounded end one side and tapered tail the other, and found it pleasingly weighted.

"Too high a centre of gravity to be a spinning top," Stephen said, his fork poised mid-air with a cargo of mushroom, bacon and black pudding.

He could skewer his breakfast with it, she thought. A medieval eating implement? A sheik's tent peg? An Arts and Crafts dildo?

She watched him take an envelope from his inside jacket pocket, slide it along the table towards her, and return to his paper and his food.

It was addressed to Mr Oakley, 16 Park Gardens, Kingston upon Thames, Surrey. Typed on the envelope, not printed on a label; in old-fashioned indented lines, not left-justified in a block. She pulled out a single, small sheet of paper, typed on both sides.

Dear Mr Oakley

Regarding your recent letter to the editor of the Westmorland Gazette, I am certainly in a position to answer enquiries about past personalities in the Westmorland Labour Party – my father made me learn the names of all the standard bearers in order. Reverend Mills, for instance – one of the first Labour county councillors in the whole country. Reverend Graham – fought for agricultural workers and was an ardent trades unionist. They all were in those days, especially the ministers. Father was a minister too and over the years held every office in the Party. Reverend Brown was another, in the nineteen-thirties. His wife was the only woman ever to stand for Westmorland in parliament and she put up a good fight. Father campaigned for her on women's suffrage and the peace movement. He used to boast about winning the Quakers over from the

Liberals, though he wouldn't want to be thought of as a proud man; it was the righteousness of his arguments that did the winning. They were a valued lot to have on your side and widely respected, though I don't remember any John Wellington among them, reverend or otherwise.

One of my earliest memories of my father as an orator, however – outside the pulpit – was quite early in the war, after Dunkirk and the Battle of Britain but before things started going our way. He took me to a meeting of the Kendal Debating Society. The motion was 'It's the Nazis, not the Germans we are fighting' and there was a fierce debate. Among the speakers in support, alongside my father, was a chap who'd had a difficult drive to Kendal in the blackout, possibly from as far away as Arnside. He spoke with passion and reached poetic heights, but was rock solid with his logic and morality and ferociously insistent. He impressed me hugely and might well have been your John Wellington because I remember my father telling him he was obviously kindred to the Iron Duke – which he took exception to, though good humouredly. The motion passed at the vote and that caused quite a stir I can tell you, with letters to the Gazette continuing the argument for many weeks.

Yours sincerely

There was no signature. She looked at the envelope. No return address.

"Yes, I presume he forgot," Stephen said from behind his newspaper. "Or she. But it didn't matter. I picked up on the mention of Quakers, and wrote to all the meetings in the area. That's like their parishes. Quakers being members of The Society of Friends. And they don't have ministers but they have *overseers* who kind of keep an eye on things pastoral." He passed her another letter, written with a ballpoint pen that rolled and swerved its way across numerous small pieces of pastel-blue paper, erratically numbered at the foot.

Dear Stephen

I was a pupil at Yealand Manor School and I do remember a lovely man called John Wellington reading to us from Robert Louis Stevenson's A Child's Garden of Verse. He had a market garden not far from the school and when he made a delivery to the kitchen he always asked if he could read to us. He said his garden grew verse as well as vegetables; to nurture the mind and the soul as well as the body. That was what the school was all about so I'm sure it played well with the headmistress, a truly inspiring lady called Elfrida Foulds who I rather think hijacked anyone with skills and a kind smile who came in her reach and put them to work.

The school was founded at the very beginning of the war by a group of Friends from the Manchester Meeting to provide a safe place for their children away from the bombing. They'd seen what a mess had been made of the first evacuation of children from London during the Munich crisis in 1938, and realised they could do a much better job with some sensible planning. But as you can imagine if you know anything about the Society of Friends, they soon saw this as much more than an emergency safety measure. It was an opportunity to give children an educational and social experience free from war-mindedness or, in the words of our headmistress, to create a place where as many children as possible might be gathered together during the war years and trained, however imperfectly, to live in that spirit which takes away the occasion of all wars.

So you can picture dozens of us leaving our homes in

Manchester, Liverpool or Leeds – and leaving our parents in most cases, including mine – and finding ourselves in a former guest house in beautiful countryside where Lancashire met Westmorland, not far from Milnthorpe. Some mothers stayed with their children and became volunteer staff. We had some refugee children who came to Britain on Kindertransport after witnessing who knows what horrors in central Europe. And we had CO's too – conscientious objectors. They went for their tribunal hearings and some were allowed to stay and teach us and some were sent to Lancaster prison.

I have never since enjoyed a richer experience of nature, a broader exposure to culture and crafts, or a more rewarding time of playful adventure. How odd that seems looking back on it. We had no desks or books to begin with. As time went on, cricket balls inevitably found their way towards windows, which had to be boarded up with plywood as glass was unobtainable. Later on, food was strictly rationed, though I don't ever remember going to bed hungry. The staff were worried about family left behind under nightly bombing. Some of the children were terribly upset at first, though I settled down quickly. The adults were very patient. Loving, I suppose. It was really like one enormous, slightly chaotic, eccentric family.

I'm sure we had lessons, though I can't actually picture any of them. I won a scholarship to Manchester Grammar so I must have learned something. Mr Goynes taught Geography and had been sacked by his old school because he was a CO. I made a beautiful model steam ship with him. I especially remember the carpentry and the wonderful plays we made up ourselves and then performed, and playing violin in the school orchestra. Arthur and Winifred Percival were our music teachers. He played for the Hallé

Orchestra in Manchester and was always dashing off to give a concert and she spoke fluent Italian. A couple of POWs from a camp nearby worked just outside the village and always stopped for a smoke on the bench opposite the school gate. She told us to say hello and be friendly whenever we saw them. The Percivals gave concerts in the camp, and cheered the prisoners no end with arias from their favourite operas. Everyone in the school played an instrument of some kind with lots on percussion of various inventive sorts. We played folk songs and sea shanties and Haydn's Surprise Symphony.

I didn't have great ability as an artist, but as an adult I have always been willing to have a go and before my hand became as shaky as you witness in my writing now, I used to draw my grandchildren with confidence and pleasure. I was a typical Yealander: we were taught to appreciate beautiful things by living with them. When I retired and joined the University of the Third Age I found there simply weren't enough hours in the day to satisfy my desire to look, with my eyes freshly open again, and make something of what I saw. That's typical too, I think, for the small number of us left who were nurtured at Yealand Manor.

I wrote poetry of course. A highlight at Yealand was an excursion to visit Wordsworth's cottage in Grasmere. And visitors came to read to us. Did we hear Louis MacNeice and Cecil Day-Lewis? I don't remember. J B Priestley, certainly. He had a beautiful sonorous voice and loomed over us like Ingleborough itself, bold and knowing, then confused us all by acting the crazy uncle. And Mr Wellington who brought us carrots and beetroot and read from A Child's Garden of Verse. 'Faster than fairies, faster than witches, bridges and houses, hedges and ditches...' Sometimes, after Mrs Foulds retired to her little cottage for the evening and the rest of the staff relaxed I would sneak out of bounds to the train tracks that carried the night mail from London to Scotland. I'm confusing you with Auden now, aren't I? But watching the Flying Scotsman itself was not as exciting as the way Mr Wellington read From a Railway Carriage. Mr Wellington sometimes brought Mr Oakley with him; they were both volunteers. Mr Oakley thought and spoke like a poem. He was so quiet and unassuming you didn't know what to make of him at first but then he'd surprise you with a brilliant observation or kindness. Mr Oakley used to help Mr Goynes in the craft workshop down in the cellar. One day Mr Goynes said we were running out of wood for carpentry and with the war and everything he didn't know how long he could keep the workshop open. Mr Oakley turned up in a lorry a few days later with bags and bags of offcuts in all shapes and sizes.

I left to go to the Grammar School after the summer of 1944. My parents were keen to have me home and weren't too worried about bombing raids anymore, though quite a few V-1s – the flying bombs – reached Manchester later that autumn. Yealand Manor closed soon after and I never learned what happened to the staff. I went to university down south and then got a job with BP and went all over the world. There was a reunion at Yealand years later but my wife was very ill at the time and I wasn't able to attend. I can't imagine any of the staff are still alive and we who were privileged to spend some time there as pupils will be showing our age, though the quality of childhood I enjoyed at Yealand survives inside me. I've been using my senior rail card for many years but thanks to people like John Wellington I still don't feel entirely grown up.

Yours

Daniel Stout

"How odd," she said. "He seems not to have made a connection between the Oakley who delivered free wood for his carpentry class and you – the Oakley who wrote to him asking about John Wellington."

"And because of that, perhaps, I put his letter to one side. It came at a busy time in my life."

She balanced the tent-peg-cum-giant's-toothpick across her index finger again. "But you'd been given a glimpse of the holy grail: a mention of Grandfather William. A William who thought and spoke like a poem, no less. Eventually you persisted."

"The Yealand Manor School reunion was in 1979, eleven years before I unwrapped the present you're fiddling with. But yes, eventually I found a photograph that had been taken at the reunion and managed to track down some of them. The Yealanders had become architects, booksellers, chemists, doctors and nurses, designers, engineers... accountants. I have the impression accountants are over-represented in Quaker families."

"The world needs good accountants. Civilisation depends on them."

He folded his paper. "I beg your pardon?"

"Proper auditing being essential for trust in the tax system. The pooling of individual resources to support the common good being the basis for civilisation. Don't you agree?"

"You do surprise me with your radical ideas. Does it go with the morning run and raw porridge for breakfast?"

"My grandmother was an accountant."

"Good for her. I thought you said she was a hippy painter."

"A hippy accountant who painted."

"Good for you. I love surprises."

He took another letter from his inside pocket and slid

it towards her. It was a long text in justified columns on A4 paper. Printed from a computer, then.

"Grandad William fell in love with a Jewish refugee from Poland, as it happens. She died a year before he did, in New York. A pupil from the reunion put me in touch with her daughter."

She liked surprises too, as long as she could organise them in a timely fashion. They were at the root of her best journalism. The Jewish refugee from Poland felt like it would take effort. She tried not to let her face show anything which might give Stephen a feeling of having an upper hand.

Dear Stephen

Yes, I remember Daniel Stout and I am not surprised that he should recall Mr Oakley bringing bags of wood to Yealand because Daniel loved making little boats and if the supply of wood was running out, your grandfather would have appeared to him as a saviour.

Mr Oakley was a saviour too for my mother Sura, for whom the supply of many things, tangible and intangible, was forever running out. But Uncle William – there were so many aunts and uncles at Yealand! – visited the school only in the last year or so and is unlikely to be remembered by many of the children. He became *my Uncle William* in a more meaningful way after Mrs Foulds, the headmistress, suggested my mother take a cottage in the village and I became a day pupil at the school and your grandfather moved in with us. 'Uncle' gave our neighbours a way of explaining the proprieties of our situation and heaven knows they needed help with that. But I'm roaming already. Let me explain: I am in my eightieth year and though I have no reason to believe my mind is not as sharp as it ever was – it took me to a Chair in Marine Biology at NYU among other things – the same cannot be said for my eyesight. Without technology I would be lost to the world. With it I can listen to novels, enjoy music, talk with my grandchildren who are scattered over three continents, and dictate this letter. I talk into a machine and some rather clever software turns it into words that I can print out. But it doesn't help me to focus my thoughts; it almost demands that I indulge myself.

I suppose it's a cliché but I can remember the smell of the porridge cooking at Yealand, remember the very words the cook said as she gave the servers their instructions. I can recall exchanges between pupils word for word, see the expressions on faces. I'm sure I can. There was such a quality of life in it all. And of necessity I was a keen observer. Odd that I started life mute and am ending it blind. Not that I was mute from the very beginning: it started when my mother and I were interned on the Isle of Man when I was five. I've no idea why we ended up there. I heard children who came to England on the Kindertransport describe the legions of kind ladies in large hats who greeted them at every stage of their journey with tea and fruit cake, and a few words of welcome in their own language. But we got only curt instructions and bad-tempered curses for not understanding. That was my introduction to the language of Shakespeare, and I wasn't having it. I suppose I was labelled an elective mute but it was no more elective than is my current loss of vision. I would not speak, I could not speak, and it worried Elfrida Foulds no end. There was a refugee girl who had the most ferocious tantrums in which she screamed and spat and bit any hand that came close but the staff managed it with patience and common sense, knowing something of the traumas she had lived through. I tested their patience more. How they wished I would scream and shout! How they wished I would stamp and spit and vent my anger! They could not begin to picture the terror behind my blank expression. I was their worst nightmare because my silence gave no boundary to the horrors of their imagining.

Perhaps I did not speak in response to the humiliation I had suffered on the Isle of Man. "They can't even speak our bloody language." I would give no one cause to say that again. 'Can't' became 'won't' and I didn't speak a word for six years.

The stories we invent for ourselves as children can have great power. Who is to say why it happened, what it meant? Uncle William never asked, which is perhaps why I put up with him. My guess is that he had plenty that he couldn't talk about himself. Everybody else prodded and poked. They looked in my ears with instruments and made me listen to sounds through headphones. They talked about sending me off to London to see an even better specialist but thank goodness never managed to organise it. When we finally reached New York I told the immigration people my full name – Laja Abramowicz – spelling it out and insisting on accuracy, and then my medical history in perfect English, though with a Mancunian accent. My mother didn't bat an eye.

Uncle William drove a group of us Yealanders to Grasmere once, to visit Wordsworth's cottage, and I liked the way he looked at the furniture and then ran his hand along the edge of a sideboard, caressed a table leg, stroked the surface of the poet's escritoire, even though we'd been told not to touch anything. I'd seen him look at my mother in the same way, though not with his hands.

More often he drove a lorry full of Italians who called out "*bambini!*" when they passed us. I thought it was an indescribably lovely word. They spoke it with a lightness their faces betrayed. The other Yealanders giggled but I heard the painful beauty of it.

Mrs Percival, one of the music teachers, spoke Italian and I remember her telling us a story set in the Alps. Someone asked why Switzerland stayed neutral in times of war and she said it was because it was a small country made up of people with different beliefs and different languages and over the centuries they had learned tolerance and respect for each other. They had become *alle Brueder, tous frères, tutti fratelli*. The others giggled at that too. They made up their own version of *Funiculi funicula* using the words *Tutti-tutti fratelli-ah.*

Tutti Fratelli. My biological uncles had fallen out, some with each other and all with my father, who had brought ruin on the family with his bad investments, and shame on my mother with his bad behaviour, and then gone missing, presumed dead. Jewish families in Eastern Europe in those days suffered unprecedented threats from without, but were not immune because of that from threats within.

Have you read Ian McEwan? Don't worry, I'm not going to talk about atonement, but human organisation. His novel Solar was such a flop that to my knowledge no one produced it as a talking book. But I am an admirer of Rachel Carson, who I met several times, and find myself strangely attracted to ecological disaster stories. Solar is more of a climate science story, but the two have become so entwined haven't they? Not so much a Silent Spring as a wet one, a dry one, a frozen one, a torrid one, a tempestuous one. Take your pick. Choose multiples. I eventually persuaded my secretary to read it to me. Where was I going with this? Tutti Fratelli, yes. The key scene in the book for me is one where a group visiting an arctic station to learn something or other about climate change can't get it together to follow the rules for organising the drying of their outdoor clothing. They start off well-intentioned but eventually someone takes somebody else's piece of kit, and that person grabs someone else's – and there's a downward spiral as individual selfishness leads to chaos which threatens them all.

So what was the organising principle at Yealand Manor? We went for so many walks! There were walks for the bigs, walks for the middles and walks for the smalls. The bigs went missing more often than the others, but were always found again. And it was always raining! There were welly boots in ten different sizes; gloves and scarves and hats; and those wonderful English gaberdines! How was it all organised? I think it merits investigation by our leading proponents of climate studies. And peace studies.

Did I say that Uncle William drove us down to Morecambe one time, just me and my mother, and we went to hear the Hallé Orchestra at the Winter Gardens? I got to sit by the passenger door – so I could look out of the side window and see the sea, my mother said. But I knew she wanted to be in the middle, where he couldn't help but rub against her. There wasn't a great deal of substance to my mother – I used to think her eyes were her biggest feature – and she couldn't insulate me from the heat she was generating in him.

He had family down there and one of them saw us by chance on the promenade. He was a nephew and he was mighty surprised to see his uncle driving a truck. I've remembered it as an army truck, but that doesn't make sense: Uncle William was exempt for some reason. Soon after that, he started working for this nephew and we could pay the rent for Pease Cottage. The landlord was a Quaker and he gave us three months grace. But the Quakers are practical folk and he made it clear that rent would be expected thereafter. There were only two bedrooms and I had the small one at the back with the single bed.

So yes, I'm sure they were lovers, your William and my Sura, but I didn't think of it that way at the time. My mother was undemonstrative, your grandfather softly spoken. Children can be simultaneously totally aware and blissfully ignorant about these things. They never expressed intimacy in public: not a kiss or a hug or a hand held. I saw it in a tenderness that came into the house when Uncle William entered, that you could feel in the air. It was quite lovely, thinking back on it. But did they love each other? That's harder to answer. I think my mother's heart had been hardened too much. I think all she was capable of was recognising that she was cherished and cared for, and allowing that to be – though even there she failed in the end.

Your relatives were builders. Mine ran a canning factory. Fruit mostly, but they were always seeking winter jobs to keep the factory working through the year. My father drank and ran the business into bankruptcy with rash speculation in herring. Fitting, don't you think, that my business became marine biology?

Pease Cottage had a wild, unkempt garden. Uncle William cleared out the nettles and brambles and found beneath them a lattice of brick pathways surrounding little beds. He was always enticing my mother out of doors and I could see why – exertion brought colour to her face and sometimes a smile. The soil was beautifully crumbly and I sometimes imagined the two of them as infants, younger than me, busy at play in a sandbox. Not talking much, not interacting much. Not much by way of organising principle, yet somehow the little beds were planted with vegetables and herbs, soft fruit and annual flowers. Even that first summer, it looked wonderful. There were no rows or blocks of plants. There would be some lettuce coming along beneath a gooseberry bush, with a cabbage on one side, and then a short stick with a tomato plant tied to it. They all seemed to get along splendidly. Tutti Fratelli, eh? Uncle William had trays of seedlings coming along in the back porch and when it was time to plant them out he would wander up and down the little paths with Sura and she might point and say "Lettuce" and he would make a little hole with his index finger and plop one in. He said he was going to make a tool for her, so she could do the planting herself without damaging her nails, but I only ever remember him plunging his fingers into the black soil, and then patting it around his seedling or cutting.

One of my uncles had contrived to get a visa for the United States early in 1939. It was to visit the New York World's Fair and find new markets for a bottling plant he said he was going to build. He got tourist visas for my mother and me. We had to pretend we were his wife and daughter. We had to buy return tickets and leave things like family photographs in the rooms we rented so it looked like we would be coming back. He let me take just one toy and I chose my doll Anka who had long black ringlets. We went on the train to Gdynia and then on the SS Pilsudski for New York. It had two enormous chimneys and made a deep throbbing noise. There was an engine problem soon after we sailed and it had to put into Southampton. It was supposed to be for just a few hours but ended up being overnight. Passengers weren't allowed to go ashore but my mother had a big row with my uncle and fell down some metal stairs and was badly hurt. As an adult I have wondered if she had refused to pay for her ticket the way he expected. She was taken off the boat on a stretcher, with me gripping her hand, and we were dumped on the floor of a busy Red Cross dressing station. When no one was watching she struggled to her feet, wrapped the thin blanket round us both, and slid away in the dark. We hid in back alleys until the SS Pilsudski left.

The day I most want to tell you about, a man came to Pease Cottage driving a smart black car. He stopped at the gate and beeped his horn. It was very soon after the war in Europe ended but the noise was angry, not joyful. My mother started towards the door but Uncle William held her back. It was his son in the car. That is to say, your father.

My mother held me to her. We heard raised voices but not the words. I remember feeling my mother tremble from somewhere deep inside and then her letting me go. She sank onto the bench seat away from the window and I ran upstairs.

I looked down from the front bedroom window. The man in the car wouldn't move. And Uncle William wouldn't leave the garden. Eventually the driver – your father – got out and walked round the car and stood in front of William on the other side of the gate. It was a flimsy little wooden thing about four feet high, with a privet hedge on each side. William put his hands on top of the gate. He was not going to open it. I didn't know what he was defending – my mother and me, his honour, his vegetables – but he was standing his ground. Your father was taller and stockier and his gestures were aggressive. Though the younger and the one you would expect to show respect, he had the manner of a man laying down the law. He pointed and jabbed at the air. Then he turned away to consult with someone on the back seat of the car. She'd been hiding in the shadows but as she leaned forward to speak to your father I saw that it was the old lady, the one who had been like a mother to his son. She had come to tea one day with another old man and asked lots of questions my mother didn't answer. Now she convulsed with a hacking cough and sank back out of sight. Then another bout over the gate, more anguished than the first. It was a dramatic scene. Your father demanding and insisting. The lady who raised him convulsing in the back of the car. Your grandfather calm and still. But hurting. How could I feel his hurt so strongly, seeing only his back, hearing no words? And how did the drama end? I have no memory of either man stepping back or stepping down. Only an image of the younger man climbing back into the car and chancing to look up, seeing my face in the bedroom window and making a gesture towards me, crude and aggressive, with two fingers.

We left the next day, my mother and I, while Uncle William was working in Lancaster. We got a lift with a farmer and then a train, several trains. We sat side by side in silence, one small suitcase on the rack above us. I've no idea where she got it from. I remember thinking it was probably Uncle William's. Then weeks and weeks in a tiny bare room in Southampton. She would leave in the morning and I would sit on the suitcase and read the newspaper I picked up on one of the trains. I could recite it page by page. I never looked in the case. She would bring back some food in the evening and soon fall deep asleep, even though it was still light. Then one day she came back much earlier and grabbed me in one hand, the suitcase in the other, and within an hour we were on board the Queen Mary, along with a few dozen other civilians and thousands of GI's on their way home to New York. She never told me how she got the tickets, or our papers or passports.

Silently, I blamed the man in the black car – your father – for this traumatic upheaval in my life. But the truth is, the sadness of it dissolved away the moment we stepped on board. The GI's were de-mob happy, carefree and charming. One or two of them tried to trick me into speaking by flirting outrageously – I was only eleven – or playing practical jokes on me. But it was all very juvenile and gentle, and was soon replaced by concern for my health and my spirit. They fed me more chocolate and candy than I had ever seen. They brought me comic books and movie magazines and an unopened boxed set of Pearl S Buck novels. They told me the sun always shone stateside and Uncle Sam would open every door for me.

But your interest is in what happened to William Oakley, not Laja Abramowicz.

Have you heard of the Sugihara survivors, as they became known eventually? My father was one of them. He had fled the wrath of family in 1938, penniless and drunk, and washed up in Vilnius. His youngest brother found him there when he fled before the German tanks. When the Russians invaded Lithuania, they allowed Polish Jews escaping the Nazis to emigrate via Russia as long as they had through visas. The Japanese Vice-Consul Sugihara, against the instructions of his government, gave thousands of Jews transit visas to pass through Japan. My father and Uncle Chaim fled to Moscow and then across Siberia to Vladivostok. They crossed safely into Japan, then to Shanghai, and in 1943 reached the United States. It was a journey in which my Uncle Chaim made bonds of obligation and friendship as quickly as my father broke them. As soon as he could, Uncle Chaim used his contacts to trace my mother. I am telling you this story so you have a tiny understanding of the power of family, for good or for ill.

My Uncle Chaim wrote to my mother at Pease Cottage saying that her husband was alive and that her duty lay at his side. I believe he also said that my father's life was in her hands, for if she did not come soon he would surely die.

My mother believed that when your father drove out to Pease Cottage in his black car that day, with the ailing woman who had been like a mother to him on the back seat, he said something similar to William.

My mother died in 1959. She never spoke about our time at Yealand, or about William, and I never asked. But as I buried my mother, I thought of him fondly. I had recently become engaged to a reliable man who was loving and kind and I wanted so much to think that my mother had some experience in her life of the reliable and the loving and kind.

I wrote to William care of the Friends Meeting House in Yealand. I knew the Elders would make sure he received it. A few months later a parcel came from England. It contained my doll Anka. Her long black ringlets had faded on one side and her dress was greasy. William wrote a note apologising for her being a little grubby. He had found her the day we left, he said, and kept her close and safe to forward in due course. But safe didn't mean in a box under the bed, or at the back of a drawer. Safe wasn't always clean and tidy, he said. She had moved with him from Pease Cottage to any number of houses, here and there with different members of his family, and she had sat on a shelf in his room where he could see her and feel some contact still, and thereby hope to offer some loving thoughts, wherever we had gone and whatever mess is made of the world.

I had always thought I would return to England, for a conference or on sabbatical, but I never have. In any case, it would seem from your letter that William died not long after our brief exchange at the end of the fifties.

I'm sorry, but I am quite worn out. Enough.

Yours truly

Laja Abramowicz

She held her hand out, palm up, for the next letter in Stephen's pocket and when he didn't produce it she clicked her fingers insistently. He patted his side pockets, said he didn't carry a handkerchief, and reached over to the adjacent table for a napkin.

"I don't want a fucking handkerchief." She wiped her eyes on her sleeve and held her hand out again. "Just fucking give me the next letter."

"Why are you swearing all of a sudden?"

"I don't know. I never swear."

"There is no next letter."

"What?"

"Don't look at me like that. It's as unattractive as your language."

"But you must have written back? Or you went to visit her? Tell me you went to visit her. You lived in the States for goodness sake. Tell me that in between banging all your rock bands' adoring groupies that you treated like shit, you at least went to visit her before she died. She was almost family."

"I've got enough almost family."

"That's shameful." She pushed her chair back from the table and it screeched on the parquet floor. She shocked herself with the strength of her reaction. This was about as far from the objective journalist as she could get, but even as she asked herself why on earth she was attacking Stephen, she continued to do so. "You didn't care? You didn't want to piece it together and fill in the gaps? To know what it meant to William and where it all led?" She grabbed the three letters on the table. Then the strange wooden object.

"There's no need to get messianic with me," Stephen said, "Acting as though you're on the trail of some sort of holy grail. I did quite enough trying to know more. I received some unusual presents and I made sensible enquiries."

"And you gave up."

"I showed a healthy curiosity."

"Not what I call healthy."

"And I'd left the States nearly thirty years before he gave me the dibber."

She looked at the thing in her hand.

"It's called a dibber."

"I know it's a fucking dibber," she said, and stormed out.

BY THE TIME SHE REACHED CARNFORTH she had calmed down. If Stephen carried a phone she would have called him and apologised. At least she didn't need to worry about him disappearing – he had no money and no car. The traffic snarled to a near halt and on her right she saw bold metallic letters announcing COUNTY LIBRARY on the front of a brick façade. It looked like a bank in a cowboy movie, inviting raids. She turned off the main road and parked near a Travis Perkins depot.

First, dibber. *Another term for dibble. A pointed hand tool for making holes in the ground for seeds or young plants.* Of course it was a dibber. William made it for Sura but didn't finish it before she disappeared.

Then she checked the comments under her last post. There was a thread of mystic mumbo jumbo around yesterday's 'clue'. Shakespeare's sixth sonnet was a coincidence. The key point was that William had given his grandson twenty-three letter tablets.

23 is the smallest odd cototient prime, and a key subject for numerologists like myself who study the way numbers reflect divine vibrations. William intuited that the secret powers of numbers are eternal though their significance is periodically lost.

Julius Caesar was stabbed 23 times.

23 cycles per second make the note F#, the fundamental vibration of the reality we call Earth. 23 is also the axial tilt of the Earth relative to her elliptic.

Humans have 23 pairs of chromosomes. Blood circulates through the body every 23 seconds. The human arm has 23 points of articulation.

She quickly scanned the following contributions which seemed to be about the number 23 in various movies, and then sank further into arguments about the relative qualities of their leading actors.

And people were still speculating about how William might have speculated.

Nobody's counted culture. Agatha Christie gave her grandson the royalties to The Mousetrap. Sixty years and 25,000 performances later, how much does that come in at? What if old William had bought a Rothko in 1960? Or a Lucien Freud?

You call Agatha Christie culture? I vote for a case of Chateau Lafitte.

Nah – Napoleon brandy.

WTF coming from Drayton I bet old William drank Joules. Not much appreciation on a bottle of pale ale however many decades it was laid down.

Her Bela River post was criticised for calling the countrymen of Leonardo da Vinci, Galileo Galilei, and Christopher Columbus 'Eye-ties'. That provoked claims that one German soldier equalled ten Italians and Wagner did the best music in Apocalypse Now, Verdi in a TV ad for Peugeot. Several comments had been removed by the moderator because they failed to meet her paper's community standards.

She wrote a paragraph about Yealand Manor School and William's small but positive contribution; she suggested he had developed a close friendship with a refugee from Poland who had moved to the area, and in particular that he helped her cultivate her garden. She described the dibber, William's fourth gift to his grandson Stephen. If the map reference theory was correct, and William had laid an elaborate treasure hunt with each gift representing a numeral, they now had an eight, a six, another six, and a one.

Before she logged off, there was already a response to her post.

Wowzer! Yealand Manor – just checked my logbook. Grid ref SD 5033 7439. Waypoint B15144. There's a CBM on the right hand gatepost. It's on grey sandstone, slightly weathered. The plot thickens!

She responded using her anonymous pseudonym: *What's a CBM?* Then she opened Google Maps while she waited for an answer. She located Yealand Conyers and Yealand Manor, with Yealand Redmayne a mile to the north. A few miles north again, Beetham, where the Germans sang Stille Nacht, then Milnthorpe, where Libby's condensed the milk. To the east, the River Bela and 'HM Prison'.

Cut Bench Mark. Duh.

She googled Cut Bench Mark. Okay, she'd seen that symbol before. A perpendicular line with oblique lines either side and a longer horizontal above. Surveyors put an angle-iron into it to make a bench for a levelling rod, to measure elevation. She couldn't make the connection with William.

Half an hour later she ran her finger along the tiny lines cut into the stone gatepost of Yealand Manor. The CBM didn't exactly jump out at you but the No Entry and Private signs were in your face. There was a lodge house by the gate and she called out politely but nobody answered. She entered as far as the lodge door, which she felt was reasonable, but no one answered her knock either and she felt alienated from a place she wanted to love. She gazed uphill towards the manor and then to each side of the curving driveway as if looking for a long lost mitten or an old mangled wellie or a decaying chunk of wood that might once have been the hull of a model boat made from Oakley offcuts. Tidy lawn swept around modest specimen trees. The organising principle appeared to have become modern suburban, hygienic and low maintenance.

The same was true of the garden at Pease Cottage. The gate was now wrought iron, the side of the house laid to tarmac and the front garden to gravel. In the centre of the gravel a small circle of soil had been left around the stem of a shrub with red leaves. Or perhaps it was a tree. A slow-growing Japanese maple, she guessed.

She looked up at the bedroom window. No face, watching in silence. She knocked on the door. No one home. No one home in all of the Yealands, it seemed. She felt an urge to leave her mark: to scratch on a neat brick wall, or a sandstone gatepost, or a village noticeboard if there was such a thing, her EWH. Emily Was Here. Duh. Then she had a better idea.

On the road back south she found the Bay View Nursery. There were plenty of bedding plants for sale: winter flowering pansies and sweet williams to flower next year. She would use William's dibber and return a tiny hint of the cottage garden to the Pease gravel. But when she visualised the small circle of bare earth around the Japanese maybe-maple she knew that its sterile appearance was created by weedkiller, and the symbolism of any active residue damaging her little plantlets didn't bear thinking about. Spring bulbs were the thing. She could dib them in and cover her traces, and the soil would surely have regained its health by the time their shoots appeared. She would plant snowdrops for William, crocuses for Sura and Laja, and they would bloom together. Tutti Fratelli. But snowdrops and crocuses were both in their different ways tribal. As individuals they were vulnerable, insignificant. Tulips and daffodils would be better, dibbed in at random to create a natural living bouquet around the maybe-maple every spring. She chose King Alfred for William – *a tall grower, bold trumpet, rich yellow.* King Alfred who burned the cakes. And for Sura, Queen of the Night – *a tall, striking beauty; dark with a texture like satin.*

Only at the check-out did she read in smaller print on their packets that the one flowered in late March and early April, the other in late April and early May, and found tears welling in her eyes for the second time that day.

Back at Pease Cottage there were two vehicles on the tarmac – a four by four which loomed over the little back porch where William had sown seeds in trays, and a hybrid Toyota Prius. She knocked on the door, the dibber in one hand, packets of King Alfred and the Queen of the Night in the other.

"Hello. My name is Emily Wray and I live in London. I hope you don't think I'm mad, or terribly cheeky, but many years ago my great great grandfather lived here with his family at the time and took great pleasure in tending the garden. I would very much like to plant a few spring bulbs around the trunk of your little tree, to mark my visit."

The dibber worked a treat.

SHE FOUND STEPHEN in the bar of the Kings' Arms.

"Have you been propping that thing up all day?"

"Nope. I'm walked out. Can't you see, the bar is propping *me* up?"

"You're being ironic, but there's no need. I'm not in the least bit angry with you."

"Now you're being ironic."

"Can we start again? Believe it or not I've had a wonderful day. I sat on the bridge and dangled my legs over the River Bela just like William did that first time he rode his bike up to the camp. It's a boarding school now for children with emotional and behavioural difficulties."

"I wonder if there are still Percivals going in to sing Robbie Williams numbers by way of lifting the inmates' spirits?"

"I checked out Yealand Manor and the Friends Meeting House which is just across the road and has the kindest feel of any building I've ever been in but here's a thing: there's a graveyard and all the headstones are the same size and shape, methodically spaced, with just names and dates. Equal in life and equal in death, I suppose. It made me think of those First World War graves in Picardy. They were equal in death at least.

"I walked right over the top of Warton Crags, and then back around the foot of them, with Ingleborough bold and knowing, J B Priestley-like, in the distance before me. Then I drove back through Arnside and Silverdale, and had a brisk walk up Arnside Knott." All of which, she didn't say, gave her a good feel for William's time driving a truck full of prisoners, and a sense of the landscape where Michelangelo painted his Hilary. Nor that Warton Crag so clearly seemed to symbolize Sura, and Ingleborough William. Damn, she didn't even mention calling by Pease Cottage, which he would think was odd and bring up when she least expected it, so that she wouldn't be able to fib with conviction.

"You've climbed the lowest Marilyn in the UK, then."

"I've what?"

"It complements the concept of the Munros. They're mountains over 3,000 feet."

"I know what a Munro is."

"Course you do. You probably know people who run up a couple before breakfast."

"Up three or four actually."

"That's because you can get three or four Munro tops on the same mountain. But a Marilyn always stands on its own. It's got to be at least 500 feet above the surrounding terrain. Anyway, you can tick off the bottom of the list."

She felt disappointed. It wasn't the time for trivia. "I told you, I've had a good day. There's no need for you to be nervous."

"Good. And you're smiling, which is wonderful, though as a matter of interest did you know that the human smile began life as an act of submission? There I go again."

"When I climb a hill I do it for pleasure, not to tick it off a list."

"Quite right. Neither do I. Neither for pleasure nor to tick off a list."

"But since you have considerable capacity for trivia – are you aware of the fact that there are people who visit and log surveyors' bench marks as a competitive sport?"

"I thought you said you weren't angry with me anymore."

"I'm not. Do I sound angry?"

"You sound like you haven't quite let go. You were angry because I hadn't followed up those letters with the zeal of an investigative journalist. You were so angry you swore."

"I don't know where that came from. My grandmother used to swear – but so rarely it really shocked me. If you carried a phone I would have called and said I was sorry."

"Well, I'll take that as an apology, though it sounds more like an accusation. But in any case there is no need."

I do indeed have reason to accuse, she thought. But he does deflect things easily.

"I don't think my sense of curiosity is much different to yours, Emily. I'd seen the doll that Laja Abramowicz wrote about, you know. Here and there, in William's bedroom. I asked him about it more than once, but never got a straight answer. But you're better at the journalism. You've got dozens of people reading your blog no doubt. Hundreds maybe."

"Thousands actually. I told you this narrative would gather momentum if we paced it."

"Exactly."

"Exactly what?"

"Curiosity without some sort of organising principle doesn't amount to anything more than pace. I believe my life has been singularly lacking in organising principle."

"Isn't that what we're trying to do? Find order and sense in these presents your grandfather gave you?"

"By mapping a fantasy of hidden treasure? Come on..."

"We're identifying clues."

"To an X that marks the spot? A six-figure map reference? So you can dig up a pot of gold?"

"Where did you walk to? You said you were walked out."

Stephen shrugged his shoulders. It said she asked too

many questions.

"Don't tell me you didn't find a little bit of gold dust, rooting around your old haunts." She could see he had, however begrudgingly. "So what, Stephen? So what, if the treasure is metaphorical? A hunt makes a good story."

She followed that with a full smile with dimples, and didn't care whether he read it as pleasure or submission.

"I walked round the Castle," he said. "Where some of the Yealand COs did hard time, coincidentally. Looked in the Priory Church. Felt like a regimental museum. Then the Friends Meeting House next door. Felt like a sanctuary. God's War and Peace, rubbing shoulders."

"Then?"

"Down to Cable Street where Howard Oakley had his yard in the sixties. It was Howard who came to get me when William died, out on the sands. It's a Sainsbury's now. Then I walked through the town centre. Hardly recognised it. Shopping arcades, pedestrianized streets, chic bistros. Up to Penny Street Bridge, where Joseph started in Lancaster. I used to build ancient Rome in his sand bin."

This was her original strategy: get him on his own terrain, rich with prompts.

"Show me! I want to see where you built ancient Rome. We can drive, then we'll have dinner in one of your chic bistros."

The drive would turn out to be much longer than she anticipated, and dinner fish and chips from Joe's Plaice as they left town, but she did enjoy an instructive interlude pacing back and forth across the site of the first Oakley builders' yard in Lancaster.

"There was builders' sand, sharp sand, and at least three sizes of gravel all in mountainous heaps against a back wall that ran along here, flush with the canal the whole length of the site, with bricked-up windows and broken glass on top. It must have been an old warehouse, but it had lost its roof." She followed Stephen along the canal-side promenade as he paced across it and gestured with precision. The little promenade the council had made on the site, facing the Royal Infirmary across the canal, made his recollections easy and she fired her prompts at him:

"So why did William work in the family firm?

"Why am I not learning anything about your father?

"Tell me about the boarding school they sent you to.

"How come you don't have any money?

"Why did you never have children?"

For once her questions seemed to fan the flames instead of dousing them. She sat on a bench and tried to assimilate his snatches of response, order them, and assess their reliability, while he gave a detailed account of how the Coliseum could be recreated to scale using only the materials found in a builders' yard.

"Things changed for my grandfather when the Oakleys discovered he could drive, and was therefore useful. They found he could keep shop, too. A little simple meant not clever, and not clever to the Oakleys meant not sharp, which meant not devious, not ruthless, not financially successful. He would do simple but honest work, for a simple wage. Time eroded the historic given – that they owed him – and gradually turned it round to a tacit notion that as a family liability, he owed them.

"I have had money, from time to time. But I've never had that knack for putting it to work to multiply itself. Subconscious negative competition with my father, if there is such a thing. Never been much drawn to building houses either. Except models, out of sand.

"Prep school was strong on the service ethic. The motto

was 'I Will with a Good Will'. But from my perspective it was 'Develop survival strategies or you will be taunted, humiliated, and generally made miserable.'

"The old Oakley business worked because Frederick Oakley made it work. He commanded loyalty, he had power, his word went. His youngest son William, war-wounded, was to be looked after. Period.

"The Army made my father into a money-making machine. He was Oakley with soaring ambition. He was Oakley without bricks and mortar keeping him earthed, or a liking for the beer that washed the dust clean. He was Oakley without owing anybody anything. Until I came along. But he sub-contracted that one.

"The thing you have to realise about the Oakleys is that the key relationship in the lives of the children is not with parent or sibling but with 'family'. The Shropshire Raffia, Mary once called them. I'd hear cousins and nephews viciously slag off their mothers, or their older sisters, and then a minute later go dewy-eyed and say don't get me wrong, she'd kill for me. Ferocious loyalty, except for when it's not so loyal.

"I know they've got other ways of doing it nowadays, but in my day it took two to make a baby. The only time I was with a woman who wanted a baby, she decided I was past it and kicked me out.

"When Frederick died, and the money began to follow the sharpness, the Oakley ferocity grew and the loyalty diminished. I think William only just made it."

Emily felt the dibber in her pocket. She would quite like to return after dark to this place where William had kept shop for his nephew, with more spring bulbs to plant through the strip of unkempt grass that looked like it had once been a tiny border. She asked Stephen what he thought about the significance of the dibber as a gift to him on his fortieth birthday.

He sat on the other bench, which also faced the towering, rugged brown stones of the Royal Lancaster Infirmary over the canal.

"The digit *one* for you, I suppose. To add to yesterday's *six* from the sonnet."

She recited:

Then let not winter's ragged hand deface
In thee thy summer, ere thou be distill'd:

He joined her and together they continued reciting Shakespeare's sixth until, with a delighted laugh at their unity, she dropped out to listen to him alone:

Ten times thyself were happier than thou art
If ten of thine ten times refigured thee:
Then what could death do, if thou shouldst depart,
Leaving thee living in posterity?

She interrupted: "They sort of go together don't they, the poem and the dibber. Encouraging fertility."

And then he finished:

Be not self-will'd, for thou art much too fair,
To be death's conquest and make worms thine heir.

"I looked it up in Waterstones when you stormed out at breakfast and I charmed the pretty young woman behind the counter into photocopying it for me. I spun her a yarn about my grandfather and some Italian prisoners of war learning to read Shakespeare with little wooden letters he made for them. I learned it by heart as I paced up and down here."

"I pulled it up on my phone and learned it by heart walking over Warton Crag. Ten children would increase your happiness ten times, Stephen, since there would be ten faces to mirror yours."

"Ah, your online edition came with a commentary."

"Death would be defeated as you would live forever through your offspring."

"I am much too beautiful to be merely food for worms?" He raised an eyebrow playfully.

"You should not be selfish, but outwit death's conquering hand by making children."

"Children…? Or poems? Or wonderful stories? Or beautiful wooden carvings?"

There was a long silence.

"In any case," he said, "winter's ragged hand has well and truly been at me, I'm afraid."

He didn't look so ragged actually, she thought. She crossed to his bench and sat next to him. Now was surely the time to confront him with a story of her own.

"But you're right, whatever his frustrations William must have seen the dibber as a symbol of renewal and growth," Stephen said. "For me, for Sura and Laja, for himself. And did you admire the grain in the handle of the thing? Isn't it just the most beautiful curve of wood you've ever wrapped your hand around?"

Emily was about to wrap her hand around Stephen's, and share something else she thought was beautiful with him, when her phone rang. Her editor. Instinctively she stood and turned away.

She let her editor talk. The more he told her, the further she walked from Stephen. She limited her responses to brief prompts.

"But when?

"How do they know?

"What will happen now?

"Page one? Won't that encourage more?

"What do you want from me?

"You're asking too much.

"How can I do that?"

Eventually she took the device from her ear, broke contact, and dropped it back into her shoulder bag. She paced the length of the old Oakley yard. What had she done in her mad desire to bring an organising principle to Stephen's life? What had she done in her selfish pursuit of a story that she thought would catapult her career forward? What had she done to a key relationship in her life that might now be stillborn?

"Stephen – I think we should head back to Market Drayton."

"Why? What's happened?"

"A group calling themselves the Oakley Necromancers have been tweeting some pretty sick ideas."

"Necromancers *tweet*?"

"Around the last phrase of the sonnet: *make worms thine heir*. They've been speculating about *treasure in the tombs*. I saw their stuff this afternoon."

"And? The phone call?"

"Apparently someone's mucked around with William's grave. The police in Market Drayton want to keep it out of the media until it's tidied up. They want to see us first thing in the morning." She couldn't stop her voice from wobbling, and as it did so she felt tears welling up. "They say they've found the metal fittings of a coffin at the site. And... well... bones... among the empty beer cans."

DAY FIVE

EVEN BACK AT CHARLES' AND JULIE'S, long abed, the BMW dogged him. Emily gripped the wheel too tightly and she drove too fast. She'd had a long, emotional day. The road was wet and it was coming dark. She thought the horror they would face at the cemetery was all her fault. Should he tell her it wasn't her fault? When she had clearly whipped the whole frenzy into being?

"It really doesn't matter, Emily."

She swung into the fast lane to overtake a BMW. "Don't you dare tell me it's not my fault."

"That's not what I said. I said it really doesn't matter."

"What the hell is that supposed to mean?"

"William told me himself that he didn't want any fuss when his time came."

"Oh yes? When you were ten?"

"He said he liked the Quaker way: a gathering of a few people who knew him, sitting in silent remembrance. Welcome to say a few words if they felt so inspired. Handshakes and a cup of tea afterwards. Body cremated, ashes scattered."

"Well he didn't get that, did he?"

"Uncle Howard took over. Howard said Oakleys only burn rubbish."

"And now it's his bones that are scattered."

"And it doesn't mean a thing to him. Would you mind slowing down? You're making me nervous."

"It's a long way."

"It's a motorway."

"We need to get there."

"We can't do anything until morning. I don't know what we can do then." He wished they were on the old A6, restrained by endless traffic lights and roundabouts, weaving their way through the middle of Preston, Bamber Bridge, Chorley...

"Music?" He reached towards the radio, but she shook her head.

"William drove much much slower. We made this journey many times together. No radio also. We used to play games."

"Like what?"

"Like *I Spy*. But always with a twist. The influence of John Wellington for sure. If the other person didn't get it after three goes you'd have to say what the thing smelled like, and then after another three, what it sounded like. Then taste, I guess. Or touch."

"That's silly. It wouldn't work."

"I was only eight or nine. We made it work. You want to try?"

She shook her head again.

"When we played Scrabble you didn't count your score unless you could justify the word you put down against a theme. If it was *happiness*, say, and you put down *xu* to use your x on a triple, you'd have to say why xu makes you happy."

"And that would be?"

"Because a hundred xu make a dong and that's always good for a laugh. If you're a nine-year-old boy. We'd double the points for a particularly clever justification."

"Who decided what was clever?"

"Mutual agreement. William might say, po-faced, he dong-get it and then I'd argue for triple points. We always came to a consensus."

"Happy families."

"We played that too. William's idea of what constitutes a family made for a bizarre set of rules."

The BMW swept up on them in the inside lane and zoomed ahead, causing Emily to wobble momentarily and Stephen to wake in a cold sweat, his head off the pillow. *I'd rather cry in a BMW.* He was sleeping terribly as he relived the journey south, haunted by the oriental face that had stared at them from the undertaking car window; him telling Emily about the woman on Chinese television, asked by a would-be date if she would ride on a bicycle with him. Emily horrified by the answer. *Rather cry in a BMW than laugh on a bicycle.* Emily racing to catch up with the BMW, to see the face in the rear window, to see if she was crying.

It was still dark outside. Two or three o'clock, he guessed. He needed the loo already.

He felt his way along the corridor with a hand on each wall, knowing there were random steps laid like booby traps. He'd rarely slept upstairs at Charles' and Julie's whatever they said to Emily about always keeping a bed aired, with clean sheets, for visiting Oakleys. If he'd brought a lady-friend and they took a shine to her, she'd get the clean sheet treatment and he'd get a blanket on the couch downstairs.

Not a sound from the room where they'd put Emily. Julie either trusted him or reckoned he was past it. His pee was deep yellow. Better flush or it might be a conversation point at breakfast. Then again, it might make for easier conversation than the colour of William's bones.

Back in his room, back in his bed, back on the road.

"You can't play scrabble when you're driving a car," Emily said.

"We had car games, walking games, home games. William didn't like TV much; we played games instead. He made up games anywhere, anytime."

"It sounds exhausting."

"Even at breakfast. Cornflakes used to come with little plastic toys inside the packet; they don't do that nowadays do they? An Oakley youngster would have reached in with his snotty fingers and nicked the toy as soon as the packet was opened, so when we ate our way to the bottom William would imagine a toy and I'd have twenty questions to guess what it was. He liked games that made you think."

"Let's play a game that makes you think, then," Emily said, easing back into the centre lane. "Tell me the stupidest thing you've ever done."

Okay, he could play that game. He had plenty of stupid things to choose from.

"I was in charge of lighting for the school play, my last year. Blithe Spirit, which the headmaster thought was the funniest thing ever, even after we slow-roasted it. I was up in the lighting gantry working an ancient rheostat that dimmed the candlelight for the séance scenes. It was a long box mounted on the wall underneath the main bank of dimmers. There was a slit in the middle and a lever sticking out of it with a Bakelite handle that you moved up and down. The hall was packed with parents dutifully laughing but with a bit of a snigger. They fidgeted on their moulded plastic seats and noisily unwrapped boiled sweets which they passed to younger siblings to try and keep them awake. My way of dealing with the tedium of a scene that was limping its way towards the dramatic climax was to wiggle my little finger into the slit in the rheostat. Just like a kid with his head in the playground railings. It was a challenge getting past the first knuckle but eventually I managed and at that precise instant of mastery, I tapped into mains voltage. Predictably, I couldn't get out again. The medium, played by the drama queen of lower sixth arts, was approaching maximum concentration in his attempt to exorcise the spirits of the two dead wives when I finally managed to let out a strangled scream and gasp for breath. More like a two-hundred-and-forty-volt orgasm than anything spiritual. I jerked the Bakelite handle up and down as far as I could, which had no impact on the amount of current flowing through my body but made the candle centre-stage appear as if it too was having an orgasm. As I lost consciousness I remember thinking, I don't want to die to riotous applause."

"Hmm."

"Your turn."

She shook her head. "I'm driving."

"Your not-a-boyfriend Peter Tomkins told me you once stuck your hand up in school to answer a question about London and said the road between Buckingham Palace and Westminster Abbey was called Coronation Street."

"Apocryphal. I told you he was unreliable."

"He said your grandmother didn't have a TV. He said having the latest trendy trainers wasn't an issue for you because she never bought you *any* trainers."

"She wasn't into royalty either. Which was never an issue for me."

"That's just what he said."

"So what's the cleverest thing you've ever done?"

"Pass O level Latin?"

"Okay. If you say so. The most cowardly thing?"

"Not so fast. Peter needs a turn. He told me you were the cleverest kid in your class."

"Wrong again. Peter really hasn't a clue. My way of fitting in was to be a model student. I was organised, did what was asked of me, and got good grades. I impressed the teachers and cut myself off even more from my peers. Not clever."

She drove in silence and let him think before prompting him again. "Come on, most cowardly."

"At prep school probably – away from home, away from family, away from civilization, it felt like. Cowardice was a vital part of my survival strategy."

"Go on."

"I was up an oak tree not far from Red India, a giant sequoia in a sprawl of rhododendron that Richard Winding called The Congo. Winding's favourite territory was a rocky field covered in bracken in which his White Russians made hideouts and cells for holding prisoners. There was another gang called The Samurai but they mostly went in for group masturbation in a place called the Black Hole of Calcutta which was a low dry-stone enclosure which once had something to do with sheep. I was never in a gang, though not because of any principled objection; I was sufficiently oddball for them to be wary of me. And I knew it to be the case with Winding that when victims were in short supply he turned on his own. My favourite trick to ensure that oddball Oakley did not become a victim, at least during the interminable periods when we were turned outdoors to occupy ourselves in the grounds, was to make myself scarce by climbing trees. I liked oaks best, but there were conifers that were climbable too, so even in winter I could disappear into a world of my own. It was against school rules to climb trees and the warrior gangs always had their noses close to earth.

"So I was high in a tree in The Congo, which was mainly where the youngest played, sitting comfortably in the fork of a huge branch with my back to the trunk, daydreaming, when I heard Winding pounce on a peon - which incidentally comes from the same root as pawn - and instead of dragging him off to do unspeakable things to him in one of his bracken cells, he ordered him to strip and hug Red India, and four of his henchmen to go round the back of the tree where two grabbed the little fellow's hands and the other two crouched down and grabbed his feet and they all pulled, so he was spread-eagled naked against the rough trunk and squealing like a pig at which point Winding said to shut up or he'd have to shove his sock in his mouth and the little chap started whimpering and begging quietly to be let go but Winding had got a long length of bramble and he wrapped the chap's shirt around one end to make a handle, flicked it in the air like a whip and then lashed the boy's bum with it. He whipped him with the bramble and the louder the boy cried the harder he whipped him and I was up there in the tree but I didn't say a word. I didn't come down. As it was happening I gradually edged my way round to the far side of my tree so they couldn't see me if they looked up. Then all I could hear was deep gasping sobs and Winding saying if Matron saw the marks and asked, he had to say he was playing aborigines and fell down the north face of the Eiger."

Emily slowed down, moved into the centre lane, then slipped between two trucks as if to hide.

"The Eiger was a little rocky outcrop on the edge of The Congo. There was a poem about The Congo the English teacher liked to perform:

BOOM, steal the pygmies
BOOM, kill the Arabs,
BOOM, kill the white men,
HOO, HOO, HOO.
Mumbo-Jumbo, God of the Congo,
Mumbo-Jumbo will hoo-doo-you.

"There was lots more like that. It went on for ages. When I was older I read all the stuff about bullies having terribly low self-esteem - that if someone just stood up to them, they would collapse and be shown up for what they were. That compounded my sense of being a coward. But looking back on it now, I'm not sure I believe it. Richard Winding was no more lacking in self esteem than Hitler or Stalin. He was chock full of it."

"So where were the adults when all this Lord of the Flies stuff was going on?"

"On that particular occasion one of them was on the school terrace, close enough to fetch a telescope from the science cupboard and focus on the boy who had foolishly climbed so high on the school-ward side of a tree that he could be readily identified. I got six strokes of the cane."

Even the trucks were overtaking them now.

"They were child abusers," Emily said. "For caning you. But even more for not seeing the other stuff."

"And what were the parents? For not seeing that they weren't seeing the other stuff?"

Keele service station came and went. He told her to take the next exit.

"Last round, then. The bravest thing you've ever done."

He didn't stop to think. "I don't do brave."

Onto the slip road, down to the roundabout, and up to the traffic lights where the signpost to Market Drayton steered his mind towards the business ahead. Emily tried to push him into declaring something brave. He wondered if climbing the tree hadn't in fact been sort of brave, as well as cowardly. It was after all a risky tactic that involved challenge and danger and which proved effective in avoiding Winding's clutches.

But Emily had seen the signpost too. "Tomorrow might see *me* at my cleverest or stupidest; my bravest or most cowardly."

THE POLICE CONSTABLE who called himself The Officer In the Case spoke of Facebook and Twitter not as social media but social vices; he'd attended a training seminar – not to become a user but to learn about the harm they could cause and the criminality they could lead to in the hands of unscrupulous *pushers*. He preferred to work with tangibles, he said, and was clearly pleased when Stephen gave him, when asked for identification, the small but solid piece of pink plastic which showed his name and address, the date and country of his birth and a photographic image of his face, along with the categories of vehicle he was licensed to drive.

"And can you identify this grave?" The OIC spread three photographs on the table between them.

"It's William Oakley's."

"How do you know? The stone's been knocked down. It's half covered by all that soil."

"Because the one on the right there, with the angels on each side, is his father's, Frederick Oakley's. And the one you can see at the back with the huge urn is his brother Heaton's, and next to that with the sun dial, his brother Albert's, though they both came later. I was there when they lowered William down, in 1960. I was ten. I've been back several times."

"Are you the next of kin?"

"No. I'm his grandson. The next of kin would be my father but he's in his nineties and not fully compos mentis. In any case, they were estranged."

"And other family? Oakleys are well known in the area."

"You got all day? Why do you need to know?"

"In my experience, Mr Oakley, few incidents cause more upset for family members than those involving damage to the grave of a loved one."

"You've got a lot of experience of graves being dug up, then?"

"I have experience of youths gathering in the cemetery and drinking, swearing, leaving litter, and tossing flowers around. It causes great offence. As far as some families are concerned you'd think the world had come to an end. Even when the flowers are plastic."

"This grave is fifty years old. No one has been leaving flowers."

FIFTEEN MINUTES LATER, he was still in the interview room at the police station, sipping a cup of tea and sorting out what he had gleaned from the OIC. A local resident had made a complaint to the force control centre about rowdy noise coming from the town cemetery. By the time the CSO's had arrived the perpetrators had gone. The scene had been secured with tape. Photographs had been taken. Later today, they had planned to make house to house enquiries in the immediate vicinity to see if anyone had noticed anything untoward; to notify the vicar and other family members. But CID had become involved and a Senior Investigating Officer nominated because there was an issue involving social media and the investigation might involve specialist officers. Not exactly the vice squad, said the OIC. More a case of computer boffins in an office at force HQ. He thought a forensic investigation was unlikely and given the health and safety issues the site presented, he hoped to have it tidied up again within a few days.

The OIC had been summoned to the telephone in another room. Now he in turn summoned Stephen, and the two of them hovered over a telephone conference speaker.

"Stephen Oakley? It's the SIO here. Listen, we need you to give a brief interview to a young journalist called Emily Wray. As soon as possible, so we can tidy this thing up within the hour."

"Emily Wray is jogging somewhere. Enjoying her pre-breakfast run."

"No she's not. She's at the cemetery with a photographer from her paper. Look, her editor has given us sight of what happened, pretty much start to finish. He's got hold of video they took. Bloody distasteful business but we can see that nothing has been stolen from the site. No hidden treasure. No bones, even. We've got half a dozen males drinking beer through balaclavas and taking turns digging. To be perfectly frank, tracking them down will take time and resources I have better use for. They'll probably give themselves away online before long anyway, and we've got an eye on that. But you can imagine the outrage our local media would stir up. Better to work with one editor we can trust, who can keep it to himself, don't you agree? A few words from yourself and he's promised this young journalist will handle it all sensitively. We've got three men from the council ready to inter the remains properly, restore the grave and tidy the site. They say one hour and you wouldn't be able to tell the difference."

"I'm not sure I want anything to do with this young journalist of yours. My thoughts about the desecration of my grandfather's grave will only add to the offensiveness."

"Not an interview, Mr Oakley. Just a comment. Just a brief reaction."

"I don't believe Ms Wray does brief reaction. She likes seven days."

"Up to you. But it's only a matter of time until another family member makes themselves available. I understand there are a number still resident in the area. I think that would be regrettable."

FROM THE POLICE STATION he cut through the car park of the Methodist church. Uncle Isaac - one of Heaton's sons - had brought him to services here while Aunty Nora cooked Sunday dinner, after his own children had been expelled from Sunday school and proved incapable of staying put through the adult service. That was in the old building, before lightening struck. Uncle Isaac had been upset the Oakleys were not involved in the building of the new – whose brickwork was handsome enough – and took to The Joiners' Arms instead while the Sunday joint was roasting.

Surprisingly, the Infant School was still there on his right, with its little black-and-white timber-framed annexe which had been his first refuge from the storm of his parents' broken marriage. No fighting over custody then; more a case of each parent arguing it was the other's new relationship which should bear the baggage of the old. Until the Oakleys, in their generality, had absorbed him, rather as they had absorbed William two generations earlier. When he was old enough, it was William who had taken him to nursery, and made sure he was settled, and shown him on the big clock where the hands would be when it was time for him to come and collect him.

Beyond the Infant School, they'd pulled down the

Grammar School and put up non-descript housing. They'd squeezed more of them all around him, in the gardens of the Edwardian houses. Oakleys had probably built some of them, but he was away at prep school by then, his father sending the bursar three cheques each year from London and his mother on the other side of the world with her new family. He remembered looking over the playing field to the red brick grammar school in his holidays and wondering what it would have been like. No *Mumbo Jumbo God of the Congo* at least. More *Dare to be Wise* he supposed.

Clive Road became Cemetery Road. This was prime building land if ever there was, filled with bumps, lumps, and headstones; names, dates and biblical one-liners: *Yea, through I walk through the shadow of the valley of death... Blessed are they that mourn... The angel was waiting, he took you in his arm, so until I join you, I know you'll meet no harm...* And waiting at the far side he could see Emily with her photographer and a young lanky constable who was probably no such thing. A Community Support Officer, perhaps. Or St John's Ambulance Brigade, in case resuscitation was required.

"So am I seeing Emily Wray at her cleverest?"

"You must know this is me at my most cowardly, Stephen. Believe me - I'm up my tree looking down as the bullies do their thing."

He wondered what on earth had possessed him to take this young woman on trust and yet even now he couldn't help admiring the chutzpah of her. He wasn't even upset about the grave. Why should he be? But it surely signified the end of this odd adventure with Emily Wray and he was surprised to discover he found that disagreeable.

There was a heap of soil at the head of the grave, where William's modest stone had stood, and a corona of red soil around the gaping hole. He stepped carefully to the edge and looked down. It was deep and dark, but not neatly edged like the graves villains in cowboy films make their victims dig before they shoot them. He couldn't see any bones. Or worms for that matter.

"The men from the council have collected the remains."

"Ah. No Yorick-like moment for me, then."

"They've got them in a little wicker basket with a lid and will put them back before they replace the soil. I told them I didn't think you would want prayers."

"I'm not giving you an interview."

"It's not necessary, Stephen. My editor wanted fifteen seconds of you at the graveside and we've got that already." She nodded at the man engrossed with his gizmo opposite. "I can give it a voice over. It's only for a tiny podcast on the blog. And one still for the paper."

"*Stephen Oakley was tight-lipped this morning?* For a change?"

"*Stephen Oakley was in sombre mood this morning as he reflected on the desecrated grave of his kindly grandfather*."

"Stephen Oakley has a right to be bloody angry, not sombre, and not just at the idiots who did this but the ones who set them up for it."

"I'm not sure you do angry. And you don't blame me for this. You said *it really doesn't matter* remember?"

But he'd never said it wasn't her fault. She'd told him not to. And now she *had* made him angry. Sort of. He certainly felt he ought to be angry.

"Who would have given a toss about my poor sodding grandfather, dead fifty years and long forgotten, if it wasn't for you and your precious blog?"

"He was never forgotten by you. And this isn't really William's story. It's yours."

"No it's not - it's yours. This is how you earn your

living. It's been yours all along, from the moment you barged into my flat and more fool me for knowing that all along and still giving you everything you wanted."

"So why did you?"

"Why did I?" Okay, think. And be honest. "Because you're young. It feels good to say yes to young people."

"And?"

"And how have you got this exclusive - this deal with the police? If this is all over the web, why isn't there a scrum of paparazzi here, fighting over shots of Stephen Oakley, the new Jim Hawkins, in sombre mood as he surveys the handiwork work of today's Billy Bones and Long John Silver?"

She lowered her head and mumbled her answer: "It seems my editor's got someone inside. Inside the group that did this." Now she did look worried, and hurried to try and explain herself: "I don't mean a reporter. And not actually doing the digging. There's a bigger group... I don't know how big... and they've emailed footage of the dig to each other. From phones, I guess. Apparently you can see the whole thing as it happened. Nothing in the hole but soil and bones and some rusty coffin fittings. Our contact got them to offer the story to the paper, for cash, before they published it themselves."

"Before they published it? There's a market for that?"

"Posted it on YouTube maybe."

"Aren't we talking about a criminal offence?"

"My editor talked to the police last night, straight after he phoned me. They agreed to his suggestion because once they'd seen the footage he sent them they wanted the site put back together again before your 'scrum of paparazzi' arrived. All the nationals heading for Market Drayton... I guess they saw that as a pretty major distraction."

"Your silly season. Poor old William's bones."

"My paper isn't breaking any laws. We're reporting a great story, and the treasure hunt speculation has become a part of that. But we'll be printing repeated reminders for readers with a metal detector in the boot of their car not to break laws of trespass, criminal damage and public nuisance. Look, I've got to do the voiceover and file my story."

He was through looking.

"The men from the council won't get to work until my photographer's gone."

"I can see I'm in the way."

"Give me three minutes."

Three minutes was quite long enough for him to drop over the low wall into Prospect Road and be gone. Being gone in Market Drayton, though, was a relative business. The railway station which had seen Frederick Oakley's departure for the Potteries and his first war-time contracts, and his son William's arrival home, broken, from Bligny Hill and the trenches, had gone with the Beeching cuts of '64. Could he catch a bus? Not like on the Kingston Road, for sure. He only had a tenner and some loose change in his pocket. He could buy time by strolling over the fields to have another look at Burnet Hall, say – he was pretty sure that would still be there, minus the Burnets, converted into desirable apartments or a nursing home. He could take the same right of way William took to see his Ada; it wouldn't be gone either, though there might be a bull in one of the fields at this time of year. Nor had the Oakleys gone, of course. One of them would surely lend him the train fair back to London, and maybe even give him a lift to a station. He'd get his bag from Charles' and Julie's before Emily got back, then head for Keith's or Bruce's, if he could remember where they lived. If they still lived there. It felt like the old days before he went to the States, juggling Oakleys for meal tickets. He decided to go for a coffee first. That was like the old days too.

At the bottom of Prospect there was a new civic building of some kind; nicely proportioned, good fenestration, with an attractive double-brick arch over the doorway. He peered in the door and could see there was a café, but it looked closed. Across Cheshire Street he could see a supermarket, pretty much where the railway station used to be. Don't even look at the brickwork. But supermarket cafés often had half-way decent coffee.

The door opened ahead of his knock when he eventually reached Charles' and Julie's and he felt it close behind with a sense of foreboding that had been entirely absent at the police station earlier.

"Well look what's washed ashore at long last."

Julie nodded gravely, a step behind her husband.

"I'll just collect my bag. Then I'll be out of your way."

"You'll do no such thing. That's what you've always done; you and your father before you and his father before him by all accounts. Come and take when you need, and bugger off as soon as you've something to give. You'll sit down, Stephen Oakley, right there. And you'll listen to what we have to say."

The seat Charles indicated was a deep soft armchair and he knew that once he took it he would be captive. He'd been at plenty of Oakley family gatherings in this house even after William died and they'd never lost their touch for the slow unfolding of the business in hand. They'd start with a contract won or lost, handsome profits made, slow-payers gone to the wall. Then some personal gossip – so and so pregnant and having to marry, an in-law on the cancer ward – all circling round a decision that had to be made to keep the peace between the ever more disparate branches. They'd defer to an elder and then when he went to the toilet join in a cruel joke at his expense. The women would be enjoying their own equivalent in the kitchen while keeping the men provided with tea and sponge cake. He knew this oversized living room, now with a thirty-six-inch flat-screen TV mounted above the recessed log-effect gas fire, cut-glass fruit bowl filled with hand-painted wooden fruit, and budgerigar in a bell-shaped cage swinging from the ceiling in the corner, for the palaver hut it was. He settled in for an Oakley powwow.

Julie came in with a tray. "A piece of raspberry sponge, Stephen?"

Charles said, "Pete and Tom are away at an auction but Keith and Bruce are coming over as soon as they can get away."

"And a nice cup of tea while we're waiting?"

"And Eric's on his way down from Crewe, picking up young Douglas in Alsager on his way. You knew Douglas and Patty had moved out to Alsager?"

"Is that Uncle Douglas's son?"

"Grandson. He's got a little boy of his own now, only he's got cerebral palsy. What they used to call spastic."

"I'm sorry to hear. I didn't know."

"Eric built up a good scaffolding business. He did a lot of work for firms that fit solar panels but then the government cut the feed-in tariff and it went flat."

"Your sponge cake is as light as ever, Julie."

"It'll come back in time, the solar panel business. Before house-building probably. But there's none of us growing any younger. Bruce had a bad go with a hernia last back end."

He couldn't identify Bruce from his back-end hernia

any more than he could from memory, and there were no introductions or handshakes as this southerly cluster of Oakleys arrived. They each nodded at him in turn and told him not to get up. Sometimes an accompanying female headed straight for the kitchen without even a nod. Emily didn't nod either, though she didn't go to the kitchen. She went for the straight-backed chair in the furthest corner, occupied by Eric, and sat cross-legged on the floor beside and half behind it. Uncanny – it was precisely his place and posture, aged nine or ten, sheltered by William, while the other Oakley children mucked around in the yard outside.

"Young Emily was sulking outside," Eric said. "So I told her to come in."

Brave *and* stupid, he figured. They often went together.

"Young Emily seems to think your grandad has laid a treasure hunt, Stephen," Charles said. "And my guess is that you're not far off finding where X marks the spot."

"William liked to play games. She does too."

"Well you would say that wouldn't you? Old William liked to play the fool too when it suited. By all accounts. But from where we're sitting now the accounts seem very one-sided. Because we all know that any fortune William got his hands on can only have come from one place: the Oakleys."

Bruce said, "Hang on a minute, Charles, before you go making accusations. We all know Uncle George was rolling in it long before William died. Stands to reason he'd have done right by his old man."

"He's never done right by his son, has he? Just look at him."

They all looked straight at Stephen, who replaced his third piece of raspberry sponge on its china plate, and the china plate on the coffee table, so they could enjoy an unimpeded view.

Charles said, "Case in point: George would never have started in prefabs after the war if he hadn't heard his uncles saying that was the way it would have to be done. It was Heaton's and Arthur's idea, long before the war was over, and George as good as stole it."

Douglas said, "That's what Grandad Albert used to say."

"Heaton and Arthur would have done it right, if they'd had the same capital as the big boys. But George never knew the meaning of doing it right. He never did a proper day's work in his life. With him it was always other people's money, other people's ideas, other people's graft. Talk it up, sell it on, take a percentage - that's all he ever did."

"Messing with those Americans."

"Fly boys."

"Took his Oakley upbringing and Oakley ideas and never looked back. We've barely seen him since."

"Ditto," he said under his breath.

"You do have a radio, Charles?"

"They said we'd be on the one o'clock news."

"Julie's got one in the kitchen."

Keith went for it and gave a running commentary on his struggle to free it from the half dozen other electrical gadgets Julie kept on the counter. He came back with an eighties ghetto blaster. It was tuned to Radio Two. No one knew the wavelength for Radio Shropshire and Bruce said they'd miss it.

"Try ninety-six FM," Eric said, relaying a whispered prompt from Emily.

The interview was already underway.

"No, I never knew Uncle William personally; only through the many stories I heard when I was growing up." There was so much bass, it sounded subterranean.

"Yours was a close family?"

"You've got it. He was my grandfather's uncle, but we all called him 'Uncle William'. The Oakleys are that sort of family."

"You must have been terribly upset when you heard his grave had been dug up."

"Absolutely. It's shocking. I've never heard anything like it. And for this to happen to a man who was so trusting and straight with people. A man who looked to his family above all else, and whose family cared for him deeply."

"Let me bring in your brother, Keith Oakley. Keith, you run a business here in the town..." There was an explosive clearing of the throat from Keith, who had presumably leaned in close to the microphone.

"It's absolutely disgusting. We're gutted. And to add injury to insult, we've had no time to grieve. No chance to pay our respects. Take my word for it, this was the work of outsiders. People from out of town. And it's being covered up by people from out of town, as if nothing happened, on orders from who knows."

"He was a war hero." The microphone moved again.

"Douglas Oakley."

"In the first world war. His whole regiment won the Victoria Cross. Uncle William was badly wounded. And now this."

"You must be very angry."

"You're dead right I am, and whoever done this is going to get what's coming."

"The Oakley plots are a place of family pilgrimage."

"Eric Oakley."

"I don't know how we'll ever get over this."

The reporter demonstrated his command of the situation by thanking his collection of Oakleys individually by name and then assuring them that they did not stand alone. William's grave may have been restored and re-turfed with what some might call indecent haste, he said, but the sense of outrage was felt across the community. The secretary of the British Legion, Church leaders and local councillors were unanimous in condemning what could only be described as a very grave affair. He then apologised for the pun, reminded his listeners that they were listening to BBC Radio Shropshire, and wrapped up with a statement from the police asking for anyone with information to come forward.

Eric said, "They cut my bit about how there should be compensation."

Charles turned off the radio.

Stephen glared at Emily but she kept her head down.

Without a hint of wit Charles said, "William will be turning in his grave."

"William never wanted to be buried in the first place," he said. "He told me that himself."

"William seems to have told you a great deal over the past sixty years Stephen. But he didn't tell you Douglas here has got a young lad who has to hobble around with a Zimmer frame, did he?"

"Uncle Charles!"

"I've got a right to talk about the treasure pot, Douglas. If it wasn't for all this talk of treasure the cemetery wouldn't have been vandalised, the Oakley graves insulted, the family disrespected. Your Uncle Stephen knows a lot more secrets than he's letting on about."

"I may have enjoyed a rich inheritance," he said, "but it has not been the kind to make me a rich man."

Eric said, "He's right. He may have frittered away many talents in his life but they've never looked like coinage."

Charles said, "Your father's the bugger. Walked away from all the Oakleys, including his own son."

"Treasure doesn't always come in chests." The quiet female voice surprised them all. "As I know well." Not wobbling, just, he thought. And addressing the whole family. She became rapidly more confident: "If you've read my articles you'll know that I think William has been giving his grandson clues every ten years, and that I believe they will lead somewhere. But I have never suggested that they will lead to 'treasure' of financial value. Nor that they would lead to William's grave."

"Douglas's lad is a treasure, right enough," Charles said. "But that doesn't alter the fact that for fifty grand he could have an operation that would give him a chance of being able to walk on his own two legs. And the NHS won't pay a penny."

They've got there at last, he recognised. Now he could say something conciliatory, get his bag, and get away.

"Stephen could get his bag right now and show us all the present William gave him ten years ago, on his fiftieth birthday."

All eyes turned to Emily.

Now surely he was seeing Emily Wray at her cleverest. Her manipulation of the media's silly season about to crash, the carefully built audience about to collapse, she backs him into a corner and uses his family to get what she wants.

All eyes turned to him.

But if this was Emily Wray at her cleverest, he was left in no doubt that the young journalist who he found alternately likeable and sympathetic, puzzling and provocative, did not view herself that way. As she returned his gaze and waited for his response, he thought that she looked deeply vulnerable, desperate even. Her career was hardly on the line; the pursuit of her story had become deeply personal.

Without a word, he struggled out of his armchair and left the room. He went to the toilet then collected his bag from the bedroom he had slept in. He was not surprised when he came back downstairs to find Keith hovering in the hallway, ready to block his exit should he try to leave without saying goodbye.

The armchair was waiting for him. Teacups had been refilled and a tray of Julie's celebrated butterfly buns circulated. He put the bag down between his feet.

"I'm not at all sure that William would want me to do this."

"So?" Emily said calmly. "He'll make yet another turn in his grave?"

"He wrote a long letter – which I have here – giving a full account of the origins and significance for him of the carving he arranged to be delivered to me forty years after his own death. I will show you the gift if Emily will read the letter aloud and you all agree to listen to the end." He passed a sheaf of papers to Emily and placed on the coffee table a piece of wood about nine inches tall and five inches in diameter.

Charles picked up the carving and scrutinised it, grunted, and passed it to Bruce on his left. Bruce turned it around several times and said it was like three pieces linked together, very nicely done. Emily held it gingerly as if concerned it might speak and say something too intimate. Eric weighed it in the palm of one hand and said it was carved from a single piece of lime. Keith lifted it high as though checking the base for a price sticker. Douglas quickly passed it on, as if worried the music might stop and he be obliged to pay a forfeit.

Stephen put back on the coffee table, in the centre of the Oakley palaver hut, the small carving which had been conceived in friendship as a representation of young

William, Ada, and their as yet unborn child, George – and realised many years later as a token of self-forgiveness. Emily read fluently.

DEAR STEPHEN

So all being well you are fifty - the age at which I started to make peace with myself.

I want to take you back to the 30th of September 1918, to - let's call it Flanders. I rarely knew in those days whether I was in France or Belgium. When I first went out I was in France because the grapes growing round the foot of Bligny Hill were for making champagne. My brother Arthur had bought a bottle of champagne for our father, to celebrate winning a contract with the war ministry for some work in Crewe, but father wouldn't take it because he didn't hold with frivolous drink, especially not made by the French, who he said were a fanciful race even if they were our allies. But after Bligny they moved us north, and kept moving us one way and then another every few days, where the border wriggles this way and that and the farmhouses and villages were shelled to smithereens, and the towns weren't much better off, so in the main I remembered the landscape of it - Aubers Ridge, the Bois-du-Biez, (which meant a drink of beer according to Dickie Sowden who knew the lingo), the rivers Somme and Sambre, and more to the point on that last day of September, Layers Ditch. The attack was launched by whistle at half past seven in the morning and by quarter to eight we were in. Later in the day another trench was captured and a fair length made safe, though we lost a lot of men. But I didn't have any part in that because at Layers Ditch Dickie Sowden stumbled on a dug-out full of the sorriest-looking Jerries he'd ever seen and before anyone thought to fire a shot or say an angry word, they surrendered and he captured them.

I knew the war would be over soon - because my father had told me so and he knew all about the Americans who had come over to finish the job, and the new tanks with proper steering; but also because Ada Doley was pregnant and I'd been making her a set of chess pieces and though I'd fairly slowed down, I had a timetable in mind that I was convinced would see me home in time for the baby coming. The sight of these prisoners – gaunt, filthy, and exhausted – made me certain of it.

I always thought of her as Ada Doley though she was properly Ada Oakley since we were married before I left. She was always her own person, with her own mind and her own plan. Always Ada Doley to me. I was only seventeen.

Most of the men, though, thought the war might go on another year or two. Dickie said he'd seen our own looking as haggard and beaten as these Jerries. He'd seen them in Amiens in the summer, slouching in little groups at crossroads, without their kit, without their rifles even, without officers, begging for cigarettes with a hopeless look in their eyes as The Fourth marched past to plug a gap.

Anyway, The Fourth still had a job to do after we'd taken Layers Ditch and the lieutenant wanted these Jerries out of the way. He told Lance Corporal Sowden that since he'd lumbered himself with them, he could bloody well get them to Abbeville, where there was a big muster. He gave Dickie a chit telling him to report to the adjutant in the village we'd come through three days before and the adjutant would give him an order to report to the Town Major next along and so on all the way to Abbeville, unless he could get one of them to relieve him of his charge. The lieutenant told Dickie to make up the escort with one private and Dickie chose me. He said I reminded him of his younger brother.

We moved off straight away, Dickie in front, fourteen Jerries in Indian file, me at the rear. We were in a labyrinth of trenches and dugouts, with traverses built-in all along, and I was terrified a Jerry would duck away and make a dash for it. I gripped my rifle in both hands, ready for goodness knows what, and that made things tougher because the duckboards were old and shattered, with long gaps – some full of water – and steps up and down, though Dickie set a slow enough pace and we had to stop and press against the wall when a squad of our own men hurried along in the opposite direction. Soon Dickie led us into a communication trench and that was worse because it was narrow and reinforcements were coming up regular, some of them hauling boxes of ammunition. Dickie pressed on and then the shelling started up worse than ever and still Dickie kept going, until he reached a regimental aid post, and he pulled us to one side into a big pit that had once been a dugout.

The prisoners dropped to their haunches, Dickie lit a cigarette, and I shouldered my rifle.

"That's right, mate," he said. "This lot ain't goin' nowhere except where we take 'em. They look like the warrior class to you? Offspring of Attila the bloody Hun? A bunch of sorry sods that have had it even worse than we have, that's what we've got here, my lad. Their worst enemy is their own officers. And hunger, maybe. And lice and trench foot and dysentery. Not a lot different to us when you think about it." He tossed his cigarette butt in the mud, kicked one of the prisoners on the edge of his boot by way of a sign it was time to get moving and then grunted a couple of times "Alley-oop, alley-oop," by way of showing off his foreign languages.

I had no idea how Dickie navigated us out of the trenches and up onto a farm track and then onto a proper lane, rutted and pot-holed as it was, and into a village. I saw my job now as bringing up the rear to make sure no one collapsed and got left in the ditch. They were dirty, lousy, unshaven, and dog-tired, but not obviously wounded. I don't believe I saw a single tin helmet go, but by the time we were on the lane they were all wearing what looked like cloth caps, caked with mud like their long greatcoats and stripped of any badges. Shuffling along quietly enough, they weren't planning on going back to war. I remember whistling to myself, in my head, which I hadn't done for a long time.

As soon as we reached the village it was obvious we were not going to find the adjutant as per Dickie's orders. The place was deserted. There were piles of rubble and charred timbers. A few lengths of wall and corners of buildings still stood, including one with a sign 'Estaminet' which Dickie said was just the place for a glass of vino except it looked like they couldn't keep the staff. He banged on what was left of the door anyway. He banged on everything left in the village that had once been a door and eventually got a response. An old man with white hair came out of a hovel with part of its roof intact, shaking his head, and holding his hand out. Dickie gave him a cigarette and asked for water then motioned tipping back a pint. The old man pointed down the side of the building where we found a pump above a closed well. It had a metal tag fastened to the handle, with a four-digit number and three words in gothic print.

"When Fritz was 'ere," Dickie said, "He kindly mapped and numbered all the bloody water sources. Let's hope it doesn't say 'poisoned on retreat'." He pumped vigorously and when the water came he let the others drink first, which they did eagerly. Dickie lit another cigarette and as no one buckled up and retched by the time he'd smoked it, he deigned to drink himself. Then we trudged on.

By late afternoon the Jerries had slowed to a crawl and started mumbling between themselves. I caught the word 'bully' which I took to mean bully beef, which they would have found aplenty if they'd ever taken one of our trenches and maybe had developed a taste for. I told Dickie if they were half as starved as I was we'd have a mutiny on our hands unless we located rations soon. Half an hour later he led us into a copse set back from the road and acted out his plan: he rubbed his belly, pointed to himself then to the road he would take to scout for food. Finally, he waved his hand over all of us and put a finger to his lips to signify quiet. Within five minutes he was out of sight and the Jerries were asleep on the ground. It was the same with our lot – they fell asleep instantly wherever they were, given half the chance, though I never got the hang of it myself. I sat with my back to a tree, took out the chess pawn I was working on, and whittled away at it with the little chisel Old Armitage had given me when I left Drayton.

I quickly became absorbed in what I was doing though I was aware of background noise: insects buzzing somewhere beneath the canopy of leaves, men on the ground breathing heavily, a rumble of artillery to the east, and most surprisingly – a tractor that had started up and was methodically passing back and forth on the far side of the road. Then, superimposed, an intense silence and a sudden awareness that I was being stared at. I looked up in alarm. One of the prisoners, lying on his side some ten yards away, faced me with his head nestled on forearms folded to make a pillow and watched intently. He smiled. I slipped my handiwork back in my pocket.

Dickie returned with news that he had found a medical unit camped in a wreck of a mansion house less than three miles away. They'd seen the odd Jerry up close and discovered he was made of flesh and blood just like us; they had a kitchen tent with bread, soup and tea for sixteen to spare; and there was a barn with fresh straw for us to kip in. "It's the bloody Ritz for Fritz," Dickie said, with a smile that got them grudgingly to their feet and ready to trudge on.

When we reached the place, Dickie hurried us into the barn and sent me to fetch the victuals. He said the matron was okay but one of the orderlies was worse than a bloody staff sergeant and we'd best keep out of his way. Dickie said that's what we'd do until we got back to the front line. He said to think of it as smuggling a bit of rough through the giant bordello that was the staff corps at the rear of the British Army. He said bordello was a key French word.

When we'd finished eating, Dickie said we'd best take four hours on and four hours off and when I asked why he said again that none of them were going to bugger off, but if an officer thought to stick his head in and found no one on guard there'd be hell to pay. He said I was on first, since I'd already had a rest earlier, and I swear within thirty seconds he was fast asleep.

I sat close to the open door, where there was still some light and a bit of fresh air that I thought would help keep me awake. Even so, eventually I must have started to nod because all of a sudden one of the Jerries nearest to me was warning one of the others, quietly but firmly – "Uli" and again, "Uli!" The other was standing over Dickie, leaning down. I looked round for my rifle and scrambled to my feet, but the one who had spoken faced me and whispered, equally firmly and in perfect English, "It's all right. It's safe.

Uli means no harm. He's a smoker. We're all smokers. But he has poor self control." The Jerry standing above Dickie walked away, his back to me, holding his hands to heaven to show anyone watching that he had made an honest try to lift a cigarette, but failed. The other came towards me, his hand held out in greeting.

Awkwardly, I shook it.

"Angel Ziegler," he said. "Englebert to my father, but every Englebert in Köln is called Angel."

"Why didn't you tell us you speak English?"

"I have learned in the army not to volunteer anything unless I have to. But I have been listening. Your corporal is a good man. I did not want Uli to take advantage."

Dickie slept on.

I sat back down in the doorway, and the German who was called Angel asked if he could join me. "You mean well also, I believe. A woodcarver, like me. I will play chess with you to make sure you stay awake on your watch."

"I'm making the pieces for my wife. I only have a few pawns."

"No matter." He reached into a deep greatcoat pocket and drew out a small wad of paper, held together with a safety clip. They were chess men, drawn on inch-square paper. With a piece of broken roof tile he drew a board in the dirt floor and we set out our pieces. I had only played against Ada Doley and at first I felt he was imposing himself between us. But as we played, I came to feel more in touch with Ada and was grateful to him. He said his wife taught him to play and berated him for his timidity, which had created in him a tendency to be over-hasty and reckless. I told him Ada urged caution and as a result I often played too warily. But for all that we were well matched, and won a game each. As we started a third he scratched beneath his coat vigorously and swore in German. He said four years a *Frontschwein* was enough for any man. That's what they called a front-line infantryman: a front pig. The trenches - *Die Schützengraben* - comes from their word for graves.

An orderly came over in the morning and talked to Dickie through the barn door. He said he'd left rations of bread, jam and tea on a groundsheet by the farm pump, which we could use for washing. But we were not to approach closer to the unit for medical reasons. Angel whispered next to me: "They feed the *Frontschwein* in the *Schweinhalle.*" Dickie said out loud, "We're not bloody lepers."

Back on the road there was a lot of military – infantry, artillery, supplies – and ambulances, all moving as fast as they could and short tempered when delayed. I think it put the wind up Dickie. He said we were going to play it by the book, head for the nearest town, and report to the Town Major. That set us zig-zagging all over Picardy when we could have been in Abbeville in two days if they'd just given us a meal ticket and left it to us. But it gave the paper-pushers and seat-warmers something to feel important about, passing us from one billet to another, Dickie said. It also gave time for friendship to grow between me and Angel.

Sometimes, when I finally got back home to Drayton and the family left me alone in the yard, I would walk round and round and I'd be back on that march to Abbeville, reliving every word of our conversation, listening again for Angel's tone - was it assured, resigned, bitter? – seeking to understand the words, to comprehend the man, to find the true meaning of the friendship he offered. At other times I would wonder if I hadn't imagined the whole thing; if I weren't hysterical, inventing visits by a Germanic Angel in fevered hallucinations.

Angel told me about his last Christmas at home, and the doll's house he made for his daughters. He described the tiny chairs and tables, and the miniature place settings he carved with a scalpel. His wife made linen and tiny quilts for the beds. He talked about the Rhine and the bridge they used to cross over when they went for picnics in summer. But he spoke of misery too. Neighbours' children without shoes. Cold winters with not enough fuel. Large families with not enough food on the table.

He talked about the Friendly Society he belonged to, and worked for as a volunteer, collecting tiny weekly subscriptions that gave members the only insurance they had to protect their families from starvation should they suffer an accident or ill health.

And he came back time and time again to the co-operative movement which he always spoke of with deep respect - almost as if it was a religion. Yes, he spoke of it like a faith. He said he was not a socialist, not a Marxist, not a trade unionist, but not a capitalist either. He might as well have been talking German for all that meant to me.

The co-operative I knew about was a grocery shop, and one my father didn't hold with. The Oakleys never shopped there. The co-operative Angel talked about had sent him to London to represent the whole of his district at an international conference. It was a co-operative movement that had grown in German towns and cities over recent decades and was beginning to break the centuries-old grip of private moneylenders and the power of the banks by running what he called credit unions. Anyone could join, and by paying small but regular amounts into a communal pool they could borrow prudently at very modest rates. It meant that ordinary working people could buy tools for a craft, or rent a workshop, or invest in stock for trade.

Angel had managed just such a credit union in Köln, paying his members dividends on their deposits and offering loans to people who had never been given credit before, with interest rates and terms for repayment that allowed their enterprise to flourish. His own furniture workshop was testament, he said, to the opportunities the co-operative movement presented, because he started with nothing. His father taught English at the *Dreikönigs Gymnasium* which was obviously a source of pride to Angel but confusion to me, until I worked out it was the Three Kings Grammar School. He'd been run over by a streetcar and left his wife and son penniless.

We played chess again the second night. We were under canvas – old army tents open on all sides – but still on straw. Angel played boldly as his wife would expect of him. He said he had become convinced he would never see her again. I said I was surely going to see Ada Doley because we were having a baby. Angel had three sons and two daughters. He said he knew they would be all right if he never made it back to Köln, not just because of his credit union insurance. He said there was a community at the heart of the co-operative movement that was moral, upright, dutiful. Many of them were Christians, he said, but not papists of which there were plenty in Köln. They were more tolerant and mindful of their responsibilities. Like the English Quakers he had met at the conference in London, he said, who called themselves Friends, which didn't mean anything to me at the time, but which I have thought much about since.

After the one game, Angel dug deep in his greatcoat again – he wore it all the time – and produced a log of wood about a foot long and six inches in diameter.

"*Brennholz,*" he said. "Firewood. From the barn last night. It's a piece of lime. It could warm the hands for a few minutes in the grate, or warm the heart for a lifetime, perhaps, if you lend me your little chisel and I carve for you Ada, William, and your baby-to-be."

"You've carried that all day?"

"War effort," he said.

On the third day it rained and as we set off again, spirits were low. One of the Jerries started singing. It sounded like a hymn. Dickie told Angel to tell him to put a sock in it. He said it would draw flak. But when we left the road for a rest, Dickie had a change of heart and said they could sing as long as they were our tunes and the words were in English. He and Angel put their heads together. By the time we were back on the road we had two songs in our repertoire and we all joined in – me and Dickie along with all the Jerries who made a fair stab at remembering the words and went at it with gusto once Angel had given them a translation. The first was a real marching song, to the tune of John Brown's Body, and it kept us going at a lick:

One staff officer jumped right over
Another staff officer's back
And another staff officer jumped right over
That other staff officer's back
A third staff officer jumped right over
The two staff officers' backs
And a fourth staff officer jumped right over
All the staff officers' backs
They were only playing leapfrog
They were only playing leapfrog
They were only playing leapfrog
When one staff officer jumped right over
Another staff officer's back.

Angel told me in German they called their staff officers *Etappenschweine* – bellies on legs.

When any military came in sight, we played safe and switched to our party piece. The tune went to Pop Goes the Weasel:

Kaiser bill is feeling ill
The Crown Prince he's gone barmy
We don't give a fuck for old von Kluk
And 'alf his bleeding army.

That got Jerry many a cheer and once an ambulance full of stretcher cases stopped right next to us and we heard them inside, none too loud, saying to Dickie's delight because he was our French expert: "Encore! Encore!"

That night the Town Major kept us in a corner of the playground in a school where he'd set up shop. There was a soup kitchen under an awning by the entrance but it looked like he wasn't going to let us eat until every passing Tom, Dick and Harry had had his fill and tottered off to bed. Dickie left me in charge and went to find cigarettes. Angel sat at the back and made swift work of whittling the log to the rough shape he wanted. None of the other Jerries were interested – Angel had made them all trinkets to send home in the time they'd known him. A miniature dachshund to sit on their missus's mantelpiece and look out for her was the favourite.

I asked him how long he'd been at the front and he said as long as the front had been there. Did I know von Kluk had got within a dozen miles of Paris? No, I didn't. Did I know they had conscription in Germany way before England did? In fact, before the war started? In fact, in one form or other ever since Napoleon did for the Prussians? No. No. No, I didn't.

But I did know about the boards in both our countries that gave exceptions from military service and created another bond between us.

"I did my national service before the war," he said. "From then on I was a reserve, my fate in the hands of a tribunal that decided who stayed home to keep the vitals going and who went to the front to fight. In Köln this tribunal was in the pocket of the big banks. The central financial district hardly lost a man. In my credit union every staffer and volunteer got his call-up papers on day one. War is big business.

"Your corporal understands well, my friend, a truth common to the Frontschwien on both sides: our biggest enemy is behind us, not in front."

He said he didn't want to simply shape us in relief. He wanted William, Ada, and their child as three separate figures linked to make one piece. Father's arm linked around mother's, mother's arm around baby, baby lodged against father's chest. He could see very well how it would work, but he didn't know how much time he would have. He said that wasn't a reason not to begin.

Finally we ate, and Jerry at least thought it well worth waiting for. They were used to S*troh und Lehm* – straw and mud, which was yellow split peas and white cabbage that was half fermented. Now they had a broth with pieces of real meat in it, and a big chunk of bread made from wheat. To cap it all, Dickie had returned with an entire carton of American cigarettes – spoils of war, he said, won from a Yankee thanks to the old three-cup-shuffle trick – and he shared them round liberally. There was almost a party mood in our corner of the school play-ground, which perhaps explains why no one noticed the approach of three other soldiers, one of whom wore the red shoulder tabs and hat band of a staff captain.

'Shun!' he shouted. I was slower to my feet than Dickie, and my salute less prompt, but it was Angel the captain had his eye on. The prisoners were still sprawled on the ground. "You! What's that in your pocket?"

Angel gave no sign of understanding. He used all the mute body language at his disposal to appear harmless and ignorant. The captain ordered one of his men to escort Angel to his office and search him. I felt instantly sick to my stomach.

The captain told Dickie we were relieved of our escort duty. We were to sleep in the school hall, where some of his staff were based, and return to our unit in the morning.

"Sir, I can explain..." I said.

"My office!" he shouted. "Five minutes."

Dickie saluted smartly, instantly, and I followed his example.

"See this rabble collect their palliasses at the front gate. At the double."

The other man took the remaining Jerries to collect mud-caked straw mattresses from where they had been dumped from the back of a lorry.

"What will happen?" I asked Dickie.

He shrugged his shoulders. "He's a bastard. I'll come with you."

The captain's aide-de-camp kept us waiting. I saw on his desk Old Armitage's precious gift, its boxwood handle stained with the sweat of my own hand, its cutting edge as clean and sharp as it ever was. It was surrounded by piles of papers, maps, and office equipment - staplers, pen and ink, a crank-handle pencil sharpener – alongside an army compass and field binoculars. It looked at home. A useful piece of kit. I could hardly breathe.

Eventually the aide-de-camp opened the door to the captain's office. He was seated behind a grand, bank-manager-like desk and didn't look up from the papers he was signing. I marched forwards in Dickie's slipstream, held together, just, by his presence at my side, came to attention, saluted. Then silence. Eventually the captain looked up. "Yes?" Silence again. I heard Dickie say that Private Oakley could explain how the German came to have in his possession... and I heard the Captain cut him off abruptly.

"Rather, let me explain, Lance Corporal. A prisoner of war has been discovered harbouring a concealed weapon. A tribunal will convene directly to decide his fate. If I should discover that any British soldier knew about this concealed weapon, that soldier would face a court-martial and very likely the same fate as the prisoner. Is that clear?"

"Yes sir!" Dickie shouted his response and saluted with such affirmative insistence, again he carried me with him as if hypnotically. "About turn!" Dickie ordered. "Quick march!" and the next thing I knew, I was outside and my knees were giving way. Dickie pushed me up against the wall and told me to breathe deeply.

"What will happen?"

He shrugged his shoulders. "I told you he's a bastard. There's nothing more we can do." He leaned in against me and I felt him pass something into my pocket. "I lifted your little chisel from the desk on the way out. There's just a slight chance they might drop it if they can't produce the evidence. Get rid of it as soon as you can. I've never seen it in my life."

I broke down, I suppose. I didn't cry, or swear, or run amok. It was more a folding-in on myself. Dickie must have got me to our billet. I remember lying as if frozen, curled up, eyes fixed awake. At some point I heard a shot – a single pistol shot in the middle distance. It was dark and quiet. Then after a while I heard another shot and I thought that was hopeful. Later again, another shot. And then I couldn't tell if they weren't all the same, single shot that I was hearing over and over. That I have heard again and again all my life.

I have kept breaking down again all my life too, though I came eventually to manage it more or less, to minimize the impact and make it easier for those around me to make allowances. Dickie was a huge help in the first few days, but he caught it at a place called Jenlain near the River Sambre, along with a hundred or more from The Fourth. It was the last time we saw action in the war, as it happens. They signed the armistice just one week later.

We left the schoolroom the next morning just as our Jerries were being marched off to Abbeville. I didn't look for Angel – I knew there was no Angel any more. Then one of them called out "*Hei! Tommy!*" – it was Uli, who had tried to steal a smoke from Dickie while he slept. Like a rugby pass from the back of a scrum, he flicked something towards me and intuitively I caught it, absorbed it, spirited it away.

It was Angel's piece of Brennholz. Firewood. I studied it later when we rested up. And later again back at the front. Every time I looked at it the form of Angel's vision grew fainter. I knew where William was supposed to be, but there was barely a shadow. The baby was neither here nor there. Where had he meant? Which way round was it? And where on earth was Ada Doley?

By the time I got back to Drayton, I couldn't even see my shadow. I found it difficult to fit in with my father and brothers – solid people all – for many reasons, though I was never asked to provide one. My father had managed business so as to win exemptions from the army for three of his sons just as the bankers of Cologne had protected their own and dispatched the men of the credit unions to the front. I never spoke of the front. I felt I had been cut away from the rest of the world by what happened there, and could never be rejoined. And I never spoke of Angel and our march to Abbeville, which was an even deeper cut and of my own making, until after many years I began to experience some sunlight in my world again. I told my sister-in-law Mary, who had raised my son as her own and always made a place for me at her table. I don't know what I hoped to achieve by doing this. The sunlight I speak of flared, and Mary fretted that it would blind me. Mary meant well, even when she shared my account of the march to Abbeville with my son though I had asked her not to. It made me feel as though I had soiled him.

But I took to carrying Angel's piece of lime with me. I took it on walks along the beach at Bolton-le-Sands and Silverdale, around Jenny Brown's Point, and up to Arnside Knot. I would place it on a rock beside me when I sat, and we would gaze over the sands, or the water when the tide was in. And I began to see again the form of the man and how his arm might link with the woman's, and where the child might be, separate but interlinked: to see again the shape of Angel's vision.

The very special friend who was the cause of Mary's concern – you may well have learned something of her – left my daily life, but not my heart, which has kept some of the warmth from the way she touched my life, has kept warmth from the touch of many friends.

When you were born, Stephen, a joy I had never imagined entered my life.

On impulse, I decided to tell again the story of the march to Abbeville. I wrote it down much as I have done here. I chatted with postmen on my walks and was aware of their commitment to their job. With postmen whose fathers had thought to number and tag every well on the western front, I felt I had a chance. I addressed my story to *The surviving family of Englebert Ziegler, Co-operative Credit Union, Köln, West Germany.* If the credit union or the co-operative movement in which it was based had survived, if the people involved did indeed have something in common with English Quakers – determination, responsibility to their community, stubbornness – if any of Angel's children had survived the hunger and violence of the period following the war, the persecution of socialists by the Nazis, and the horrors of the next war – which included massive aerial bombardment of the civilian population of Cologne by our air force – then my story might find its reader.

Over a year later, I received a reply. Elisabeth Krause wrote to say that she believed Englebert Ziegler was her maternal grandfather, and that she was the only surviving member of that line of the family. She said she had put my letter on one side because she had not known how to respond. In the autumn her son Wilfred had started at a new school and surprised his parents by declaring woodwork his favourite lesson. He seemed to have a flair for it. And then she knew how to reply to the conscientious gentleman in England with his sad story from so long ago. She said that I should surely complete her grandfather's carving. She said perhaps it should no longer aim to represent the young William, Ada, and their child. She said perhaps it should look to a future, unknown family, with hope.

I have tried to do just that.

From your grandad,

William.

EMILY WOULD WANT to track down this Elisabeth Krause, or more realistically the son Wilfred. To find out what he'd done, if anything, with his love of woodwork. To ask if there had been more correspondence. The Oakley males wouldn't want to know; they'd be worried these Germans might figure they had a debt to call in. Julie would surely insist he stay for a meal.

"You'll be staying for tea, then, Stephen? I've got a lovely apple pie in the oven."

He knew his smile was both charming and impudent.

"I don't see what's so funny," Charles said.

"We'd love to," Emily got in quickly. "I just have to pop over to the library to file my story. I can't even get a signal on my phone here."

He reclaimed the carving from the coffee table. No one had picked it up for a second look but he knew it had gained stature and weight; the feel of it in their hands would be too personal now. He felt pleased after all that these Oakleys had heard William's story, however predictable their response. And he supposed he was pleased to be with Emily Wray still; when you're on a roller coaster ride it's not easy to jump off. He knew now that he wanted to bring William's story to a solid, grounded ending if he could, not leave it mid-air like a silly-season scream of scares and laughter.

In the hall he caught Emily as she left and told her the invitation to stay for tea had been addressed to him.

"Don't be silly. They think of me as family."

"They think they like you. But you're not trustworthy, are you? Give me one reason why I should stick with you."

"Because I *am* family." And she slipped out of the door, smiling.

She was bright, she could be charming, she was cheeky, she was a fantasist. He knew all these things before; after this crazy day he knew them in Technicolor. She was undoubtedly high risk.

He sought out Douglas and asked about his son. He was remarkably well informed about cerebral palsy and the pros and cons of the new operative procedure. It had put a strain on his marriage from time to time, he said. But then what child didn't?

As soon as he reasonably could, he followed Emily to the library.

The large central table with all the computers was occupied by children in school uniform presumably doing homework. He found Emily at a small desk hidden round the back of the fiction shelves and sat down opposite her, the raised screen of her laptop like a barrier between them. There was plenty of background noise. A group of infants rifled noisily through a wooden trough containing picture books. An argumentative trio of adults was hanging an exhibition of watercolours on the wall above teenage fiction. The homework gang at the desktop computers gave off a kind of white noise, accompanied by chewing gum and body odour.

"I'm afraid you're going to have a serious problem with your six-figure map reference."

"Tell me about it." She kept tapping away, didn't look up. "Your birthday tomorrow. You think you'll get the sixth present?"

"On past form it seems likely. But it's not as simple as you think."

"I think it's simple? Take the carving you just showed us. The fifth digit. Is it a one – one family, one piece? Or is it a three – three individuals, however linked? Then we've got the whole issue of which hundred kilometre square the six-figure reference sits in. You think there hasn't been plenty of speculation about that online already?

There are twenty-five options in England, and at least four covering the places we know William lived in at some time or other, not counting his wartime experience."

"Your bloggers are web-savvy. They can easily search for all the options in four squares. They can try both one and three for the fifth digit. They hardly need the sixth. Your paper's probably got someone on it, if only for a heads up on where more truly silly stuff might be about to happen."

"But what if we've deliberately allowed a false clue to go through earlier?"

"What do you mean?"

"Let's recap. Starting with your tenth birthday, you have received *eight* chess pawns, *six* wooden coins, twenty-three wooden letters which lead via William Shakespeare to the numeral *six*, *one* dibber, and for the sake of argument let's go with *three* figures in a family formation."

"*Three* French hens, *two* turtle doves and a partridge in a pear tree."

"But what if there were more than six wooden coins, Stephen? No one else could possibly work it out, could they?"

"What makes you think that there were more than six coins?"

"I'm right, aren't I?"

"I'll rephrase that. How on earth do you know that there were more than six coins?"

She looked him straight in the eye.

"I know it because I'm your granddaughter."

"Don't be ridiculous."

"Why do you think I called you a week before your sixtieth birthday and asked if I could pop round and have a chat? You don't really think one of these Oakleys tipped me off, do you? You think any of them would have cared a damn? You have any other reporters calling? You have anybody else in the whole world remotely interested in your sixtieth birthday?"

She reached for her bag on the floor, rummaged around in it, and produced one of the wooden coins he had shown her on day two. She slapped it down on the table next to her laptop, causing a momentary failure of white noise on the central table. "Number seven." She placed a rouleau of six more coins next to it.

"Where did you get that?"

"From my grandmother. On her deathbed. Where did she get it? From Stephen Oakley, her English lover with the hippy-dippy birthday present from his dead grandfather, San Francisco, 1970. It's as good as my mother's birth certificate."

"It's no such thing. What was her name, your grandmother?"

"What was her name?" There was a flash of anger in Emily's voice now, causing a few stretched necks as the homework club tried to locate its source. "You mean *which one* of your circus of lovers with flowers in their hair? How many were there, for goodness sake?"

"They weren't lovers. We didn't have lovers in those days, on the west coast. They weren't girlfriends. They weren't fiancées or partners. And they certainly weren't mothers of my children."

"So how many were there of these non-categorised female entities whose beds you shared? Please tell me you didn't call them *chicks*."

"No, I didn't. And only three as it happens. There were only three women I gave coins to."

"Three special payments then, in duff coinage. For services rendered."

"That was not the spirit in which they were given or received. Read what it says round the edge – JOY IN FELLOWSHIP. It was a perfect token for the times."

"Yes, and look at the image on the face – children at play. You sowed your seed, left the memento, and buggered off."

"I did nothing of the sort."

"And three at once!"

"Not at once. One after the other. With gaps."

"I might have a whole army of half cousins out there on the west coast."

"You are not my granddaughter."

"Oh yes I am."

"No you are not."

"I am."

"Not."

"Am."

Ping pong over the vertical screen of her laptop. Giggles from the homework table.

"You're impossible."

"It's in the blood."

A librarian scowled vaguely in their direction.

"This is the way young people talk to their parents," he said.

"I wouldn't know. I never knew mine."

"Grandparents are supposed to be the allies you confide in."

"Then start acting like one."

"I think we're about to be told off."

"This is where you toss out some frightfully interesting arcane anecdote."

"I'm not the slightest bit nervous."

"Well there you go. Because you know I'm right."

"And you are smiling disproportionately."

"I am not."
"You are."
"Not."
"Are"
"So are you."
"With dimples."
"Ditto. And dimples are inherited. It's in our genes, Stephen."
His smile vanished.
"So. We are the only two in the world who know that your grandfather's second digit is nine, not six. We have the delights of an evening meal with the extended family ahead of us. And tomorrow morning on the long journey back to London you can tell me all about your three joys in fellowship."
"I guarantee, sadly, it will pop the fanciful balloon of your imagining."
"And if there is enough light left after dinner, I want to walk over the fields to Burnet Hall and ask to see if Frederick Oakley's prognosis regarding the crack across the wall of the breakfast room has stood the test of time. We might seek out Ada's grave in Burnet churchyard too."
"What?"
"You've never wondered where your grandmother was buried? I checked in the cemetery this morning and couldn't find her anywhere among the Oakleys."
He wondered why he had never wondered. He could think of worse things to do on the eve of his sixtieth birthday. And however vexing Emily was with her juvenile, left-field ideas that she put such an organised weight of welly behind, her agenda seemed full enough to preclude her probing into his sexual history round the Oakley dinner table.
"Crikey, these tweeters are fast! There's a new hashtag:

#williamsangel." She bent the screen of her laptop to lessen the glare from a ceiling light and read out: *Famous Dreikönigsgymnasium alumnus – Georg Ohm, physicist, discovered Ohm's Law.*

"The current flowing through a conductor between two points is directly proportional to the potential difference between them. That's poetry, not an anecdote. It does sound more like poetry than physics, don't you think?"

"And listen to this: *UK military tribunals as bad as German. 102 of 104 staff of one Co-operative Society sent to trenches. Rival shopkeepers' sons all exempt.*"

DAY SIX

SHE CAUGHT A SIDEWAYS GLANCE of her grandfather as the road south opened up beyond Newtown and she shifted into fifth gear. Was that the right word – grandfather? It sounded a little formal, now it came to it. But she didn't like 'grandad' any more than he would. Or the American 'grandpa', though that would capture some of their joint folklore. Joint folklore and the shared memories of elders were staples of family she had always hungered for and now was getting in jumbo portions. She could go the whole hog and call him 'pops'. Or she could follow his example – he called his grandfather 'William' most of the time – and call him Stephen. She'd called Jeannie by her first name after all, when she insisted, and eventually hardened herself to odd looks from her peers. She quite liked Stephen. The name. Well, the man too, on the whole, now she was pretty certain he really was her grandfather. You made allowances for your grandfather. The random anecdotes, the scattiness and lack of direction, the occasional obstinacy – you found ways of accepting them without condescension. Wasn't this what she had hoped for? She stole another glance. He was even rather handsome. Distinguished looking; that was the expression at his age. Even sitting he had something of an Oakley chimney to him. He was someone she could feel proud to take along to, say, an awards ceremony. The NUJ annual conference in fact, if he'd let her dress him up a bit. "Let me introduce you to Stephen, my grandfather."

And would he feel proud to accompany her? To sit beside her as her name was announced from the stage and she stepped forward to collect her award? To circulate at her side, champagne flute in hand, during the reception afterwards, her next of kin, her only close relative?

She was determined not to push the pace. He'd passed the interview; no need to keep up the roles. You could relax with family, that was one of the givens. She would sit and drive all the way in silence if that's what it took. He'd probably put the radio on and then fall asleep, especially after all the pancakes he'd eaten. She needed to concentrate on driving anyway, needed to make good time if they were going to reach the Kingston sorting office before one o'clock. She still had to get her story. Thank goodness she'd thought to check if they closed early on Saturdays. Of course they closed early on Saturdays, just as surely as the Oakleys rose late on Saturdays. Still, making American pancakes for the entire family had been a masterstroke. Julie even said she wished she'd had a daughter after all. Auntie Julie. Uncle Charles. He'd fallen in love with her a bit, too. Not sure she was ready for that. When they finally heard who she was, they'd tell everyone they'd adopted her anyway. Amazing that Stephen had been able to find real maple syrup in Market Drayton, even if Charles did say it was just like golden syrup.

"I suppose I'd better tell you then, seeing as we've become partners in crime as it were."

What? After all these miles down the M54, the M6, the M42 – what did he just say?

"I have to admit I was less than totally honest in not owning up to there being more coins. I've been too carried away by the prospect of adventure."

Partners in crime. She felt a little shiver of excitement. In it together. Keep quiet and let him talk.

"But I have to say, last night when that dipstick of a Burnet showed us the crack in the plasterwork running right across the wall of his kids' playroom, and you ran your hand along the length of it and then sat and questioned him, and squeezed out of him pretty much everything he knew about his family history, including the fact that it used to be his great grandma's breakfast room, I just watched your face. And when we found Ada Doley's headstone in the Burnet churchyard and you stood in front of it prayer-like, I stared at you again, willing it to be true, but I just couldn't do it. I couldn't find the remotest resemblance. I summoned up Francine and Leila and Jeannie and I scrutinised the four of you and I couldn't find a trace of a match, for all your quaint village-England vocabulary is peppered with *going to the movies*, and *getting good grades* and *doing a liberal arts degree*. God knows where you got *G Rover Cripes* from. And you surely made the best blueberry pancakes.

"But I'm going to tell you about those three women I gave my coins to anyway. Just don't turn analyst on me, okay? This has been a bit of a Boy's Own adventure ever since our escape up the rope ladder into the royal park and I don't want you turning it into a psychodrama about lack of attachment in childhood and an inability to sustain relationships in adult life, okay?"

She nodded, eyes on the road.

"You okay to keep driving, then?"

She nodded again, and he began:

"Francine was a slip of a woman with an angelic face

and long blond hair that she piled up, twirled around her head, and kept in place with sparkly metallic pins so it looked like a messy halo. She was a singer-songwriter and she carried a guitar on her back like a dysfunctional wing. It probably had a peace sign on it, and a flower or two. Yes, the broken angel was an appealing image for me, though I came to realise the only dysfunctional thing about Francine was her musical ambition.

"I don't recall where we met, but it almost surely wasn't at a club or a bar and certainly not in a concert hall. When I was looking after bands I was looking after bands not picking up groupies and anyway Francine wasn't like that. It was almost certainly in a city park, on the grass in the sunshine, or on a beach round a campfire. Come to think of it, I must have met Leila in the same kind of place. Leila played Frisbee not guitar. It was surprisingly athletic and organised, with teams, but remarkably friendly. If you accidentally committed a foul everyone gathered round you in a circle and you indulged them with sincere apologies and self criticism. Only in a west coast city park! Leila's team wore shirts embroidered with peace signs; the others with flowers or eagle feathers or maybe a dope leaf.

"Jeannie I definitely met indoors though; the circumstances were memorable. It was a party in someone's basement. Piped music. The Dead, I think. They were already getting to be the grandaddies on the scene, but were much loved. I was on my own and she obviously picked up on that because she came straight over to me and said something about being a moon spirit ascending and needing a Leo to ground her.

"You're probably thinking these are such caricatures I've got to be making them up. I'm thinking, which of them could possibly have given you one of my coins?

"Jeannie knew very well that I was a Leo because it

turned out she was friends with Leila and I'd recently moved out of Leila's place, not long after my August birthday. I'm sure I was an interesting topic of conversation. Looking back, I'd have to say I represented a form of modern chivalry that was not typical. I was clearly available for damsels in need, if not distress – with my kindly English accent and my enthusiastic pennant aloft. I was courteous and considerate. I was faithful and true, at least for the term of our association. And above all I was responsible and came properly equipped: I always had a condom, and I always used it, which was so unusual as to be eccentric. It was the era of free love courtesy of the contraceptive pill and long before HIV but the fact of the matter was, I would occasionally imagine William looking down on me – don't laugh – and I wanted to do right by him. I always thought of William as doing the responsible thing, however much he trusted or didn't trust the people he was with. And in my own feeble way I wanted to live up to that. Astonishing when you think about it. I wasn't in the least religious or spiritual. I suppose it was something to do with feeling the archetypal in the intense new experience that was sex and relating it to other juvenile archetypal instincts, like imagining our ancestors are looking down on us to see if we pass muster. Don't you think? Do you mind me talking like this? We're adults after all. I suspect you're far more adult than I am.

"Actually, I didn't use a rubber when I was with Leila because she only ever wanted oral sex. She chucked me out after she went to a feminist encounter group and decided she was lesbian.

"I've kept expecting team Frisbee – they call it Ultimate Frisbee nowadays – to turn up at the Olympics. I'm sure it will one day. A competitive spirit is expected but never at the expense of respect between players and the sheer joy of play. It's a bit like touch football but there's no physical contact, except for the multiple group hugs at the end, and no referee. Isn't that lovely? Players call their own fouls and resolve their own disputes. It's beautifully counter-culture and summer-of-love, and genuinely sweet. Like all the three young women under current discussion, come to think of it.

"Jeannie told me it was started by loutish Yale undergrads eating tuck made by the Frisbee Pie Company and then throwing the empty tin trays round the quad, but she was mainly having a dig at Leila.

"Jeannie was gorgeous and endearingly dippy. She said she was taking me to a Latino music festival in San José once and we ended up at a Native American powwow in Seattle. Her mind was always on higher things – the stars, the future, the planet's karma. She was English as it happens but the least likely person on the west coast to morph into an accountant. You see, I remember. You said your grandmother was an accountant. It's a concept that stayed with me. But we can also rule Jeannie out for another reason. She told me I didn't need to use a rubber because she couldn't get pregnant. I always used one anyway, for reasons already stated, and because Jeannie would have happily believed she couldn't get pregnant when Venus was in the House of Mars or some such, if one of her charts told her so. But it was also the case that she had a condition called endometriosis, which I eventually learned about from a paramedic who'd been in the Peace Corps. She used to get terrible pains twice a month and he gave her all sorts of herbs and hands-on healing but he always said it was just to help with the symptoms – there was nothing to be done about the cause and she would never have children.

"So that leaves Francine. Francine was certainly the one

that would have most liked to get pregnant – but not with me. She finally discovered her musical forté when a kindergarten teacher invited her in off the street and she captivated everyone under the age of seven with her energetic version of *I'll take you for a ride in my car car*. It was one of Woody Guthrie's, not her own, but she wrote some lovely little songs for children thereafter, when the captivation proved mutual. We broke up when she moved back to South Dakota where she'd grown up and was therefore entitled to free tuition at the state university and could get her teaching certificate in three years. I didn't see myself as a three-years-in-South-Dakota sort of person.

"She wrote several times telling me what a great time she was having and why didn't I join her, and I'm sure if we'd had a baby on the way she'd have used that to pull me in.

"That's why I stopped handing out the coins. There were plenty more women with whom I celebrated joy – it was the fellowship part where I came unstuck. Their idea of fellowship was something more mature and enduring than mine. I suppose you could say I was playing the field. Yes, for two decades or so I would say sex was a game for me. It was playful and stimulating, obviously. I was not promiscuous in the sense of being indiscriminate. I certainly selected. And I did so with enormous pleasure. I just found women endlessly fascinating. They had so many different qualities, different charms, and being intimate with them was like opening a secret box. Yes, all this talk about William and his games makes me think of myself more kindly in those years. Each time it was like mastering a new set of rules, playing the most exciting game in all creation. Hardly surprising with those first three that I should feel so immensely grateful, and that it should feel entirely right to pass on to them one of William's beautiful creations."

"I need a pee." She swung onto the exit for the service station just beyond Oxford. She didn't, but she was pretty sure Stephen would, with his sixty-year-old prostate he banged on about.

She made herself accompany him through the food mall, feeling nauseous. As soon as the gents' door swung shut behind him, she walked briskly back to the car and got back on the motorway heading south.

HAD SHE BEEN A SCREAMER she could have turned up the radio, floored the accelerator, and hollered herself less hostile. If she was a crier she could have opened all the windows, pushed down the accelerator, and let the wind clear her vision as the tears flowed. Instead, she fumed: she kept a steady foot on the pedal and her anger smoked. *Did she mind him talking like this?* Was he kidding? To his granddaughter! A third his age! About the grandmother who raised her! His pennant up, running around opening secret boxes! The exclamation points accumulated as she seethed, flaring now and again when she fired off expletives – at Stephen, at the trucks that pulled out in front of her without warning, at the flash cars with game show contestants crying on the back seat that zoomed up behind her and stabbed with their lights, until she saw eventually that life in a road movie didn't work for her, at least not on the M40 heading for the Chilterns. He couldn't be her grandfather; he was right. Jeannie was a storyteller. A bad storyteller. Jeannie had her head in the stars, yes, even if her nose was in people's books. Jeannie who had loved her granddaughter so much she simply couldn't bear the thought of dying and leaving her alone, a three-hundred-and-sixty-degree orphan, account closed.

So she had spun her a crazy story around a memory from forty years ago triggered by a hippy medallion she found at the back of a drawer in her painful tidying up of her messy life.

She drove another mile on the thought of the account closed. Memories of Jeannie came at her like bugs on the windscreen and she drove on regardless, knowing that wiping would merely smear. Jeannie the necessary breadwinner. Jeannie the self-employed accountant, fully qualified, with printed letterheads and letters after her name. But plenty dippy for all that, yes. Phone calls from clients on the answer machine when she got back from school: Ms Ganymede was expected at 2pm and the Managing Director had come in specially. Had there been some emergency? Yes, there had often been an emergency – Ms Ganymede had lost her diary, Ms Ganymede had decided it was the perfect day for taking her watercolours out into the park, Ms Ganymede's spirit guide had advised an afternoon of Bach and lavender-scented candles. Come to think of it, wasn't Ganymede the name of one of Pluto's moons? Yes, and Jeannie the right-on playmate: younger at heart than any of the mums at the school gate, for all her wrinkles and grey hair; organising them like American cheerleaders on sports day; badgering them to sign her petition in favour of dungarees over the school uniform's girly gingham dress. Jeannie the explorer, who arranged fantastic trips to the United States for the two of them every summer. Always a different place and always something new. Often friends to stay with – where had she made them? How had they kept in touch? – in ramshackle log cabins down long rutted tracks, or flaking wooden town houses with porches and swings. Never with family. There was no family. There was a faded newspaper clipping about a young couple in a headlong collision and an autopsy report pointing to excessive alcohol. That was all she had of Pete and Kim Wray, high-school lovers, runaway newlyweds, her supposed parents. Pete from the wrong side of the tracks, perhaps, with a family as transient as Kim's, with no home base and no written records. Only the notice of live birth: Emily Wray, daughter of Pete Wray and Kim Wray née Ganymede. Wasn't that where they signed the Magna Carta? Was that Jeannie the fantasist, creating a document convincing enough to satisfy a ten-year-old? Nowhere to be found in the clearing of Jeannie's things from the bungalow? But neither was there a scrap of evidence that either Emily Wray or Kim Ganymede before her had been adopted. Did they give you documents like that? And how on earth had she been given a passport? She wished she'd found out while she could. Jeannie was an accountant. Even dippy accountants kept accounts.

Or made them up.

She took the next exit and pulled up on the edge of the slipway. Jeannie never made them up. The world needs good accountants, she always said; as much as it needs Oxfam and Water Aid and Medécin Sans Frontières. As much as it needs the United Nations and the World Cup. What if Stephen was the storyteller? She crossed her arms over the steering wheel and lowered her head onto them. What if he had spun her a yarn about always using a condom, and Jeannie's endometriosis?

Five minutes later there was a gentle tap on the side window and she turned her head without lifting it. A young woman not much older than herself gave her a concerned smile. A policewoman, stepping back a half pace, asking for contact.

She wound down the window and was jolted by the noise of the world outside. The woman in uniform bent down and leaned towards her.

"Can I help you?"

She shook her head.

"Problem with the car?"

She shook her head again. She couldn't believe the noise the traffic was making. There were few cars coming up the slipway behind her but fifty yards away on the freeway a great press of vehicles hurtled about their business.

The policewoman followed her gaze and leaned back casually against the wing of the car. "Everyone's in such a hurry, huh? Get to the airport, get to the coast, get to the garden centre, get back home again." Crossing her legs and slouching, the woman watched the speeding cars and sighed.

"I've got to collect a parcel in London. It's my grandad's birthday."

"That's nice."

The woman reached into the breast pocket of her uniform. The little book then, with a pen tucked in the spine, to write the ticket. But she brought out a packet of chewing gum, unwrapped a piece for herself, and offered the pack through the driver's window.

She shook her head. "I left him at the service station."

The woman chewed.

"Just south of Oxford."

The woman kept chewing, watching the traffic on the motorway.

"I don't know what to do."

"They can be aggravating," the woman said, her eye still on the traffic. A radio clipped to her belt burst into life: a male voice talking too loudly. She seemed to ignore it.

"I think I'd better go back and get him."

"Sounds like a plan."

Neither of them moved. The policewoman lifted her

face to the sun, her eyes closed, chewing slowly.

"I have to check a couple of things first."

The gently pulsing blue light from the police car on the hard shoulder thirty yards behind her was joined by a single note of its siren.

"Gotta go," the policewoman said. She leaned down to the window again. "So you take a minute or two if you need to, then up to the roundabout and take the second exit onto the slipway to head north, okay? And you don't stop on the hard shoulder unless it's another emergency, right?"

SHE FOUND STEPHEN at the start of the slip road from the service station heading south, looking uncomfortable and far too sorry for himself to get a lift. He was holding a piece of cardboard on which he had written in red felt pen: London?

"Get in," she said, leaning over to open the passenger door. "What's with the question mark?"

He scrambled inside and she sped south again.

"I thought it might have the effect of suggesting gentle enquiry. *Anyone heading towards London by any chance?* I'm too old for exclamation points. The girl I borrowed the pen from offered to add a smiley, but I declined."

"I thought I'd find you reading a newspaper over a cup of coffee. I spent ages looking for you."

"I suppose celebrating my sixtieth birthday in a motorway service station would have made a good line in my autobiography. I wasn't expecting your return."

"If I am not your granddaughter, would I have been upset enough to leave you?"

No response.

"If I am not your granddaughter, would I have come back for you?"

Silence.

"Anyway, I've got a story to finish. By that I mean William's final gift to you, not your history as a condom-carrying fornicator."

"We'll have missed the mail for today, I'm afraid."

"Not so. The sorting office has a bag full of stuff for you. The head man is a fan; he says he reads my blog every day. He's going to bring everything he's got for you round to your place mid-afternoon on his way home."

And then perhaps because something about the turn of events brought out the competitive in her, she said, "And don't think I'm shocked – I don't want you imagining I'm a virgin."

As if she could ever compete with him in that regard! What on earth was she thinking of? But she didn't. She didn't want him imagining that.

Here came the Chilterns again.

She could have expressed it better.

"Or a prude. I don't want you imagining that I'm a prissy prude. As a matter of fact, I arranged to get over the virginity business some time ago. When I heard everyone my age boasting about having sex I wanted to find out what it was like."

"You do make it sound rather clinical."

"So I took the initiative. I made the moves, extended the invitation."

"Lovely. So who was the lucky guy?"

"That's not the point. I have to say I found it all a bit of an anti-climax."

Unfortunate choice of vocabulary. He was not convinced, she could tell. He thought she was making it up.

"As a matter of fact it was at music camp, the summer before my A levels."

"A romantic context, potentially."

"He played the clarinet. Very well, as a matter of fact. And was quite handsome." That was enough detail to support her veracity. "But more interestingly, I've been busy catching up on my homework while you stood there with your thumb out. I can now tell you about at least a half dozen famous alumni of Angel Ziegler's school in Köln. As well as Georg Ohm there was Carl Schurz, for example, who was a revolutionary until he emigrated to the States where he became a general in the Union Army, a US senator, and Secretary of the Interior."

"A deliciously quirky anecdote."

"Then there's endometriosis. Depending on the extent of it, according to Wikipedia, the link with infertility remains 'enigmatic'. I think we can agree, Jeannie went with enigmatic.

"And finally, same source, the typical pregnancy rate among condom users varies as to the population being studied but ranges from between ten and eighteen per cent per year.

"The perfect-use rate, which means among people who use condoms properly and consistently, is two point five percent.

"I am more than content to live my life as beneficiary of a two point five percent failure rate. My grandmother used to make a point of saying that she was proud of being in the two-and-a-half percent. It came up quite often.

"Now you can put the radio on."

AS SHE PULLED INTO PARK GARDENS she felt apprehensive, wondering how they would deal with paparazzi on the pavement now they were no longer behaving like a team, then wondering if they weren't more of a team than ever. Apprehension turned to disappointment when she saw there were no hacks relaxing on fold-up seats in the shade of fishermen's umbrellas, or snappers stripping down and reassembling their telephoto lenses like soldiers readying weaponry for action.

"I'd forgotten what a dump you live in."

"I'll open a window."

"It'll take more than that, Stephen."

"Give me an hour. Go for a walk in the park. Pick up a bottle of wine. We can get something to eat later. I'll make space for you in my other room if you don't want to worry about driving."

He wanted to make up, then.

"You must promise you won't leave the flat. You must be here when the postman arrives. And you must be here when I get back." She took a tenner from her purse. "Give him this and tell him to have a drink on us. He's probably breaking the rules."

She drove straight to her place, which took longer than she'd hoped it would. She wanted to change clothes and pack a few more things just in case. She couldn't see the endgame but wanted to be prepared. Maybe the endgame had happened already, if Stephen decided to go to earth with the postman's tip in his pocket.

She showered, dealt with her email, spoke with her editor. He said the timing was diabolical and wanted her to hold the endgame over 'til Monday if possible. Otherwise she was to give it all on her blog and promise new photos and a double-page interview with Stephen in the paper on Monday. She tried to picture Stephen tidying his flat, scouring the sink, cleaning his bathroom, but she couldn't make it work. She couldn't imagine him even owning a vacuum cleaner. But she was determined she was not going to take him out for a meal, like a mother visiting a teenage son in a student rental, frightened of picking up an infection. She put her own vacuum cleaner in the boot of her car. Plus a duster and dustpan. Next to her sleeping bag on a shelf in the hallway closet she saw her flute case, long unopened, and on impulse put that in too. A real relationship has to have content, he'd told her. Maybe she could try giving it some beyond the job in hand.

As soon as she stepped inside his open front door, three hours after she had left him there, she could tell he hadn't lifted a finger as far as cleaning went. He was exercising them well on the piano, though. Jazz nineteen-fifties style, or sixties, or even seventies: she'd never got to grips with jazz. He was improvising, she supposed. She recognised These are a Few of my Favourite Things after a while, and then he was away again, so confident and playful she regretted bringing her flute and quickly popped it down by her dustpan and bag of groceries.

He stopped as soon as he became aware of her in the doorway.

"Ah, at last! We can get down to business." He waved his hand over two tall piles of mail on the coffee table and a heap of parcels on the floor beside it. "I've sorted them into the ones that are obviously cards and ones that look like letters. Your postman chap wouldn't take the tenner. He wanted my autograph for his wife instead. She's a teacher's assistant and her class is doing The Great War."

"You should have made a start."

"I used to get a birthday card from a woman I lived with in my forties but she gave up a long time ago. I was so surprised when the postman gave me this lot I clean forgot about cleaning."

"Forgiven. You definitely need a little organising principle in your life, but your birthday is *your* day."

"And you're thinking, not instantly ripping open his

mail doesn't sound like the selfish, egotistical Stephen you have come to know and love."

"There's nothing to love when you're being nasty about my grandmother."

"*My* day, remember. I'm capable of acting excited for the benefit of the younger generation present. Isn't that what older people do on birthdays?"

She told him to get on with it. She wished she'd thought to buy a cake and candles.

He started on the cards.

"Wouldn't it be lovely if a postal order for five shillings fluttered out? I remember the thrill of it at prep school, even though there was no cash economy."

"Fatherly love?"

"Motherly actually. For three birthdays on a row. I used them as bookmarks."

It was soon clear that the common factor in these cards was a request for money, not a bequeathing of it. She felt embarrassed for Stephen. She should have seen it coming. *Dear Mr Oakley. Many happy returns. I hope your final birthday present from your grandad leads to treasure and that you give some of it to my grandad who is very poorly and wants to go to Blackpool again, like we used to do when I was a baby. Love from Ashley.*

She took the card from Stephen and put it on the window shelf as he opened the next. "At least he didn't send a photograph."

Plenty of them did, though. There were photographs of children in wheelchairs; of gaunt, shaven-headed teenagers hugging outsized teddy bears; and taking up most of a double bed, an enormous woman who would die if she couldn't go back to a miracle-working dieting clinic. She filled up the window shelf and then the little mantel above the gas fire.

They weren't all requests for money. Some simply offered good wishes, beneath a printed greeting:

Count your life in smiles, not tears
Count your age by friends, not years.

She gave these cards preference in her display, relegating the begging ones to a stack behind the clock that didn't work.

Birthdays are filled with yesterday's memories
today's joys and tomorrow's dreams.

"Just think, Stephen: someone chose that on purpose especially for you."

The letters were longer and he asked her to help him get through them. After each one they would categorise it for the benefit of the other, and occasionally give a précis. Sometimes they read a passage aloud and once or twice passed the entire letter over.

"You could have a new career as a public speaker. This is an invitation for Stephen Oakley Esquire to address a WI meeting in Cumbria. They want to know your fee and availability mid-October."

"Another begging letter. From a local history group. They want me to sponsor a research project. The 'brief' is fifteen pages."

"An offer to become your financial adviser."

"Did I know that a Catholic priest was recently charged with removing a corpse from a grave contrary to common law? Something to do with a Polish schoolboy who died in Mexico... his mother smuggled his body into the UK in a suitcase... they wanted to make him a saint but the body went missing."

"Investment advice. Ten pages of it, plus application forms. For only 5 percent commission."

"And did I know that Robert Kennedy Jr acted illegally when he dug up the coffin of his estranged wife and moved it seven hundred yards across the cemetery?"

"A numismatics society has sent you a treatise on wooden medals. They want to make an appointment to come and photograph William's coins."

"Here's a treatise on buried treasure. He seems to be comparing William Oakley with William Kidd – the only pirate known to have buried treasure, he says. He hid a chest containing gold and diamonds on an island near New York to use as a bargaining chip should he ever be caught. Apparently a local dug it up and presented it in court as evidence, condemning Kidd to the gallows. But I must distinguish between buried treasure and a hoard, he says. You want to read why?"

She shook her head. "This sounds more interesting. It sounds in fact amazingly like a marriage proposal. What do you think?" She held up a photograph.

"Definitely a treasure. Recently dug up."

She smiled despite herself.

"This is not so funny." He passed her a letter composed of words cut from magazines and pasted together: *You give twenty per cent. I give protection. Not negotiable. PS I know where you live.*

"Stephen, that's terrible! We should tell the police."

"It's just a kid's fantasy. It's an offence to waste police time. Time for a glass of wine."

He turned back to the piano while she located glasses, washed them, found a tea towel, rejected it, opened a fresh roll of loo paper, dried the glasses, poured. He was revisiting Favourite Things and he vamped a sequence of chords with his left hand as he took a gulp of wine then ran the fingers of his right hand up and down the keyboard with renewed energy.

"So, you're just going to sit there and look at it?"

She thought he meant the pile of birthday packages

until he nodded towards the stuff she'd brought.

"I thought we'd made up," he said. "You surely haven't used a flute case to smuggle in your grandmother's Derringer? Along with a duster and vacuum for cleaning up afterwards?"

"Sorry. I thought we might play a duet later, after dinner."

"A duet? How quaint."

"But I need notes. Even quainter, I suppose. You presumably don't believe in anything as organised and helpful as sheet music?"

"No problem. We can work something out."

"Why are you putting off opening William's last gift?"

"Can't you download some music from the internet? Don't kids do that? I mean don't they delay the unwrapping to savour the expectancy?"

"I'd have put you down as a rip-them-open-on-the-spotter."

"How about Satie's Gymnopédies?"

Against her better instincts, she opened her laptop and within seconds found a free download.

"You know them?"

Of course she knew them, though she'd never played them. She shook her head nervously, though the top line of number one didn't look too difficult. It was in 3/4 time all the way through.

"What key is it in?" He looked over her shoulder. "Okay. You play the melody. I'll get the alternating chords; two major 7ths, on the subdominant G and the tonic D."

She made room on top of the piano for her open laptop. He'd established his credentials and made her even more nervous. She took her flute out of its case, slid the head onto the body and let her fingers run tic-like over a notional scale, the keys begrudging her attention.

"Been a while since you played."

"Not much since I left Keele." So why on earth had she thought bringing her flute was such a good idea? Trying to meet him on his own ground. That's what she'd been doing all along.

"Nice and slow then."

Nice and slow. So slow, in fact, that she struggled with her breathing. But even with poor phrasing from the flute it sounded slow and nice and strangely beautiful. It reminded her of her grandmother.

"It reminds me of Jeannie," she said, when they finished.

"The dissonance? Against the harmony it produces such a gorgeous melancholy."

"It's too beautiful for melancholy."

"Ageing, then."

"Yes."

"Aged well, I'd say."

"I don't really mind you saying Jeannie was gorgeous. She was."

"Let's try number two. I might embellish a little this time."

"She would get up early when the weather suited and take her watercolours into Gladstone Park. She loved to paint the sunrise. Not sunsets. She said you always knew how sunsets ended."

She lost her concentration halfway through the second gymnopédie and wanted to start over, but he told her to just pick it up again and he'd find her.

"I've always felt like I live on the edge of a precipice. I asked Jeannie about my parents once and she said not to worry, she was all I needed. I thought if I asked again I would be saying no, she wasn't all I needed, and she would feel hurt. Jeannie was my only anchor."

"Pick it up wherever you like," he said.

A bar before the end he told her to repeat from the beginning and she impressed herself by keeping time as she did so, though she was aware that he was right there with her, guiding from behind without touching, like a parent crouching with hands at the ready as a toddler launches ahead. Not exactly jamming together then, but promising.

Half way through the third there was a sharp knock on the front door. She welcomed the interruption because Stephen was being very clever at both ends of the keyboard simultaneously and she was struggling to stay on her feet in the middle, but he was annoyed and kept playing. "Keep going. It's not like it's two in the morning or we're amped up." But it was not a complaint about noise.

"That's bloody brilliant!" A head of youthful hair peered round the room door and smiled at them. "Your front door was unlocked. I thought I'd sneak in under the radar." It was the guy from the ground floor flat with a six pack of beer. "I love ambient."

Stephen looked amused. "Blood Sweat & Tears covered it in '68. With a flute, as it happens. Please join us."

"Great!" He sank into the collapsed armchair and opened a beer in one deft movement.

"I meant join the music. I heard on the TV you play in a band."

"You saw my ace interview."

"I've invited Emily's friend Peter too. We can have a session: I asked him to bring his clarinet."

The guy in the armchair opened another beer and thrust it at her: "That kind of friend, huh? You look like you need first aid."

"He seemed keen but didn't think he'd make it."

She punched Stephen in the shoulder. It was becoming a habit. She'd never punched anyone before in her life.

"They played Benny Goodman on the radio in The Merry Kettle. He said it was his instrument, that was all."

The guy in the chair started cheerfully on the beer he had opened for her.

"What do you play?"

She willed him not to say bongos. Please whatever you say, don't say bongos.

"We don't really make music. More of a noise. I drum. Y'know – hit things. It's sort of retro punk with aggro against bankers. I only do it to give me a chat-up line with the ladies."

Stephen re-filled his wine glass. "Does it deliver?"

"I'm working on it. Better than saying I'm an accountant."

"Hey, don't knock accountants," Stephen said. "The world needs good accountants."

"What?"

"Civilisation depends on them. Civilisation needs taxes and taxes need collecting. Something like that. Don't you agree?"

The punk bongo from the ground floor looked as though he thought he was being made fun of. He asked her if she agreed.

She squirmed. She punched Stephen on the same shoulder and reached for the wine bottle in one deft movement.

"I don't think anyone would treat their grandfather like that," he said, rubbing his arm.

The reluctant accountant from the ground floor said he didn't know about that. If only he dared: his grandfather was a right old bastard.

* * *

IT WAS NINE O'CLOCK by the time Gordon made his way back to the ground floor on his way to the pub where his band was playing.

"I don't think punk bands can hack it without their drummer, however unmusical he is. He'd have left long ago if you'd agreed to go with him."

"You knew very well that was not going to happen. Not before the end of time."

"Why ever not? He's a handsome enough young man. A little short on the social graces, but that would give you something to work on."

"Out of order Stephen."

"Surely not if I was your grandfather? I bet Jeannie dabbled in a little gentle match-making."

"Only on her deathbed. She didn't want to leave me alone in the world. She gave me a coin and a story."

"A made-up story."

"And if you are *not* my grandfather, the way you pushed me at ground-floor Gordon was tantamount to pimping."

"Sorry. I was enjoying myself. It felt almost like a party. Too bad Peter couldn't make it."

"You've got a nerve."

"He told me your grandmother also took the view that *you* were all *she* needed. That's the trouble with anchors, isn't it? They're fastened securely at both ends."

"I wish."

"Peter said he tries to remind you that you do have friends, but you don't make it easy."

"Peter always has a big family meal to go home to, or a clan gathering in Cornwall for Christmas, or a wedding in Scotland."

"And he says there's a mutual friend called Robert."

"Rover G..."

"Cripes!"

"What do they put in the tea at The Merry Kettle? Why couldn't you have talked about football or real ale or something, like ordinary men?"

"Sounded like Robert offered you a lifeline."

"Robert doesn't mean a thing to me."

"There you go again. Robert's Dad then."

"What? What did he tell you about Robert's Dad?"

"That when you dropped out of college to look after your grandmother and then she died and there were only three people at her funeral and you nearly fell off your precipice it was Robert's Dad who offered you a six month apprenticeship on his paper."

Lengthening pauses before her responses took the place of punches to his shoulder.

"Just because I'm not paid doesn't mean I'm not a professional."

"Join the club."

"This week should earn me a place on the staff."

"I hope so. You deserve it."

"Or I could go freelance."

"That sounds more like it, for a two-and-a-half percenter."

She tidied ground-floor Gordon's empty beer cans into the empty groceries bag. "He'd have left ages ago if *you'd* agreed to go with him for that matter."

"My prerogative not to. It **is** my birthday."

"Only by a few hours. Time you opened your presents."

"No need." He turned his chair back to the keyboard. "William's have always been addressed to Mr Stephen P Oakley." He started playing with his foot on the soft pedal. "I opened it while you were gone."

He was infuriating. He was unpredictable, undependable, un- a lot of things. She would have punched him again, but she had been keeping back a secret of her own: a paternity test cost a mere £99 and gave 99 per cent certainty, one way or the other, within three to five working days. The website was less clear about its 'grandparent index' and it cost twice as much. But all it would take was a swab from his mouth and a swab from hers.

"I suspected opening William's last present would be disappointing for you, and I was right. I'm afraid I was selfish for your company. I didn't want you dashing off."

"But you tried to push me off with Ground Floor."

"I was having fun. I knew you wouldn't go."

"I need to write up my story, if nothing else."

"If nothing else." He picked a parcel from the pile and handed it to her.

She could see where he had carefully pulled off the tape and then pressed it down again afterwards. "We could do a DNA test by mail," she said as she unwrapped the present from William. "You just rub a little brush gently against your cheek inside your mouth for a few seconds. They tell you whether or not about three days later." But she was too distracted to see how Stephen reacted to the whether or not because out of a small cardboard box in the parcel tumbled half a dozen chess pieces. Six pawns. Hand carved, from some kind of blanched wood.

"There's a brief note from William," Stephen said, sounding his own disappointment.

She unfolded the single sheet of paper, handwritten in pencil.

Dear Stephen

You don't need many more words from me after all these years. I'll just say that this is Something Different.

These pieces were sent to me quite recently, in the post, just as I am now arranging for them to be sent to you. But they came to me with no note, no explanation. At first I was intrigued and wanted to know who sent them, and why. I studied the postmark, which was smudged; the stamps, which were British; the wrapping and the string and the cardboard container, which could have come from Woolworths or from Harrods. So few people knew enough about my past to understand the significance of chess pawns. I asked Mary, and drew a blank. Your father, for all his cleverness, has not the wit. I thought of Angel's great-grandson in Cologne, who had taken up woodwork. Then I thought of you and our walks together on Arnside Knot, your quick-witted way with words, your child's sense of wonder and delight in things as they are, and it encouraged me to think of these chess pieces as what they are rather than where they had come from.

They are nicely fashioned, I think you will agree. I believe the wood is lime. It's blanched naturally, and pleasingly so. These pieces would stand against my darker pieces, which I carved from a table leg of cherry wood. Or perhaps I should say stand with them. And of course they are pawns, not officers or royalty or clergy. I decided not to write to the German boy. If whoever sent me these pieces wanted to get in touch with me, he or she could presumably do so. I decided to accept them for what they are and in doing so I felt more in touch than usual with the sense of grace which is my silent partner. Spending time with you has similarly helped me achieve this, Stephen. I hope it is something you have come to understand and appreciate, not only about my life but also in your own. It will mean, perhaps, that my occasional presents have in some small way helped to keep me present.

With love from your grandfather and your friend
William

"There's only six of them. Please stop playing the piano, Stephen."

"It's the way I keep in touch with my sense of grace."

"Why are there only six? There should be eight. Eight pawns. But he only sent you six. He only sent you six because the last digit of his six-figure map reference is a six!"

"Grace, Emily."

"Purpose, Stephen!" She opened her laptop. "We've got a six-figure map reference." She opened a site showing the ordnance survey grid for the UK. "We just need to know which hundred kilometre square it sits in. They're identified by two letters." She took a second package from Stephen's pile of 'presents' then scrutinised her screen. "Market Drayton is in SJ. Heading north, like the Oakleys did, we've got SD, then possibly NY. Here, open this." She tossed the package into Stephen's lap without taking her eyes off her screen.

"There's no point in opening any others," he said. "They'll just be more requests for money, with evidence of need in 3D. Propositions for investments, protection, nuptials..."

"Open that one. It's from me."

"It says it's from Amazon."

"SD... " She snatched up the letter from William and read aloud: "'This is Something Different, Stephen.' He's used capitals for Something Different. He's telling us we're in SD!" She opened a site she'd saved in her favourites and typed in the map reference: SD896136. She clicked a button and in a flash had the corresponding post code. Another button and she had a shortlist of addresses.

"*Cascada Bathrooms, Elegant Interiors, Paradise Fruit and Veg*," Stephen read aloud with a little smirk.

"*The Baum*," she read. "*A pub with great ale and good food* – and *The Rochdale Pioneers Museum*. What's that?" Her fingers swept over the keyboard. "The Rochdale Pioneers Museum, 31 Toad Lane Rochdale, is *The birth-place of the modern Co-operative Movement*. We've found it! X marks the spot – mark my word!'

Stephen was stunned.

"*Open Monday to Saturday, 10am to 5pm*. Damn, we're four and a half hours late. Unless they have a social on a Saturday. I'll try anyway."

Stephen was stunned and bowled over. "You really are something."

She dialled the number on the website. There was a call tone and as she glanced quickly upwards at stains on the ceiling, as if to heaven, there was a beep then a pause and then the call tone again. It was answered promptly.

"Hello?"

"The Rochdale Pioneers Museum?"

"The museum is closed. Who is calling, please?"

"Mr Stephen Oakley would like a word."

"Ah. This is why I have had calls diverted to my home this evening. I have been expecting his call."

But Stephen was not quite ready to have his word. First, he needed to give Emily Wray – who really was something, granddaughter or not – a big hug. To do so he put down the present which he had opened while she completed her detective work: a set of six wood-carving chisels, a mallet, and a voucher for a beginners' course in the Forest of Dean.

DAY SEVEN

HE LAY IN BED IN THE DARK, too alert to noise – from his spare room, outside the flat, inside his head – to sleep, despite the wine he'd been drinking all evening.

He tried to remember the last time someone had slept over. It was after his business failed. Roast tamari nuts, fifteen years ago. All six staff laid off with two weeks' notice. Sylvia knowing that he'd refused to file for bankruptcy and was running his assembly line himself in a rented garage to pay off creditors, and volunteering to work for nothing. Putting her up in his spare room the least he could do, but even that a mistake. Hearing her sighing theatrically when she went to her room for the night. Then crying theatrically. Then crying for real, wanting far more than just to help on his assembly line and he – what? Too busy? Too selfish? Too bogged down in the mess of his life? No sighing or crying from Emily, but he thought he could hear the dabbing of fingers as they flitted across the keys of her laptop. At two, maybe three in the morning? Emily also wanted much more than he had thought at first.

Outside, Gordon from the ground floor delivered home by someone whose car pulsated with drum and bass. A fan, perhaps. Or someone in the band. It sounded like

Gordon had drunk too much, but not enough to cause collapse. His attempts to coax his driver indoors were not successful and Stephen was glad his light was out, or he would surely have had another visit.

Inside his head, so many voices, all of them whispering, most of them with just a sentence or two, or a question, and then fading away before he could explain himself:

"Press down gently on the accelerator, Stephen, and then ease your left foot back on the clutch until you hear it engage. Don't worry about anything else; just listen to the engine."

"I have five children, Stephen; twelve grandchildren; and now my first great-grandchild. She's so bright, and so musical. I'm teaching her some of those first songs I ever wrote, for kids in the kindergarten. Every summer we rent a big house in the Black Hills and all the generations go skinny-dipping together in the creek."

"Whatever our faults, we Oakleys make things. Out of bricks and mortar. What have you ever made Stephen? What have you ever made that will last?"

"Funny how these things come around... my nephew is trying out for a place on the Revolver team – their mission quest: *to shape Bay Area Ultimate with Intensity, Humility, and Discipline*. I guess I was never so hot on the discipline, with a Frisbee or anything else."

"Stephen always was a charmer. Good looking and good company. But he never seemed to achieve anything."

"My daughter died so young. You never met her did you? She left me with a baby granddaughter and I was blessed with a second chance."

"You don't need to know what's under the bonnet, Stephen. You don't have to know how it all works. You just have to listen. Can you hear it purring? Can you hear it say I'm ready now, I'm ready to go, let's do this together?"

"Did you know our daughter died so young? Our baby granddaughter has been a blessing; she kept me alive."

He swung his legs out of bed and sat on the edge of it in determined silence. Eventually he stepped up to his door and listened closely. He opened it knowing that the hinges squeaked. Then he listened at Emily's door.

"Stephen?"

"Yes. Sorry. I can't sleep."

"Me neither. You can come in. I'm decent."

"I'm not, I'm afraid." Better not show himself in tee-shirt and underpants, even in the dark.

"You don't have a dressing gown?"

"I wanted to ask you about Jeannie."

"Well if you must know, she used to like to sleep naked. But she always kept a dressing gown handy."

"What did you call her?"

"I called her Mom when I was young. Not quite Mum. But she didn't really approve. Jeannie to other people. She liked the equality of it."

"Why did she never try to find me? I was in the phone book for years."

Emily was silent.

"You said she moved back to London when you were two. She only lived forty minutes away on the north circular."

No reply.

"I mean, if she was so sure I was your mother's father..."

Another long silence. Then, "Perhaps she felt she had healed around your absence. People do, don't they? Like you with your mother and father?"

AT NINE O'CLOCK he knocked on her door and went in with a cup of tea. She groaned and then rubbed her eyes with the knuckles of her index fingers. He thought only children in Walt Disney movies did that.

"After I talked to you through your door in the night, I thought I might as well get dressed and go for a walk in the park. They lock it at night and I liked the idea of having it to myself. I thought the rope ladder would be a doddle second time round, after you'd showed me how to climb up it. Then I nearly came to get you and drag you away back north to Bolton le Sands, where William died, so we could speed on the beach with the world to ourselves, and write our names in the sand in tyre tracks before heading back down to Rochdale."

"How delightful. A little Walt Disney, perhaps."

"Then I fell asleep."

"Just as well. I think we'd both drunk too much."

"I'll make coffee in a minute. Tea in bed then coffee in the kitchen: the start-up routine of a civilized life."

"Tea in bed, twenty minutes jogging, invigorating shower, coffee in the kitchen. Then we need to talk business."

"What business?" Whether she meant the giving and receiving of instructions or the making of compromises and the striking of deals, he thought it to his advantage to press home the matter while he was standing, dressed, and she was lying down sipping the tea he had so considerately brought her.

"What we are going to do in Rochdale."

"I was rather hoping that you wouldn't be inviting all and sundry."

"I haven't invited anyone. I wrote up yesterday for the blog but held back the clue, the number of pawns. And I still haven't come clean about the number of coins. Our merry band of treasure hunters have no way of knowing that we are heading for Rochdale."

"Thank you."

"But you do owe me, Stephen."

"I owe you some sort of ending for your story, yes."

"You owe me the whole story, start to finish! You don't get it, do you? If I hadn't come along you would never have got it. You would never even have twigged that William had set you a puzzle, with a prize at the end."

"With something at the end."

"A solution, then. A conclusion."

"With whatever we find in Rochdale."

"If I hadn't come along..."

"... perhaps I would have had to invent you."

"Oh, that's brilliant. You won't have me for your granddaughter but you're happy for me to be your alter ego."

"So if you think I owe you, what's your idea of payback?"

"You let me stream it live on the blog: an interview with me first, your meeting with the curator, then your opening of the package he said he's holding for you."

IT WAS A SURPRISINGLY SOLEMN JOURNEY north to Rochdale. Just beyond High Wycombe he registered her saying something about one of the female Oakleys – she thought it might have been Eric's wife – telling her that he was a nice chap, but he'd never amounted to much.

He offered to drive and when they reached the service station near Oxford she took him up on the offer, sliding over from the driver's to the passenger's seat while he got out and walked round. Perhaps she was worried he'd have a flashback to his experience here just twenty-four hours earlier and leave her behind to see how well she coped with long-distance hitchhiking.

On the M42 going round Birmingham, he said he remembered so clearly the driving lessons William gave him at Bolton-le-Sands. He thought Emily should know that there were numerous Boltons up and down the land and it was only when the railways were built that people felt the need to distinguish them and started referring to Bolton upon Dearne, Bolton-on-Swale and so on. The one in East Lancs, not far from Rochdale, became Bolton-le-Moors. Maybe William knew he had a weak heart and had intimations of his end. He said he wished he had been more observant, more enquiring. He wished he'd asked William more about his life and times. "But you don't when you're young, do you? The world was all about me." She said she agreed. She said for her this whole week had been about her, really. But hopefully Stephen wasn't going to die on her any time soon and deny her the chance to rectify the situation.

On the quietly pleasant stretch of the M6 between Stafford and Stoke, in the company of light Sunday traffic, Emily mentioned what appeared to be a significant grouping of religious types in the twitter-sphere surrounding her blog. She said she knew that he had not been following her posts and the quirky comments and passionate contributions they had attracted. She took no offence at this. She liked to think of it as a sign of his trust, she said, but she was aware it could just as well be laziness. Anyway, she thought he might be interested to know that one group was holding séances in an effort to contact William's spirit.

It wasn't until they reached the M62 that he wondered if he should try to contact Francine and Leila. Not through a medium. It was easy these days, apparently, using sites like Friends United, as long as they were still alive. Emily would know how to do it.

"I wonder if Leila and Francine will read about me and William's coins, and remember that I gave them one? I wonder if they have children? Grandchildren?"

"The idea makes me jealous. And not just for my sake. For Jeannie."

"I wish I had known her. I mean, other than in the biblical sense. Your grandmother. I wish I had known her as a mother, as a grandmother."

He left the final stretch of motorway heading north from Oldham and drove under a railway bridge which announced in bold capitals: BIRTHPLACE OF COOPERATION.

"That's pushing it a bit, don't you think?"

Emily's fingers flicked across the screen of her phone. "It's because of the principles the Rochdale pioneers agreed on, before they opened shop. They were good shopkeepers, I guess. But it was their principles that the movement looks back to."

He thought he might quite enjoy a little lecture from Emily Wray and her smartphone on the origins and principles of the Co-op. But he suspected there would not be time. Ahead loomed seven residential tower blocks in cream and brown, like monumental memorials to the old British Railways. Close beyond them, Pennine moorland so bare it looked rude. Far from the secure place William had presumably sought for the finale of his long-playing game, this felt like a town turned sideways and shaken every decade since the nineteen-sixties. They would have to search for the Pioneers' museum among random retail malls, peeling bingo halls and impromptu parking lots.

"Take the first right."

Phone in hand, she gave directions with the precision and authority of air traffic control.

"Right again. Pull up on the left, then we'll make a slow loop round these two streets. We've got ten minutes before we meet the curator."

It was an odd place to adopt a holding pattern. On

their left, a yard littered with large moulded plastic forms, a rotting boat, windblown plastic bags and empty bottles, nettles and thistles; all contained by a tall metal railing topped with vicious spikes. No comment from Emily, still absorbed with her phone. Round the corner, a short terrace of two-storey houses. Stone sills and lintels to the windows but plain brickwork; nothing an Oakley would write home about.

The second house along had an estate agent's sign in its tiny front garden and Emily had presumably gone to their website. She read from the screen in her hand: *"This property briefly comprises a lounge with feature fireplace, modern fitted kitchen with base and wall units and integrated oven and hob, integrated fridge-freezer, two double bedrooms with fully fitted wardrobes, and three-piece family bathroom suite with shower over bath.* The point being, Stephen, that Pioneer Street and Equitable Street behind it were built by the Rochdale Equitable Pioneers Society. In 1867."

"Complete with combi boilers and UPVC double-glazed windows no doubt."

"The point being, Stephen, that these were well-built houses. Not ostentatious, but always worth doing up when times changed."

"Times have changed, for sure," he said as he turned back towards the town centre and looked up at the transparent domes of an Islamic building that towered over Equitable Street. He started reading from a motto which ran around the eaves of the building in roman capitals: *SAY O PEOPLE OF THE BOOK COME TO COMMON TERMS AS BETWEEN US...*

"We need to get going. Turn left."

The museum, when they finally reached it, was locked.

"We're late," he said. "So much for our tour of

Equitable Street."

"He said he was expecting us. Given that it's half a century since William set this up, I think our curator will have waited ten minutes."

He knocked loudly on the door. He cupped his hands to the glass and peered inside. It was a small room with not much in it. An enormous slab of yellow substance with the unlikely label *butter* sat on a broad wooden plank laid across two wooden barrels. A black metal weighing balance was suspended from the ceiling above the centre of the plank. Leaning against the barrels were three hessian sacks with labels painted on in stencilled letters declaring the contents to be oatmeal, flour, and sugar. The floor was bare flagstones. There were two straight-backed wooden chairs against the opposite wall, whose brick was beginning to show through the covering whitewash.

He stepped back and looked up at the second and third storey windows. Then he knocked again. He was about to send Emily round the back to see if there was another way in when an elderly gent emerged from the building next door and told them to hold their horses. He said he knew that appeasing the impatience of clients was de rigueur for contemporary retailers but he would like them to know that back in the eighteen-forties, the period of his chief historical interest and expertise, things were different. On divi night, when the trading surplus was shared among the shop's customers, he said, people were perfectly happy to wait in line for extended periods. He stopped speaking as he removed his spectacles and rubbed their lenses on the lower part of his tie, which looked like something his wife, or even his mother, might have made from homespun material. Stephen savoured the waiting, divi day or not.

“My specs always steam up when I’m excited.” The warden held out his hand. “Mr Oakley, I presume? Long expected. And your personal assistant.”

“His granddaughter.”

“Our journalist. With a vivid imagination.”

“Mr Howarth. No relation to Charles Howarth, a founding member of the Rochdale Equitable Pioneers Society.” He unlocked the door and let them in. “This is what the shop looked like on the day it opened.” He led them through into the next room and showed them a photograph on the wall. “And that’s what it looked like just twenty-two years later, when they opened the new central store fifty yards up the street.” He removed his glasses and wiped them again on his tie.

He was surprised to hear Emily say “I do hope we’re not over-exciting you, Mr Howarth.”

“Not you, my dear. I still tend to get excited when I’m talking about the Co-op. J Alfred Prufrock may have measured out his life with coffee spoons, by which T S Eliot meant to indicate ennui, but I have measured out my life with parcels of flour and oatmeal and butter and sugar, which indicate purpose because there is no trade more honourable and worthwhile than providing the members of one’s community with wholesome, unadulterated foods at fair prices, and I think your grandfather would agree, Mr Oakley, though I know he also had a particular interest in the building of decent housing.”

Mr Howarth pointed at the photograph of the grand central store in which he had worked himself as a younger man. “You can see the different departments on the ground floor, each with a display window: drapery, grocery, shoes. On the first floor, the offices. On the second floor, a library: education for its members has always been important to the Co-op. Two-and-a-half per cent of trading surplus went to supporting it. I've always been thrilled by what can be achieved with life's two-and-a-half-percents. Members' social lives revolved around the society too: there were lectures, magic lantern shows, amateur dramatics groups. I doubt I would ever have discovered T S Eliot without the second floor. The top floor was given to meeting rooms. Before it opened the only place working men could meet was in a pub, and some of our members were teetotal."

"But not yourself, Mr Howarth? And this towering wedding-cake of a central store has also gone, in turn. To make way for the road we drove in on."

"Are you are trying to provoke me, my dear?"

Stephen looked daggers at her.

"I occasionally enjoy a drink in a social context. A pot of tea, as it happens, in this instance, which The Baum does very well."

"She spoke out of turn, Mr Howarth. It's part of her game plan for getting a good interview: intimidate the warden to make sure he holds back enough not to get in her way and push me into polite mode, compensating for her rudeness, so I'll be more obliging."

"Goodness, that sounds rather Machiavellian."

"She's good at her job."

Emily was arranging seating for the interview, but he could tell that she was flattered. She preferred that he had acknowledged her tradecraft, he suspected, than that it had worked.

"So tell me," she said, "Mr... may I know your first name?"

Mr Howarth took off his glasses and wiped them for a third time, stepped backwards, and observed her closely. "I am old enough to get away with saying that you can look forward to significant experience of over-exciting people, my dear. No, you may not know my first name. I'm not sure I can trust you with it."

Emily positioned three stools in front of a wall-mounted display that featured an Edwardian bicycle with a wicker basket on the handlebars and a sign beneath the crossbar advertising *Co-op Men's Ware*. Around the bike was an array of plates celebrating the coming of age and golden jubilee of various co-operative societies. It was a toss-up between that and the life-sized photograph of the Chartists, Owenites, Methodist Unitarians, and proselytising teetotallers who made up the original Rochdale pioneers. She clipped her tiny webcam to the edge of a display case opposite and manoeuvred the stool with her laptop on it so she could monitor the output without showing her equipment. Stephen returned from the loo looking more at ease. She briefed Mr Howarth on the kind of questions she would be asking him, and encouraged him to relax.

"A day of surprises for all of us then – I've never been streamed before." His right hand moved infinitesimally towards the flap end of his tie, and then froze in the glare of Emily's full-beam stare. She called her editor, who they could all hear answering in confident monosyllables, then spoke likewise to a techie on the paper's web team. At a private signal from him she slipped her phone into the bag at her feet and with no script or scrap of a note turned her body minimally towards Stephen, faced the webcam, and spoke without hesitation.

"This is Emily Wray at the end of an extraordinary week, streaming live the climax of what many followers of this story have come to see as an intriguing treasure hunt set more than fifty years ago. I'm with Stephen Oakley and Mr Howarth, who is no relation of Charles Howarth, a founding member of the Rochdale Equitable Pioneers Society in whose original shop, which opened in 1844, we are now sitting. In 1931 the premises became a museum and for many years Mr Howarth, starting as a volunteer in his spare time from the day job he held with the Co-op groceries department, has guided and instructed visitors from all over the world who come here to learn about the principles, practices, and people who inspired the co-operative movement. Stephen and I have come with a different purpose, led by clues we identified in the birthday presents Stephen has received from his grandfather William every ten years since his tenth birthday. Stephen, remind us please just what these presents consisted of, and how they have brought us here."

We. Us. Of course she was justified. Without Emily he doubtless wouldn't be here. Without Emily he would wake to discover this last crazy week had never been. But he never quite knew the extent of what she was up to. There was always a slightly uncomfortable edge. Always a sense of challenge.

"Stephen?"

"Eight chess pieces. Pawns. That was the first present. Carved in the trenches. The first one at the top of Bligny Hill while my grandfather was lying terrified in a scraped-out hollow being shelled by his own and German artillery. The last, waiting to be demobbed while his older brothers, exempted from conscription thanks to the influence of William's protector Lady Burnet, salvaged unused supplies at rock bottom prices and shipped them home for private profit.

"The second present consisted of nine wooden coins carved with legends of hope and comradeship and given – by a man who felt he had no right to be alive – to a kindly, hardworking fellow carpenter who was turned out on the road by those same brothers with nothing except a ragged wife and nine hungry children.

"Is this enough? You look discomforted. Too much?"

"It's up to you, Stephen. It's your story."

"No. Let's be honest. The story is yours. You're the journalist. I'm just the man who's been getting these gifts from his grandad."

"The gifts *are* the stories. And as any orphan will tell you, stories from relatives are powerful gifts."

"I don't need lectures from you on being an orphan."

In a whispered aside, Mr Howarth – on the other side of Emily – suggested that her strategy for encouraging polite cooperation from Stephen appeared not to be working. He offered to swap seats with her and act as intermediary.

"But perhaps you need a lecture on honesty. You told me there were six wooden coins, and I told my readers there were six wooden coins."

Mr Howarth faced the camera and silently raised his bushy grey eyebrows and shrugged his thin shoulders.

"Though you yourself, Emily, knew all the time that there were more."

"Oh yes, there were also the coins you left like tips – tokens as they were of all that hope and comradeship – with three of your many lovers, including the one who subsequently gave birth to the woman who subsequently gave birth to me."

The phone in Emily's bag beeped. Stephen didn't know this signalled an incoming text. He suggested she might want to answer it, while turning straight to camera and giving her time to do so.

"Ms Wray has believed for some time that I am her grandfather, despite the solid reasons I have given her why the notion is fantastical. I suspect she has not included this significant subplot of our week's adventures in her published accounts."

Emily held the screen of her phone towards him and he read: '50k hits and climbing.'

"Nine coins it is," Emily said to camera, with a conciliatory smile. "And though our mutual elderly relative would, in his fifth present, give Stephen a carving of three figures in a family unit which harked back to the most painful experience of his life, when his friendship with a POW led to the man's execution, his third and fourth presents surely represent positive experiences in a life that was making atonement and finding renewed purpose."

Mr Howarth brought his hands together in three exquisitely timed gentle claps.

"A set of wooden letters," Emily continued, "Giving us a six but made to help Italian prisoners of war make sense of what was happening to them in this strange cold country so far from home, and in one case to express the yearnings of his heart. Then a gift that expressed the yearning of William's own heart, giving us a one."

Mr Howarth made another quiet contribution: "For I am the one who loves changing from nothing to one," which Stephen knew, however unlikely, to be a line from a Leonard Cohen song and which served as a warning to Emily that she may yet have a wild card in her hand with the excitable seventy-five-year-old.

"And yesterday we received a sixth gift," she said.

That *we* again. She was incorrigible and he was drawn up sharp, yet again, by the realisation of how much he liked her.

"On *my* sixtieth birthday," he said.

"Six white chess pieces. Pawns again, but not carved by William," Emily said. "This gift, as William himself remarked in a brief note, was something different. Something truly enigmatic. Something that raises a multitude of questions. Who made them, and when, and why? And why six? What story, what message, what lesson lies behind them? Can we be so sure that William, who loved the challenge of games and puzzles, did not in fact make these pawns himself in later life? To bring the treasure trail he was laying for his grandson to the conclusion he wanted?"

"It's probably because you're only twenty-one," Stephen interrupted.

"I beg your pardon?"

"You're full of questions. You can't see beyond the questions. That's what young people do. It's an attribute of youth."

"And old men have all the answers?"

Her phone beeped again and she tilted the screen towards him: *UR trending big time*.

"Perhaps William did," he said. "Some of the big ones anyway, in the end."

"Your grandfather was something of an orphan too. Unattached."

"I don't agree. I think he found his family in unexpected places, and they didn't need to be blood relations. Ada Doley, Angel Ziegler, John Wellington, Sura and Laja... he put trust in them all."

"And had pretty serious unfinished business with most of them. You know there is a group of spiritualists in contact with William's spirit, trying to help him find peace by bringing closure to all his unfinished business?"

"Sometimes I wonder if *I'm* not William's unfinished business," he said. "Though he said in his last letter that he had found grace."

Mr Howarth said, "I rather think everyone alive is

unfinished business."

In the brief ensuing pause Emily's phone beeped yet again and he wondered why she didn't have one of those little earpieces you see interviewers fiddling with on television. Before she could hide it, he read: *enough with the philosophy already.*

"And isn't it toddlers who run you ragged with questions?" Mr Howarth said. "I thought by their mid teens young people nowadays knew everything."

"What we do know for certain," Emily said commandingly to camera, "Is that the six gifts which William gave to his grandson Stephen over the last half century also gave him the map reference SD 896136, which is the location of the museum in which we are now sitting, and that when we telephoned you last night, Mr Howarth, you said that you had been expecting our call. Please explain why."

"Because the diary said so."

"Whose diary?"

"The museum's. It's our appointments diary. It lives up on the wardens' table on the first floor. Or in the cupboard if the table's being used for a meeting. We have school groups, you know, on educational visits, WI coach parties, that kind of thing. The diary has a list of frequently used phone numbers at the front that we copy forward every year into the next diary. And underneath that, a note to check storage box WO at the beginning of the first August in each new decade.

"William Oakley!" Emily exclaimed for the benefit of followers online.

"So nine years out of ten, the note was simply copied forward. But this is my third first-August-of-the-decade as an assistant curator, and the timing has been perfect because we're closing the museum at the end of the month for a major refurbishment. We're packing up everything to go into store. Three hundred and fifty plates for a start. Dozens of Women's Guild Banners. All being wrapped in acid-free tissue paper then bubble wrapped and into specially constructed boxes. Packing a museum, I can assure you, is a skilled art."

Another text on Emily's phone: *Enough museum*. She dropped the phone back into her bag.

"Box WO would have found itself cocooned in deep storage. But here we are. Ready to empty it."

"So *you've* been forwarding William's presents to Stephen."

"I located box WO in 1990, as directed in the diary, and there were four packages in it, one of which had a note attached saying to make sure it reached Stephen Oakley by August 21st 1990. There was a loose scrap of paper saying he was last known at an address in Kingston upon Thames. In fact, I learned from tenants at that address that he was living on a smallholding near Eccleshall in Staffordshire. It wasn't difficult. Package in the mail. Job done. For another ten years."

"So you did the same again in 2000?"

"And the same again just a few days ago."

"But you said there were four packages in the box when you first found it."

"Yes, I've got the fourth here." He eased himself from his stool and shuffled towards the far corner, where Emily could see the process of packing smaller exhibits for storage had already begun. He came back with a large, bulging envelope and Emily asked him to hold it up to the camera while she provided the words.

"It's one of those sturdy brown foolscap envelopes that lawyers use for bulky important documents. My grandmother was an accountant and she used them too. Closed with a little metal fastener that you pass through a hole in the flap and then open out like a butterfly. And there's some writing."

"A legend!" Mr Howarth exclaimed like a schoolboy.

Stephen clarified for the benefit of junior followers online, with enough sarcasm, he hoped, to register with Emily: "That's explanatory wording on a map or diagram, such as one showing where 'X' marks the spot."

"It says: *On or shortly after 21st August 2010, you can expect Mr Stephen P Oakley to make contact with a representative of the museum. When he does so, please give him the contents of this, my final package. Should he not contact you within the month, you may dispose of the contents as you see fit. In either case you will have executed the terms of our agreement, for which I am grateful. William Oakley.*"

Mr Howarth unfastened the clasp, took out of the envelope a wooden box, and handed it to Stephen. Emily asked him to hold it up for the camera and describe it.

"It's beautiful." He held the box forward on the flat of his open hands.

"In a little more detail, please, for the benefit of the many viewers and readers who have followed the trail that has brought us to this dramatic conclusion."

"It's about eight inches by five by two. I can do that in centimetres if you want. Or in hands and fractions of a cubit for that matter, if you want me to use my imagination and milk the treasure-hunt angle." He turned it over, lifted it to the light. "Most significantly, I'd say, it has no obvious opening. It's wonderfully crafted." He inspected each plane of the box closely, first with his eyes and then with the pad of his index finger. "Not so much as a hairline crack. My grandfather made a few wooden puzzles that were the dickens to open, but I don't think this is one of them. It's hornbeam at a guess. William said hornbeam was the best when you wanted rigidity and strength. He'd warn me not to cut myself on the edge of it. See – there's no jointing on the corners, just the finest straight line where the two hard edges meet. He must have made it in two halves, with hidden mitred dovetail joints. Glued together on inaccessible surfaces. And look at this beautiful top!"

"But what's inside?" Emily asked.

He was speechless for a moment.

"We all want to know what's inside," Emily said.

"No. That's not what this is about."

"Of course it's what it's about, Stephen. It's William's final gift to you."

"Then perhaps this is my moment of truth," he said, sounding shocked and looking in credulous appeal to the camera and his live audience of many thousands, all over the world. And then with a visibly relaxing expression: "Perhaps this is my epiphany."

Mr Howarth asked if he could get him a glass of water.

"You cut me off, Emily, before I could describe the stunning decoration on this lid. Around the edges he's made a border in bas-relief, cutting down into the hornbeam to fashion what looks like a string of roses – dog roses." He looked up towards the camera and said he might have a go at something like that himself one day. "Emily here gave me a set of chisels and a mallet yesterday, for my birthday. How thoughtful was that?" Then down to the box again. "William's hedgerow roses are framing a handsome piece of marquetry. I believe it's a stylised view across Morecambe Bay towards the Lake District, perhaps from Bolton-le-Sands. I suspect he's used fruit-wood veneers that he cut himself. Apple, pear, cherry. Maybe alder for this sweep of sand in the foreground. Perhaps birch for the washed-out sky."

"And inside?"

"You asked me to describe the box."

"Yes – and inside?"

"Oh, an odd sock, I should think. Or a handkerchief."

"You're joking."

"No – it would be William's joke. Or William's considered commentary on the pre-eminence of the quest over the find, the observation and examination over the answer."

"We can have both."

"I think William's experiences in life suggested a more complicated view. The War Office always had answers. The Church of England had answers. His family had answers. I think he found that those who always had the answers seriously discouraged questions. I think he came eventually to an appreciation that he could live happily in a state of not having answers. But still asking questions."

"Can we get back to the box?"

But he was sticking with the questions, and he turned towards Emily to ask her directly, "Isn't it all about context, in the end? Haven't William's gifts given me a sense of the context of his life, to set against mine? If he had given me them all at once, in 1960, or 1990, or today, I wouldn't have seen what they amounted to. I see now, though, that they don't point to a moral. They give me a sense of his journey. Isn't the key to a great treasure hunt in the hunt, not the treasure, Emily? I believe we pick up the treasure on the way. Sometimes in the very places where we stumble."

"This is unfair. You're hijacking my story."

"I know what I'm going to do with my box. But you have a box of your own, don't you Emily? That's why you're so keen on the opening of the box. A simple DNA test – that's your box. Ninety-nine pounds sterling off the shelf. A swab from me to match a swab from you."

"Unfair. Mixing up our stories."

"Then you leave me alone with my box and I'll let you get on with yours. I'll give you my swab. You can open your box if the answer is so important to you. But let me warn you that there are more puzzles than William's that are not necessarily made for opening. There are many gifts that can be broken by the act of looking inside."

For the first time since the interview began, he could see that Emily was entirely focussed on him and what he was saying, not on her audience.

"But being a grandfather is about who you are," she said.

"No, I think not. I believe it's about what you do. Nobody else makes me a grandfather. I do that."

"What about me?"

"What about connectedness as a beginning, not an end?"

Unnoticed by Emily, Mr Howarth was urgently wiping condensation from his glasses with the wide end of his tie. "It's like Take Your Pick, with Michael Miles," he said. "I can hear the audience yelling *Open the box! Open the box!*" Unnoticed too, another message on her phone: *going viral. what's in the box a meme on reddit*

Stephen lifted his box to his ear and shook it gently. "Actually, I know exactly what's inside." He passed it to Emily and asked her to listen.

She shook his box. Then she put it in her lap and considered and her eyes became distinctly moist.

"I suppose it could be in a sheath of some kind," she said eventually. "I suppose you think that it's the little chisel Old Armitage gave him."

"The chisel my grandfather used to make all my

presents, including this one. For sure it is."

MR HOWARTH MADE THEM A CUP OF TEA while Emily packed up her kit and spoke with her editor.

Stephen said, to neither of them in particular, that he had some understanding now of why Jeannie never tried to contact him back in England. He said he thought we all had our little Mount Blignys, our marches to Abbeville.

Beyond the photographs of the founding members there was a display about the houses on Pioneer Street and Equitable Street and when it caught his eye and he went to scrutinize it, Mr Howarth followed at his elbow.

"The first aim of the Rochdale Pioneers was to open a grocery store, the second to build a number of houses for members. The impetus to do that came when a local landlord who was also a shopkeeper raised some of his rents. He put them up only for those tenants who were Co-op members, who didn't buy their groceries from him."

"I suspect my grandfather knew the story."

"I feel honoured to have played a small part in his."

As they were leaving, Mr Howarth asked him if he would ever open his box. He said of course not. To open the box, he said, he would have to destroy it.

"In that case," Mr Howarth said, "will you please step back inside again?"

Stephen and Emily sat on the two chairs in the replica of the original shop, facing the bags of wholemeal flour, sugar, and oatmeal. Emily wanted to get her webcam out again.

Mr Howarth advised against.

"But it's classic!" she said. "You hide a lesser treasure on top of the real thing. So the dilettantes walk away with the consolation prize and leave the real treasure for the smart and determined. We've got to video it!"

Mr Howarth said he found it strangely gratifying that she had managed to misread the situation to the extent she had; that she had become so excited about what was no more than the explanatory wrapping up of loose ends that comes after the climax of so many engaging stories.

"Inside the envelope that contained the box you choose not to open, Mr Oakley, there was another, smaller envelope addressed to the presiding official of the museum. That's me, for our current purpose. It contained a letter from the warden who handled this business at the start, in 1960. Please bear in mind that the Co-operative Union as it was then – which bought these premises in 1925 and opened the museum on behalf of the whole movement – was not a charity. Nor was it a bank. Fifty years ago managers would undoubtedly have exercised their individual judgement in ways unlikely today. Allow me to read:

To Whom it May Concern

Today I received a visit from Mr William Oakley, currently residing with his sister-in-law Mrs Mary Oakley of 1 Hinkson Street, Skerton, Lancaster. Mr Oakley presented to me in some detail his plan for the delivery of five packages to his grandson Stephen P Oakley (the son of Mr George Oakley) currently resident at a boarding school in Westmorland but frequently resident with Mrs Mary Oakley during school holidays, each package to be delivered on or near to the first 21st August in each decade. Although Mr Oakley purported to have no agenda other than to provide a novel and protracted amusement for the grandson with whom he had in recent years clearly enjoyed many stimulating and educational excursions, it was evident to me that together with the first gift, which he would deliver himself, the series in fact constituted, or had the potential to amount to, a significant instruction, or illustration, or perhaps even illumination; that Mr Oakley had sought out the Co-operative Union, via the agency of the Rochdale Pioneers Museum, to facilitate his scheme because he trusted our offices in preference to those of lawyers, bankers, or any other – indeed, he said more than once and in a way that made a deep impression on me, that he had faith in us; and that he was subject to heart failure which his doctor had said could take his life at any moment.

When he understood that I was sympathetic, Mr Oakley produced a draft for five thousand pounds, untouched since his father, on his deathbed, had pressed it into his hand some fifteen years previously. A small fortune at that time, it remained a significant sum when Mr Oakley in turn pressed it upon me. He thought it likely we would incur expenses over the decades. Although not actively seeking donations, I could immediately identify a number of projects which would benefit from a cash appropriation. I explained to Mr Oakley that the basis on which I would undertake his unusual bequest was not a commercial one and that half of the sum he was offering was the most that I would be able to accept by way of covering expenses. Mr Oakley put up no small argument and made clear that he wished to leave with the matter concluded.

Seeking a solution that I felt was fair and equitable, I suggested that the other half of the money could be invested on behalf of his grandson. Mr Oakley finally agreed, on this condition: that Mr Stephen Oakley leaves the museum with the box he is due to receive in 2010 intact, and having expressed the intention of not opening it.

If events should unfold otherwise, this part of Mr William Oakley's bequest shall also fall to the Rochdale Pioneers Museum, for use as the museum sees fit.

"It's signed and dated," Mr Howarth added. "And there is an account number." He passed the letter to Stephen.

"WHAT NEXT?" Stephen asked when Mr Howarth had disappeared back into The Baum leaving them on the deserted pavement, Emily with her bag of communications kit and Stephen with his wooden box in hand.

"I didn't start out looking for money or status. I'm not the type for crying in a Mercedes."

He wanted to invite her to laugh with him on a bicycle. It struck him as exactly the kind of celebratory thing he would love to do with a young person who believed she was his granddaughter. Instead he said, "I hardly think that two-and-a-half grand, left in a bog-standard deposit account with interest reduced annually by the standard rate of income tax will have accumulated to the price of a Mercedes."

"Actually, I was thinking of myself. Even while I was packing up I saw a couple of job offers on my phone."

"You can take your time. I always have."

But neither of them took notice of a moped as it pulled into the cul-de-sac which was the tiny remaining length of Toad Lane containing the Pioneers Museum and the period public house called The Baum next door. They didn't remark the abrupt halt, the engine left idling; the swift dismount of the two riders; the simultaneous unsheathing of weapons. They didn't have time to grasp that one of the men had circled behind them, blocking their exit round the wall at the end of the cul-de-sac.

"The box," said the one facing Stephen.

In slender-fitting jeans and white tee-shirt, his globular helmet with its heavily tinted visor – which he had not removed – made him seem unsustainably top-heavy. Like an alien whose enormous brain and observational apparatus had out-developed an underused, or undernourished, body. But he bore arms – a knife – and he clearly expected prompt appeasement. It bothered Stephen that Emily had taken up what seemed more like a defensive than a submissive posture. She stood close to him, but with her back to his, and as he turned she turned with him.

"You can have the money! You can have all my money," he said quickly, as much to make Emily aware of his strategy as the man in front of him, at whom he waved the details of his new bank account.

"Give me the box!"

Nice and slow, he knew. The last thing you wanted to do was to trigger an impulsive reaction. It was all about adrenalin. About status. About *not* being alien. Not so different from prep school except for the lethal weapon. He proffered his little box like favourite tuck.

And then the worst happened, at breakneck speed. Emily grabbed the box from him and yelled for help at the top of her voice. Holding the thing in both hands she thrust it at the helmet in front of her, bashing him where it hurt least, but making him yell too: "Fuck you! Back off! Fuck!" The knife came up and caught Emily's hand before she bashed it away with the box. Stephen saw blood. He had no idea how you went about fighting a man who had a knife. The other man pushed him aside and made to grab Emily from behind, his knife hand flailing the air. Stephen stumbled. He thought some of the blood may be his own, though he could see no wound and no glint of a steel blade flashing towards him. He could see only the true meaning of the real treasure that lay underneath, for the determined seeker. "Emily!" he shrieked, throwing himself at her, throwing himself between her and the danger that threatened, knocking both her and the man to the ground. He pushed the box away as he crumpled down on top of her, his arms around her. He hurt somewhere. He hurt everywhere. There was more blood. There was far too much blood. There was more noise too. A revving bike. More voices. More swearing. A siren off in the distance. And then something like oblivion, tempting him.

AS SOON AS HE SAW STEPHEN ON THE PAVEMENT Mr Howarth ran back into the pub and called for an ambulance. The request went via a call centre in Manchester and there were more questions than the curator anticipated. Yes, the assailants had left. No, the police had not yet arrived. Yes, the victim had suffered multiple stab wounds. Yes, he had lost a lot of blood. Yes, he was breathing and still conscious, though he kept saying things that didn't make sense.

But the ambulance station was less than a quarter of a mile from Toad Lane and a vehicle with blue light flashing pulled across the entrance of the road within minutes.

Seeing a disorderly scrummage of people on the pavement and no police presence, the driver and technician followed their protocol and assessed the scene to make sure their own lives were not at risk. As they approached, those leaning over Stephen's prostrate body did not immediately give way. They were holding tea towels from the pub against stab wounds to his chest, arms, and thigh. The lower wound spurted blood as soon as Emily relaxed her pressure against it and the technician swiftly wrapped an orange belt round the top of Stephen's thigh and twisted a lever until it tightened and the flow stopped. His teammate had put a cuff round Stephen's left arm and soon it started beeping. He called out numbers.

“Close to the litre,” the man next to Emily said.

“What do you mean?”

“He’s lost a lot of blood. He mustn’t go into shock.”

“What can I do?”

He handed her a pair of sewing sheers. “Cut his trousers away. From the ankles up. We need to check if there are any more wounds.” Then he moved swiftly to Stephen’s right arm and chest, peering under the tea towels the others were holding against his torso. The man in charge of the blood pressure cuff slid a needle into the back of Stephen’s hand and set up a drip, with a little bag of clear liquid on a tiny metal frame – all on the pavement outside the Rochdale Pioneers Museum where members had waited patiently on divi night for their monthly share of trading surplus.

Stephen’s exposed legs were deathly pale, thin, defenceless. Emily looked up and saw that his face was the same – pale and gaunt, but sweating. Beads of sweat stood out on his forehead. And then he started shivering.

The wounds to his chest were less serious. The knife had glanced, not penetrated. Tea towels were replaced by sterile dressings one by one.

One of the medics brought up a stretcher on wheels. It was a couple of feet above Stephen. He organised the team – Emily, Mr Howarth, two men from The Baum – and together they lifted at his command. Then swiftly to the vehicle, Stephen sliding inside, the medic sitting beside him steadying the pouch of fluid, listening to the electronic bleeps.

Mr Howarth said the infirmary was only two minutes away.

The ambulance driver said Stephen’s injuries were life threatening and they would take him to the A and E in Bury.

Emily climbed into the passenger seat.

The driver told her to get out; that she had been very helpful but her own injury was superficial.

"I believe she is the wounded gentleman's granddaughter," Mr Howarth told him.

The ambulance pulled away, blue light flashing, siren blaring.

The wooden box made by William Oakley, which may or may not have contained the gouge given to him as a young man by Old Armitage, had been taken and though Emily's paper offered a substantial reward for its return undamaged, it was never seen again.

"YOU DO BRAVE AFTER ALL," Emily said.

He wanted to play possum and let her say more.

"But just in case you're playing possum - for the record, I've already paid you back for saving my life."

He opened one eye but the light hurt and he closed it again quickly. She pretended she hadn't seen.

"Sundays in August not being the most convenient of times to bleed just about to death on the pavement and need a transfusion so urgently they don't have time to type you."

Okay, he was blood group O, rhesus negative. He knew because once in the States he'd been so hard up he'd sold a pint of it for cash. They gave him fifteen dollars and an awareness that he could only take blood from other O negatives.

"So they reach straight for the deluxe stuff from their universal donors, group O rhesus negative, which in this particular place and at this particular point in time they have not got, for reasons that are mostly forgivable and involve fate at its conspiring worst."

Unlikely. Storytelling alert.

"Except running through the veins of yours truly, who is of course willing and able."

He felt the corners of his mouth twitch with the faintest hint of a smile, though that hurt too.

"Turns out we're both O negative as it happens. Fancy that. Both singular receivers, both universal donors."

In this day and age they surely screened for dozens of other factors. They wouldn't take her donor card's word for it.

"And I know you'd enjoy hearing, if only you weren't still hovering at death's door, that I've been seeing the promise of treasure in the most unlikely places. X marks the spot. The police drew an enormous one with chalk on the pavement outside the museum, marking where you fell protecting me. And a surgeon drew another one with something like a green felt pen, pretty much right above your heart. He was concerned about one of your cuts and wanted to investigate."

She cupped her bandaged hand gently round his and whispered, "Anyway, I've decided against the DNA test. You're right: it could be the end of a promising story. I know it could be the beginning of another, but beginnings can be so... indefinite."

He slept deeply on that.

She was still there, or there again, when he woke the next day, or the day after that.

"I've been thinking we should play together again. When you're home. I've got some beautiful arrangements of Schubert for flute and piano."

"I'd like that."

"Of course you'll have to learn to play from a score. I can teach you."

"And we can try some Brubeck. I think you'll like it. Of course you'll have to learn how to improvise."

"You can teach me."

"I might invite Peter to bring his clarinet. I can provide the continuo for the two of you to improvise over. As it were."

It was quiet on the ward the next time he surfaced. There were empty beds on both sides of him, no visitors, and the solitary nurse was absorbed in paperwork at a desk some distance away. He ran a mental inventory of his body parts and functions and decided he was more-or-less all there. More all there, actually, than he'd felt for a long time. A bag of clear fluid hung from a metal hook on a pole above his bed and when his eye slowly tracked the course of the tube from the bag to a drip chamber and then on down and along, he was surprised to see that it led via a needle taped to his inner arm into his own vein. Surprised and reassured. He couldn't see any tubes leading in the reverse direction, taking fluid away from his body, and that was also reassuring.

Eventually his line of sight came back to the little table beside his bed and he noticed for the first time a bouquet of flowers. It was not like anything you would see in a florist's window or on a garage forecourt. It was artless but confident. It was not so strong on organising principle – or was it? It reminded him of himself. He couldn't identify the flowers, but he recognised the glass pitcher she had poured lemonade from earlier. They were the kind of flowers William might have grown in his cottage garden at Yealand. She'd arranged them, if that was the word, in a way that was simple and honest, though he suspected she had picked them from here and there around the hospital grounds. Some of them were drooping a little already. But they undoubtedly belonged, and contributed to the composition.

There was a note leaning against the pitcher. She'd

written on the back of the card they gave out to remind people of visiting hours: "From your granddaughter, or whatever."

ACKNOWLEDGEMENTS

For help in creating the historical context for this work of fiction I would like to acknowledge particularly Susan Vipont Hartshorne's The Story of Yealand Manor School, Winifred Percival's Not Only Music Signora, Renata Laxova's Letter to Alexander, Bob Matthews' The Bengel has Landed and Matthew Barry Sullivan's Thresholds of Peace. I am also grateful for conversations with and the assistance of staff at The Shropshire Regimental Museum, Shrewsbury, and curator Peter Duckers; Robin Greaves, daughter of Elfrida Foulds, Headteacher of Yealand Manor School; staff at The Rochdale Pioneers Museum, Toad Lane, Rochdale, and Gillian Lonergan, Head of Heritage Resources at The Co-operative College; Local History Librarians at Kendal Library and the descendants of Italians held prisoner at Bela River Camp and their local employers with whom they put me in touch.

Thanks to Nancy Stewart for assistance with editing and cover design.

The photograph on the back cover shows a paper knife and hand-bell. They were made from .303 cartridges and the nose of a mortar shell towards the end of the First World War by a German prisoner of war as my grandfather escorted him away from the battlefield. Both men were carpenters and leading lights in their local co-operative societies. They became friends.

John Hargreaves, Market Drayton, 2015

18802503R00156

Printed in Great Britain
by Amazon